IRISH MASTERS OF FANTASY

IRISH MASTERS OF FANTASY

An Anthology

with introduction and biographical essays

edited by

PETER TREMAYNE

ILLUSTRATIONS BY JEANETTE DUNNE

WOLFHOUND PRESS

© 1979 Peter Tremayne
Published by
Wolfhound Press
98 Ardilaun Portmarnock
County Dublin

Cover portrait of Le Fanu by Robert Ballagh
Courtesy of the Arts Council of Ireland

Typeset by
Gifford & Craven
50 Merrion Square, Dublin 2.

Printed in Great Britain by
Redwood Burn Limited, Trowbridge & Esher

Acknowledgements

I am most grateful to Jon Wynne-Tyson of Centaur Press, Arundel, Sussex, England, the literary executor of the estate of M. P. Shiel, and to Katia Gould of Dr. Jan Van Loewen Ltd., literary agents, for permission to republish 'Xélucha'.

I am similarly grateful to the 19th Baron Dunsany of Dunsany Castle, Co. Meath, for permission to reprint 'The Ghost of the Valley' and 'Autumn Cricket'.

Portraits: Charles Maturin from drawing by W. Brocas; Joseph Sheridan Le Fanu from photograph by E. Walker; FitzJames O'Brien from drawing by Sol Eytinge Jr.; Bram Stoker from photograph by W. D. Dromey; Lord Dunsany photograph courtesy *Independent Newspapers Ltd.*; M. P. Shiel photograph from *The Listener* 1947.

CONTENTS

ILLUSTRATIONS

For my friends
Jane and Tony O'Malley

THE IRISH AND FANTASY LITERATURE

ONE OF THE OLDEST AND STRONGEST emotions of mankind is fear of the unknown. Fear is such a primal emotion that the horror tale has endured as long as human thought and speech itself. Especially today, people, for whatever psychological motivation, have a constant urge to free themselves from the commonplace of their lives and experience that strange tingling fear of the the spectrally unknown. Even the bulwark of the sophistication of our modern age is no barrier to the addiction of mankind to the weird. The popularity of horror-fantasy, in books, comics and movies, is still increasing.

Irish writers have had a profound effect on the field of fantasy writing and, in particular, on the horror-fantasy tale. Indeed, *Dracula*, the creation of Dubliner Bram Stoker, has become, with *Frankenstein*, almost synonymous with the horror tale.

The first exponent of fantasy as a serious modern literary form was the Dubliner Jonathan Swift (1667-1747) whose *Travels into Several Remote Nations of the World by Lemuel Gulliver*, more popularly known as *Gulliver's Travels*, had a world wide impact. An ardent admirer of Swift's form of fantasy was his fellow Dubliner, Samuel Derrick, who is best known today for his translation of the work of Cyrano de Bergerac, especially *Voyage dans la Lune* (1657) which was published as *A Voyage to the Moon* in Dublin in 1753.

As an identifiable literary medium, fantasy writing is now generally accepted as a sub-genre of Science Fiction, a Science Fiction story being one built around human beings with a human problem and a human solution which would not have happened at all without its scientific content. But, I would argue, that fantasy writing is not really a mere sub-division of Science Fiction, as critics would have us believe. The reverse is true. Fantasy, and especially the horror-fantasy, is a far older form of story telling. It offers either a co-universe ruled by laws openly presented as magical (in other words, fairy tales for adults in close affinity with the concepts of ancient mythology and legend) or it is presented as a disturbance in the fabric of our own universe, a suspension of natural laws. This latter form of fantasy is usually the essence of the horror tale whose pattern was firmly established by Edgar Allan Poe (1809-1849).

Is there any reason for the prominence of Irish writers in this particular genre? Aodh de Blacam, in *A First Book of Irish Literature*, thought there was and indicated it to be the cultural background of the writers. He went so far as to see a particular school of Irish horror-fantasy writers which he designated the 'Maturin School', naming it after Charles Maturin the first writer featured in this anthology.

De Blacam was not the only critic to see an 'Irish school'. H.P. Lovecraft (1890-1937), regarded as the most important American horror-fantasy writer since Poe and who has had an incalculable effect on all horror-fantasy writing in recent decades, also mentions this school but does not include Maturin in it. Writing in his superb essay *Supernatural Horror in Literature*, Lovecraft says:

'Somewhat separate from the main British stream is that current of weirdness in Irish literature which came to the fore in the Celtic Renaissance of the later Nineteenth and early Twentieth Centuries. Ghost and fairy lore have always been of great prominence in Ireland, and for over a hundred years have been recorded by a line of such faithful transcribers and translators as William Carleton, T. Crofton Croker, Lady Wilde — mother of Oscar Wilde — Douglas Hyde and W. B. Yeats.

Brought to notice by the modern movement, this body of myth has been carefully collected and studied; and its salient features reproduced in the work of later figures like Yeats, J.M. Synge, 'A.E.', Lady Gregory, Pádraic Colum, James Stephens and their colleagues.

'Whilst on the whole more whimsically fantastic than terrible such folklore and its consciously artistic counterparts contain much that falls truly within the domain of cosmic horror. Tales of burials in sunken churches, beneath haunted lakes, accounts of death-heralding banshees and sinister changelings, ballads of spectres and 'the unholy creatures of the Rath' — all these have their poignant and definitive shivers, and mark a strong and distinctive element in weird literature. Despite homely grotesqueness and absolute naivete, there is a genuine nightmare in the class of narrative represented by the yarn of Teig O'Kane, who in punishment for his wild life was ridden all night by a hideous corpse that demanded burial and drove him from churchyard to churchyard as the dead rose up loathsomely in each one and refused to accommodate the newcomer with a berth. Yeats, undoubtedly the greatest figure of the Irish revival if not the greatest of all living poets, has accomplished notable things both in original work and in the codification of legends'.

Having observed this distinct stream of horror-fantasy in Irish literature, emanating from Irish mythology and folklore, it is strange that Lovecraft does not point out its significance when he writes about the work of the six writers featured in this book. Having made his point about the separateness in English literature of Irish horror-fantasy, Lovecraft reviews the work of these six as individuals and barely mentions the fact that they had an Irish nationality in common.

Is it a mere nationalist indulgence to attribute some cultural influence to the fact that these six giants of macabre fantasy writing were Irish? I think not. That element of cosmic horror and fantasy has appeared as an ingredient in the earliest folklore of Ireland and it is crystallised in the ancient written mythology, in folk tales and ballads. From the time of the Irish myths and sagas, fantasy has ever been a strong tradition in

Irish story-telling. From the cycle of Finn and the adventures of Cuchulain the idea of swords and sorcery, of ghosts and gods, and the break in the natural laws of our universe, has been a 'stock-in-trade' of Irish writers; more so, I would argue, than their 'down to earth' Anglo-Saxon counterparts. It is this exploitation by Irish writers of folklore and traditions, the ability to present breaks in natural laws as vivid and realistic, which have produced such classics of fantasy writing.

Some critics have gone so far as to see Irish cultural influence in the work of British and American writers of Irish descent. Pádraic Colum, writing of the fact that Edgar Allan Poe was of Irish parentage and that his parents brought him to Ireland as a boy, comments: 'Certain peculiarities of his work have been put down to racial tendencies for his father though American born was of Irish descent.' In this he was taking up a point made by Aodh de Blacam. Colum, quite rightly, dismisses the idea of *racial* tendencies in writing. However, there is an argument for the observation of *cultural* influences.

The Brontë family, for example, displayed a strong element of Gothic fantasy in their writing. Lovecraft has said of Emily Brontë's *Wuthering Heights* (1847) that it stands 'quite alone both as a novel and as a piece of terror-literature'. This fantasy element is attributed by biographer Phyllis Bentley, in *The Brontës* (1947), to the fact that their father Patrick Prunty came from Co. Down. 'Both Brontë parents,' says Miss Bentley, 'belonged to a race, or if that is too strong an expression, let us say a form of civilisation, definitely Celtic.' She adds: 'Patrick, who was an admirable raconteur, told his children Celtic legends which actually moulded the structure and incidents of *Wuthering Heights* and -*Jane Eyre*.'

Miss Bentley goes further:

' . . . there is a peculiar quality in the Brontë presentation of Yorkshire; a quality of wild poetry, of arrogance, of melancholy, of stern intransigence and fiery intensity, of passionate scorn for material values, which is not native to that robust and practical county. This is the Celtic strain which mingles with the Yorkshire to produce so strange a blend. There are no other Yorkshire writers like the Brontës for all other Yorkshire writers hitherto lacked the Celtic strain. There are no other Irish writers like the Brontës for all other Irish writers lacked the Yorkshire strain.'

Miss Bentley makes it clear, therefore, that she sees an Irish cultural influence in the Brontës' writing.

W.B. Yeats claimed that he saw that cultural influence in the fantasies of the great genius William Blake (1757-1827) for Blake, too, was born of Irish parents. In the early 18th century John O'Neil married Ellen Blake who kept a shebeen in Rathmines, Dublin. To escape financial trouble John O'Neil changed his name to that of his wife — Blake. His son James also adopted the name and eventually emigrated to England. He settled in London where he opened a business as a hosier and where his son William was born. Through his art and poetry Blake revealed a fantasy world with a mysticism both metaphorical and symbolic. Was that fantasy world, as Yeats suggests, nurtured by the cultural background of his parentage? It surely had some influence.

This tradition of literary fantasy makes itself known in writers who do not consider themselves to be exponents of that style of literature. Oscar Wilde's most powerful tale, in my estimation, was that produced by his foray into the realms of horror-fantasy: — his frightening story of moral degeneracy *The Picture of Dorian Gray*, first published in the July, 1890, issue of *Lippincott's Monthly Magazine*. And one must also pay literary tribute to his exquisite fairy fantasies such as 'The Selfish Giant', 'The Happy Prince', 'The Birthday of the Infanta' and others.

James Joyce, Nobel Prizewinner Samuel Beckett, and Flann O'Brien, have all utilised the traditional fantasy element. O'Brien's *The Dalkey Archive* (1964) is regarded as 'almost Science Fiction' and *The Third Policeman* (1967) is an exceptional piece of fantasy writing.

Although the Belfast born and bred Clive Staples Lewis (1898-1963) was best known for his religious and ethical works, he has been described by the critic Marcus Crouch as 'a writer in the mainstream of English fantasy, and he contributes to it his own clear and original spring'. Of his 49 books, three in particular have marked him as one of the most influential writers in the adult fantasy genre — the trilogy *Out of the Silent Planet* (1938); *Voyage to Venus* (1943) and *That Hideous Strength* (1945). Yet C.S. Lewis strongly denied being part of any Irish school. He wrote: ' . . . the Celtic origin seems never to have affected my imagination which is Germanic through and through . . . Norse mythology having been my first love and perhaps my strongest.'

Today, Ireland's best known writer in the mainstream of the fantasy form is, perhaps, James White, born in Belfast in 1928, whose first story 'Assisted Passage' appeared in *New Worlds* in 1953. His first novel, *The Secret Visitors*, was published in 1957.

Therefore, we can observe that fantasy, and especially the fantasy of the macabre, has an interesting tradition in Irish writing dating from early mythology and folklore to modern times. This cultural influence, I believe, has contributed to the rise in prominence of the six Irish masters of the macabre who are the subjects of this anthology.

They are, indeed, masters of fantasy.

CHARLES ROBERT MATURIN (1780-1824)

CHARLES ROBERT MATURIN is regarded as the author who concluded the early Gothic horror-fantasy cycle which began with Horace Walpole's *The Castle of Otranto* (1764) and reached its peak with Mary Shelley's immortal classic *Frankenstein* (1818). Of his work Brian Cleeve has written: 'He was one of the strangest among the many strange characters in Irish letters, and deserves more attention than he has ever received'.

He was born in Dublin on September 25, 1780, of Huguenot stock. He entered Trinity College in 1795, graduating in 1800. His father held a prominent position in the Irish Post Office but Maturin rejected a career as a civil servant to take Holy Orders in the Anglican Church. He was ordained in 1803 and went to serve as a curate in Loughrea, Co. Galway. In the following year he secured the curacy of St. Peter's in Dublin, a small parish in the then heart of Dublin's slums. Soon after, in October of that year, 1804, he married Henrietta Kingsbury. And it was to escape from the poverty and degradation in which he and his family had to eke out a living on £90 a year that Maturin turned to writing.

He published his first novel, *Fatal Revenge; or The Family Montonio* in 1807, at the age of 27. As with most of his novels, it was of the Gothic horror-fantasy genre. A typical example of this style of tale usually featured a young heroine pursued by a wicked villain. Her flight takes her to a variety of dismal

Drawn by W.Brocas.   Engraved by H.Meyer.

THE REV. C. R. MATURIN.

or dangerous places such as subterranean caves, vaults, crypts, secret rooms and graveyards. There is always the element of threatening supernatural. Invariably the heroine is rescued by the handsome hero.

Such writing began with Walpole's *The Castle of Otranto* and became refined with works such as *The Mysteries of Udolpho* (1794) by Ann Radcliff, *The Monk* (1796) by Matthew G. Lewis and *The Vampyre* (1819) by John Polidori. But of all the Gothic horror-fantasy novels of this period it is Mary Shelley's *Frankenstein* that remains the classic of the age.

Maturin's *Fatal Revenge* appeared under the pseudonym of Dennis Jasper Murphy, a name which Maturin was to use for most of his works. It attracted the attention of Sir Walter Scott who, in the May, 1810, issue of the *Quarterly Review* was fulsome in his praise of its 'strong and vigorous fancy, with great command of language'. But, he added, the writer would have to learn discipline.

Maturin did not see the review until 1812 and wrote, on December 18, to Scott and thanked him. Scott replied and the correspondence between the two men continued until Maturin's death. Scott's letters are full of advice and moral support and once he helped Maturin financially.

The year after *Fatal Revenge* was published, Maturin published *The Wild Irish Boy*. This was a tongue in cheek answer to Lady Morgan's *Wild Irish Girl* (1806), a novel in which everything polite England wished to hear about Ireland is contained. It has a beautiful windswept heroine playing a harp on the ruined battlements of a romantic castle plus a dispossessed Irish nobleman and so forth.

But now began a bad period for Maturin. His father was unjustly dismissed from the Post Office over allegations of corruption and misuse of funds. Maturin supported his father and the family knew acute poverty before the real culprit was identified and Maturin's father was reinstated. But not long afterwards Maturin stood security for a relative who defaulted and he had to pay the sum guaranteed.

In 1812 Maturin was paid £80 for the copyright of his new book entitled *The Milesian Chief*. His friend Scott reworked the idea in his more celebrated *The Bride of Lammermoor.* It was in *The Milesian Chief*, in a preface, that Maturin accurately summed up his ability: 'If I possess any talent,' he wrote, 'it is that of darkening the gloomy, and of developing the sad; of painting life in extremes, and representing those struggles of passion when the soul trembles on the verge of the unlawful and the unhallowed'.

Maturin now turned to the stage and, in 1814, wrote his first play *Bertram*. He sent it firstly to Walter Scott who recommended it to John Kemble for production. Kemble declined it and, in June of 1815, Scott sent it to Byron who shared Scott's praise. On May 9, 1816, *Bertram* was produced at Drury Lane with Edmund Kean in the title role. The play was a great success and earned about £1,000 for Maturin.

Maturin wrote three more plays. *Manuel*, a tragedy, was produced at Drury Lane on March 8, 1817, but proved a failure largely due to Edmund Kean's indifference to his part. The second play was another tragedy entitled *Fredolfo* and was produced at Covent Garden on May 12, 1819. Again, it was a failure. His last attempt was *Osmyn the Renegade* which was put into rehearsal in Covent Garden in 1822 but never given a public performance there. The play was finally produced in Dublin in 1830.

Maturin returned to the novel form and, in 1818, he published *Women; or Pour et Contre* which was to be the only one of his novels to deal with contemporary Irish society. In his preface to the novel, he reflected his disillusionment at his failure as a writer and complained about the lack of interest in his work. He was 'not at all surpriz'd', however, at the unpopularity of his work since it now seemed 'to want reality'.

He was 40 years old when he published his masterpiece *Melmoth the Wanderer* in 1820. His publisher, Archibald Constable, advanced him £500 for the work, mainly due to Scott's influence. *Melmoth* was seen as the rival to *Frankenstein*. It combined all the Gothic terrors, hinging its theme on the haunting of Faust and the misery of the legendary Wandering Jew. Leonard Wolf (professor of English at San Francisco State University, in his *Annotated Dracula*, 1975) says of

Melmoth that it has 'the most sustained and certainly the most complex vision of any Gothic fiction — not excepting *Dracula*.' H. P. Lovecraft maintained that it made 'the Gothic tale climb to altitudes of sheer spiritual fright which it had never known before'.

Melmoth is a vast work of nearly unrelieved sombreness that follows the adventures of its hero who, at the cost of his own soul, purchases 150 years of life to learn, in the most bitter way, that he had only purchased an opportunity for more and more loathsome experiences in a world that was monstrous from the start. The book is replete with Gothicisms, dungeons, castles, ghosts, cannabalism, monsters both real and imaginary, and truly monumental instances of personal dismay.

Wolf comments: 'What gives profundity to the fiction is the way in which Melmoth's long adventures into the abyss that is the world becomes an apparently accurate chart of the cost to mankind of original sin.'

Two French translations were made in 1821 and the story had such an effect on Honore de Balzac, the celebrated French novelist (1799-1850) that he wrote a whimsical sequel to it entitled *Melmoth Reconciled*. On July 14, 1823, a dramatisation by B. West was produced at the Royal Coburg Theatre and was an instant success.

Scott, Rosetti, Thackeray and Baudelaire also recognised the work as a literary milestone.

It is ironic to note that Oscar Wilde chose for his last days in Parisian exile the pseudonym Sebastian Melmoth.

Aodh de Blacam (in *A First Book of Irish Literature*) describes *Melmoth* as 'manifestly in the tradition of Swift'. He continues: 'In works like this we see a definite vein of Irish genius, a horrific imagination which dramatises the insane universe of the sceptic'.

De Blacam sees Maturin as the founder of a school of horror-fantasy writers in which he includes Sheridan Le Fanu and Bram Stoker.

Maturin was never to repeat the success of *Melmoth*. He wrote only one more novel in the Gothic vein entitled *The*

Albigenses, which was published in 1824. Scott wrote to him: 'there is in *The Albigenses*, as in all you write, the strongest traces of the *vis poetica*, enough to make the stock in trade of a dozen modern rhymers'.

On October 30, 1824, Maturin died at the age of 44 in Dublin, leaving a widow and four children, the youngest only five years old. His widow wrote to Scott on November 11: 'he laboured with incessant assiduity for his family even after it had pleased the Almighty to deprive him of his health — his sufferings with regard to pecuniary circumstances preyed on a constitution naturally delicate, till at last it put a period to his existance'.

Of his children, his son Edward, born in Dublin in 1812, continued the literary tradition. Educated at Trinity, he emigrated to America and became professor of Greek at Charleston and then at New York. His novels included *The Irish Chieftain* (1848) and *Bianca* (1852). He died in New York in 1881.

Charles Robert Maturin was once described as a tall, slender, handsome man with large melancholy eyes, who dressed well when income allowed. He prided himself on his skill in dancing and always insisted that his wife wear rouge in spite of her naturally high colouring.

He preferred to compose his stories in a noisy room full of people, saying that a noisy argument was especially inspiring. He would cover his mouth with a paste made of flour and water, indicating that he was in the throes of composition and not to be disturbed.

If the weather was good he would compose on long walks. He once wrote: 'I compose on a long walk but the day must neither be too hot, nor cold; it must be reduced to that medium from which you feel no inconvenience one way or the other'.

Maturin was a lover of antiquity with a strange passion for exploring old and desolate houses. If, when out walking, he saw some ancient building that attracted him he would knock at the door and find some excuse for examining the interior.

Melmoth the Wanderer has not enjoyed the continued widespread success that its rival *Frankenstein* has. Critics and morticians of literature, such as myself, pay tribute to it but it is hardly ever read nowadays except by ardent fans of the genre. The last time it was published was in 1968.

Brian Cleeve has stated that Maturin is deserving of popular attention even today. 'Even during his lifetime,' Cleeve points out, 'when his books created a considerable stir of interest, they were comparatively little read, none reaching a second edition before his death in 1824 in Dublin'. Certainly, Maturin influenced very closely Sheridan Le Fanu but whether one could go as far as Aodh de Blacam and see a 'Maturin School' is a matter of debate.

In introducing his work I have decided to use an extract from *Melmoth* which I consider to be one of the most potent passages from the book, one which even today has not lost its power to evoke dread.

Melmoth begins with a deathbed scene; an old miser is dying of sheer fright because of something he has seen, coupled with a manuscript he has read and a family portrait which hangs in an obscure closet of his centuries old home in County Wicklow. The miser, old Melmoth, sends to Trinity College, Dublin, for his nephew John. When John Melmoth arrives he sees many uncanny things. The eyes of the portrait in the closet glow horribly and twice he sees a strange figure which resembles the man in the portrait. Under the picture is inscribed the name 'J. Melmoth, 1646'. The dying miser claims that this 'J. Melmoth' is still alive! The miser dies and John Melmoth is told, in his will, to destroy the portrait and a certain manuscript which he will find in a desk drawer.

Instead of destroying it, John Melmoth sits up in bed late one night to read its fading 17th century script . . . . .

from
MELMOTH THE WANDERER
Charles Maturin

Apparebat eidolon *senex.*
Pliny

HE MANUSCRIPT WAS DIS-coloured, obliterated, and mutilated beyond any that had ever before exercised the patience of a reader. Michaelis himself, scrutinizing into the pretended autograph of St Mark at Venice, never had a harder time of it. Melmoth could make out only a sentence here and there. The writer, it appeared, was an Englishman of the name of Stanton, who had travelled abroad shortly after the Restoration. Travelling was not then attended with the facilities which modern improvement has introduced, and scholars and literati, the intelligent, the idle, and the curious, wandered over the Continent for years, like *Tom Coryat*, though they had the modesty, on their return, to entitle the result of their multiplied observations and labours only 'crudities.'

Stanton, about the year 1676, was in Spain; he was, like most of the travellers of that age, a man of literature, intelligence, and curiosity, but ignorant of the language of the country, and fighting his way at times from convent to convent, in quest of what was called 'Hospitality,' that is, obtaining board and lodging on the condition of holding a debate in Latin, on some point theological or metaphysical, with any monk who would become the champion of the strife. Now, as the theology was Catholic, and the metaphysics Aristotelian, Stanton sometimes wished himself at the miserable Posada from whose filth and famine he had been fighting his escape; but though his reverend antagonists always denounced his creed, and comforted themselves, even in defeat, with the assurance that he must be damned, on the double score of his being a heretic and an Englishman, they were obliged to confess that his Latin was good, and his logic unanswerable; and he was allowed, in most cases, to sup and sleep in peace. This was not doomed to be his fate on the night of the 17th August 1677, when he found himself in the plains of Valencia, deserted by a cowardly guide, who had been terrified by the sight of a cross erected as a memorial of a murder, had slipped off his mule unperceived, crossing himself every step he took on his retreat from the heretic, and left Stanton amid the terrors of an approaching storm, and the dangers of an unknown country. The sublime and yet softened beauty of the scenery around, had filled the soul of Stanton with delight, and he enjoyed that delight as Englishmen generally do, silently.

The magnificent remains of two dynasties that had passed away, the ruins of Roman palaces, and of Moorish fortresses, were around and above him; — the dark and heavy thunder-clouds that advanced slowly, seemed like the shrouds of these spectres of departed greatness; they approached, but did not yet overwhelm or conceal them, as if nature herself was for once awed by the power of man; and far below, the lovely valley of Valencia blushed and burned in all the glory of sunset, like a bride receiving the last glowing kiss of the bridegroom before the approach of night. Stanton gazed around, The difference between the architecture of the Roman and Moorish ruins struck him. Among the former are the remains of a theatre, and something like a public place; the latter present only the remains of fortresses, embattled, castellated, and fortified from top to bottom, — not a loop-hole for pleasure to get in by, — the loop-holes were only for arrows; all denoted military power and despotic subjugation *á l'outrance*. The contrast might have pleased a philosopher, and he might have indulged in the reflection, that though the ancient Greeks and Romans were savages, (as Dr Johnson says all people who want a press must be, and he says truly), yet they were wonderful savages for their time, for they alone have left *traces of their taste for pleasure* in the countries they conquered, in their superb theatres, temples, (which were also dedicated to pleasure one way or another), and baths, while other conquering bands of savages never left any thing behind them but traces of their rage for power. So thought Stanton, as he still saw strongly defined, though darkened by the darkening clouds, the huge skeleton of a Roman amphitheatre, its arched and gigantic colonnades now admitting a gleam of light, and now commingling with the purple thunder-cloud; and now the solid and heavy mass of a Moorish fortress, no light playing between its impermeable walls, — the image of power, dark, isolated, impenatrable. Stanton forgot his cowardly guide, his loneliness, his danger amid an approaching storm and an inhospitable country, where his name and country would shut every door against him, and every peal of thunder would be supposed justified by the daring intrusion of a heretic in the dwelling of an *old Christian*, as the Spanish Catholics absurdly term themselves, to mark the distinction between them and the baptised Moors. — All this was forgot in contemplating the glorious and awful scenery before him, — light struggling with darkness, — and darkness menacing a light still more terrible, and announcing its menace in the blue and livid mass of cloud that hovered like a destroying angel in the air, its arrows aimed, but their direction awfully indefinite. But he ceased to forget these local and petty dangers, as the sublimity of romance would term them, when he saw the first flash of the lightning, broad and red as the banners of an insulting army whose motto is *Vae victis*, shatter to atoms the remains of a Roman tower; — the rifted stones rolled down the hill and fell at the feet of Stanton. He stood appalled, and, awaiting his summons from the Power in whose eye pyramids, palaces, and the worms whose toil has formed them, and the worms who toil out their existence under their shadow or their pressure, are perhaps all alike contemptible, he stood collected, and for a moment felt that defiance of danger which danger itself excites, and we love to encounter it as a physical enemy, to bid it 'do its worst,' and feel that its worst will perhaps be ultimately its best for us. He stood and saw another flash dart its bright, brief, and malignant glance over the ruins of ancient power, and the luxuriance of recent fertility. Singular contrast! The relics of art for ever decaying, — the productions of nature for ever renewed. — (Alas! for what purpose are they renewed, better than to mock at the perishable monuments which men try in vain to rival them by). The pyramids themselves must perish, but the grass that grows between their disjointed stones will be renewed from year to year. Stanton was thinking thus, when all power of thought was suspended, by seeing two persons bearing between them the body of a young, and apparently very lovely girl, who had been struck dead by the lightning. Stanton approached, and heard the voices of the bearers repeating, 'There is none who will mourn for her!' 'There is none who will mourn for her!' said other voices, as two more bore in their arms the blasted and blackened figure of what had once been a man, comely and graceful; — 'there is not *one* to mourn for her now!' They were lovers, and he had been consumed by the flash that had destroyed her, while in the act of endeavouring to defend her. As they were about to remove the bodies, a person approached with a calmness of step and demeanour, as if he were alone unconscious of danger, and incapable of fear; and after looking on them for some time, burst into a laugh so loud, wild, and protracted, that the peasants, starting with as much horror at the sound as at that of the storm, hurried away, bearing the corse with them. Even Stanton's fears were subdued by his astonishment, and, turning to the stranger who remained standing on the same spot, he asked the reason of such an outrage on humanity. The stranger, slowly turning round, and disclosing a countenance which —— (Here the manuscript was illegible for a few lines), said in

English —— (A long hiatus followed here, and the next passage that was legible, though it proved to be a continuation of the narrative, was but a fragment).

. . . .

. . . .

The terrors of the night rendered Stanton a sturdy and unappeasable applicant; and the shrill voice of the old woman, repeating, 'no heretic — no English — Mother of God protect us — avaunt Satan!' — combined with the clatter of the wooden casement (peculiar to the houses in Valencia) which she opened to discharge her volley of anathematization, and shut again as the lightning glanced through the aperture, were unable to repel his importunate request for admittance, in a night whose terrors ought to soften all the miserable petty local passions into one awful feeling of fear for the Power who caused it, and compassion for those who were exposed to it. — But Stanton felt there was something more than national bigotry in the exclamations of the old woman; there was a peculiar and personal horror of the English. — And he was right; but this did not diminish the eagerness of his . . . .

. . . .

The house was handsome and spacious, but the melancholy appearance of desertion . . . .

. . . .

— The benches were by the wall, but there were none to sit there; the tables were spread in what had been the hall, but it seemed as if none had gathered round them for many years; — the clock struck audibly, there was no voice of mirth or of occupation to drown its sound; time told his awful lesson to silence alone; — the hearths were black with fuel long since consumed; — the family portraits looked as if they were the only tenants of the mansion; they seemed to say, from their mouldering frames, 'there are none to gaze on us;' and the echo of the steps of Stanton and his feeble guide, was the only sound audible between the peals of thunder that rolled still awfully, but more distantly, — every peal like the exhausted murmurs of a spent heart. As they passed on, a shriek was heard. Stanton paused, and fearful images of the dangers to which travellers on the Continent are exposed in deserted and remote habitations, came into his mind. 'Don't heed it,' said the old woman, lighting him on with a miserable lamp; — 'it is only he.

. . . .

. . . .

The old woman having now satisfied herself, by ocular demonstration, that her English guest, even if he was the devil, had neither horn, hoof, or tail, that he could bear the sign of the cross without changing his form, and that, when he spoke, not a puff of sulphur came out of his mouth, began to take courage, and at length commenced her story, which, weary and comfortless as Stanton was, ...

. . . .

'Every obstacle was now removed; parents and relations at last gave up all opposition, and the young pair were united. Never was there a lovelier, — they seemed like angels who had only anticipated by a few years their celestial and eternal union. The marriage was solemnized with much pomp, and a few days after there was a feast in that very wainscotted chamber which you paused to remark was so gloomy. It was that night hung with rich tapestry, representing the exploits of the Cid, particularly that of his burning a few Moors who refused to renounce their accursed religion. They were represented beautifully tortured, writhing and howling, and 'Mahomet! Mahomet!' issuing out of their mouths, as they called on him in their burning agonies; — you could almost hear them scream. At the upper end of the room, under a splendid estrade, over which was an image of the blessed Virgin, sat Donna Isabella de Cardoza, mother of the bride, and near her Donna Ines, the bride, on rich almohadas; the bridegroom sat opposite her; and though they never spoke to each other, their eyes, slowly raised, but suddenly withdrawn, (those eyes that blushed), told to each other the delicious secret of their happiness. Don Pedro de Cardoza had assembled a large party in honour of his daughter's nuptials; among them was an Englishman of the name of *Melmoth*, a traveller; no one knew who had brought him there. He sat silent like the rest, while the iced waters and the sugared wafers were presented to the company. The night was intensely hot, and the moon glowed like a sun over the ruins of Saguntum; the embroidered blinds flapped heavily, as if the wind made an effort to raise them in vain, and then desisted.

(Another defect in the manuscript occurred here, but it was soon supplied).

. . . .

'The company were dispersed through various alleys of the garden; the bridegroom and bride wandered through one where the delicious perfume of the orange trees mingled itself with that of the myrtles in blow. On their return to the hall, both of them asked, Had the company heard the exquisite sounds that floated through the garden just before they quitted it? No one had heard them. They expressed their surprise. The Englishman had never quitted the hall; it was said he smiled with a most particular and extraordinary expression as the remark was made. His silence had been noticed before, but it was ascribed to his ignorance of the Spanish language, an ignorance that Spaniards are not anxious either to expose or remove by speaking to a stranger. The subject of the music was not again reverted to till the guests were seated at supper, when Donna Ines and her young husband, exchanging a smile of delighted surprise, exclaimed they heard the same delicious sounds floating round them. The guests listened, but no one else could hear it; — every one felt there was something extraordinary in this. Hush! was uttered by every voice almost at the same moment. A dead silence followed, — you would think, from their intent looks, that they listened with their very eyes. This deep silence, contrasted with the splendour of the feast, and the light effused from torches held by the domestics, produced a singular effect, — it seemed for some moments like an assembly of the dead. The silence was interrupted, though the cause of wonder had not ceased, by the entrance of Father Olavida, the Confessor of Donna Isabella, who had been called away previous to the feast, to administer extreme unction to a dying man in the neighbourhood. He was a priest of uncommon sanctity, beloved in the family, and respected in the neighbourhood, where he had displayed uncommon taste and talents for exorcism; — in fact, this was the good Father's *forte*, and he piqued himself on it accordingly. The devil never fell into worse hands than Father Olavida's, for when he was so contumacious as to resist Latin, and even the first verses of the Gospel of St John in Greek, which the good Father never had recourse to but in cases of extreme stubbornness and difficulty, — (here Stanton recollected the English story of the *Boy of Bilsdon*, and blushed even in Spain for his countrymen), — then he always applied to the Inquisition; and if the devils were ever so obstinate before, they were always seen to fly out of the possessed, just as, in the midst of their cries, (no doubt of blasphemy), they were tied to the stake. Some held out even till the flames surrounded them; but even the most stubborn must have been dislodged when the operation was over, for the devil himself could no longer tenant a crisp and glutinous lump of cinders. Thus Father Olavida's fame spread far and wide, and the Cardoza family had made uncommon interest to procure him for a Confessor, and happily succeeded. The ceremony he had just been performing, had cast a shade over the good Father's countenance, but it dispersed as he mingled among the guests, and was introduced to them. Room was soon made for him, and he happened accidentally to be seated opposite the Englishman. As the wine was presented to him, Father Olavida, (who, as I observed, was a man of singular sanctity), prepared to utter a short internal prayer. He hesitated, — trembled, — desisted; and, putting down the wine, wiped the drops from his fore-

head with the sleeve of his habit. Donna Isabella gave a sign to
a domestic, and other wine of a higher quality was offered to
him. His lips moved, as if in the effort to pronounce a bene-
diction on it and the company, but the effort again failed;
and the change in his countenance was so extraordinary, that it
was perceived by all the guests. He felt the sensation that his
extraordinary appearance excited, and attempted to remove it
by again endeavouring to lift the cup to his lips. So strong was
the anxiety with which the company watched him, that the
only sound heard in that spacious and crowded hall, was the
rustling of his habit, as he attempted to lift the cup to his
lips once more — in vain. The guests sat in astonished silence.
Father Olavida alone remained standing; but at that moment
the Englishman rose, and appeared determined to fix Olavida's
regards by a gaze like that of fascination. Olavida rocked,
reeled, grasped the arm of a page, and at last, closing his eyes
for a moment, as if to escape the horrible fascination of that
unearthly glare, (the Englishman's eyes were observed by all the
guests, from the moment of his entrance, to effuse a most
fearful and preternatural lustre), exclaimed, 'Who is among us?
— Who? — I cannot utter a blessing while he is here. I cannot
feel one. Where he treads, the earth is parched! — Where he
breathes, the air is fire! — Where he feeds, the food is poison! —
Where he turns, his glance is lightning! — *Who is among us? —
Who?*' repeated the priest in the agony of adjuration, while his
cowl fallen back, his few thin hairs around the scalp instinct and
alive with terrible emotion, his outspread arms protruded from
the sleeves of his habit, and extended towards the awful
stranger, suggested the idea of an inspired being in the dreadful
rapture of prophetic denunciation. He stood — still stood, and
the Englishman stood calmly opposite to him. There was an
agitated irregularity in the attitudes of those around them,
which contrasted strongly the fixed and stern postures of those
two, who remained gazing silently at each other. 'Who knows
him?' exclaimed Olavida, starting apparently from a trance;
'who knows him? who brought him here?'
    The guests severally disclaimed all knowledge of the English-
man, and each asked the other in whispers, 'who *had* brought

him there?' Father Olavida then pointed his arm to each of the company, and asked each individually, 'Do you know him?' 'No! no! no!' was uttered with vehement emphasis by every individual. 'But I know him,' said Olavida, 'by these cold drops!' and he wiped them off; — 'by these convulsed joints!' and he attempted to sign the cross, but could not. He raised his voice, and evidently speaking with increased difficulty, — 'By this bread and wine, which the faithful receive as the body and blood of Christ, but which *his* presence converts into matter as viperous as the suicide foam of the dying Judas, — by all these — I know him, and command him to be gone! — He is — he is —' and he bent forwards as he spoke, and gazed on the Englishman with an expression which the mixture of rage, hatred, and fear, rendered terrible. All the guests rose at these words, — the whole company now presented two singular groupes, that of the amazed guests all collected together, and repeating, 'Who, what is he?' and that of the Englishman who stood unmoved, and Olavida, who dropped dead in the attitude of pointing to him ....

....

The body was removed into another room, and the departure of the Englishman was not noticed till the company returned to the hall. They sat late together, conversing on this extraordinary circumstance, and finally agreed to remain in the house, lest the evil spirit (for they believed the Englishman no better) should take certain liberties with the corse by no means agreeable to a Catholic, particularly as he had manifestly died without the benefit of the last sacraments. Just as this laudable resolution was formed, they were roused by cries of horror and agony from the bridal-chamber, where the young pair had retired.

They hurried to the door, but the father was first. They burst it open, and found the bride a corse in the arms of her husband.

....

He never recovered his reason; the family deserted the mansion rendered terrible by so many misfortunes. One apartment is still tenanted by the unhappy maniac; his were the cries you heard as you traversed the deserted rooms. He is for the most part silent during the day, but at midnight he always exclaims, in a voice frightfully piercing, and hardly human, 'They are coming! they are coming!' and relapses into profound silence.

The funeral of Father Olavida was attended by an extraordinary circumstance. He was interred in a neighbouring convent; and the reputation of his sanctity, joined to the interest caused by his extraordinary death, collected vast numbers at the ceremony. His funeral sermon was preached by a monk of distinguished eloquence, appointed for the purpose. To render the effect of his discourse more powerful, the corse, extended on a bier, with its face uncovered, was placed in the aisle. The monk took his text from one of the prophets, — 'Death is gone up into our palaces.' He expatiated on mortality, whose approach, whether abrupt or lingering, is alike awful to man. — He spoke of the vicissitudes of empires with much eloquence and learning, but his audience were not observed to be much affected. — He cited various passages from the lives of the saints, descriptive of the glories of martyrdom, and the heroism of those who had bled and blazed for Christ and his blessed mother, but they appeared still waiting for something to touch them more deeply. When he inveighed against the tyrants under whose bloody persecutions those holy men suffered, his hearers were roused for a moment, for its always easier to excite a passion than a moral feeling. But when he spoke of the dead, and pointed with emphatic gesture to the corse, as it lay before them cold and motionless, every eye was fixed, and every ear became attentive. Even the lovers, who, under pretence of dipping their fingers into the holy water, were contriving to exchange amorous billets, forbore for one moment this interesting intercourse, to listen to the preacher. He dwelt with much energy on the virtues of the deceased, whom he declared to be a particular favourite of the Virgin; and enumerating the various losses that would be caused by his departure to the community to which he belonged, to society, and to religion at large; he at last worked up himself to a vehement expostulation with the Deity on the occasion, 'Why has thou,' he exclaimed, 'why hast thou, Oh God! thus dealt with us? Why hast thou snatched from our sight this glorious saint, whose merits, if properly applied, doubtless would have been sufficient to atone for the apostacy of St Peter, the opposition of St Paul, (previous to his conversion), and even the treachery of Judas himself? Why hast thou, Oh God! snatched him from us?' — and a deep and hollow voice from among the congregation answered, — 'Because he deserved his fate.' The murmurs of approbation with which the congregation honoured this apostrophe, half-drowned this extraordinary interruption; and though there was some little commotion in the immediate vicinity of the speaker, the rest of the audience continued to listen intently. 'What,' proceeded the preacher, pointing to the corse, 'what hath laid thee there, servant of God?' — 'Pride, ignorance, and fear,' answered the same voice, in accents still more thrilling. The disturbance now became universal. The preacher paused, and a circle opening, disclosed the figure of a monk belonging to the convent, who stood among them. .

. . . .

After all the usual modes of admonition, exhortation, and discipline had been employed, and the bishop of the diocese, who, under the report of these extraordinary circumstances, had visited the convent in person to obtain some explanation from the contumacious monk in vain, it was agreed, in a chapter extraordinary, to surrender him to the power of the Inquisition. He testified great horror when this determination was made known to him, — and offered to tell over and over again all that he *could* relate of the cause of Father Olavida's death. His humiliation, and repeated offers of confession, came too late. He was conveyed to the Inquisition. The proceedings of that tribunal are rarely disclosed, but there is a secret report (I cannot answer for its truth) of what he said and suffered there. On his first examination, he said he would relate all he could. He was told that was not enough, he must relate all he knew.

. . . .

'Why did you testify such horror at the funeral of Father Olavida?' — 'Every one testified horror and grief at the death of that venerable ecclesiastic, who died in the odour of sanctity. Had I done otherwise, it might have been reckoned a proof of my guilt.' 'Why did you interrupt the preacher with such extraordinary exclamations?' — To this no answer. 'Why do you refuse to explain the meaning of those exclamations?' — No answer. 'Why do you persist in this obstinate and dangerous silence? Look, I beseech you, brother, at the cross that is suspended against this wall,' and the Inquisitor pointed to the large black crucifix at the back of the chair where he sat; 'one drop of the blood shed there can purify you from all the sin you have ever committed; but all that blood, combined with the intercession of the Queen of Heaven, and the merits of all its martyrs, nay, even the absolution of the Pope, cannot deliver you from the curse of dying in unrepented sin.' — 'What sin, then, have I committed?' 'The greatest of all possible sins; you refuse answering the questions put to you at the tribunal of the most holy and merciful Inquisition; — you will not tell us what you know concerning the death of Father Olavida.' — 'I have told you that I believe he perished in consequence of his ignorance and presumption.' 'What proof can you produce of that?' — 'He sought the knowledge of a secret withheld from man.' 'What was that?' — 'The secret of discovering the presence or agency of the evil power.' 'Do you possess that secret?' — After much agitation on the part of the prisoner, he said distinctly, but very faintly, 'My master forbids me to disclose it.' 'If your master were Jesus Christ, he would not forbid you to obey the commands or answer the questions of the Inquisition.' — 'I am not sure of that.' There was a general outcry of horror at these words. The examination then went on. 'If you believed Olavida to be guilty of any pursuits or studies condemned by our mother the church, why did you not denounce him to the Inquisition?' — 'Because I believed him not likely to be injured by such pursuits; his mind was too weak, — he died in the struggle,' said the prisoner with great emphasis. 'You believe, then, it requires strength of mind to keep those abominable secrets, when examined as to their nature and tendency?' — 'No, I rather imagine strength of body.' 'We shall try that presently,' said an Inquisitor, giving a signal for the torture. ....

....

The prisoner underwent the first and second applications with unshrinking courage, but on the infliction of the water-torture, which is indeed insupportable to humanity, either to suffer or relate, he exclaimed in the gasping interval, he would disclose everything. He was released, refreshed, restored, and the following day uttered the following remarkable confession. ...

....

The old Spanish woman further confessed to Stanton, that ....

.... and

that the Englishman certainly had been seen in the neighbour-hood since. — Seen, as she had heard, that very night. 'Great G—d!' exclaimed Stanton, as he recollected the stranger whose demoniac laugh had so appalled him, while gazing on the lifeless bodies of the lovers, whom the lightning had struck and blasted.

As the manuscript, after a few blotted and illegible pages, became more distinct, Melmoth read on, perplexed and unsatis-fied, not knowing what connexion this Spanish story could have with his ancestor, whom, however, he recognised under the title of *the Englishman*; and wondering how Stanton could have thought it worth his while to follow him to Ireland, write a long manuscript about an event that occurred in Spain, and leave it in the hands of his family, to 'verify untrue things,' in the language of Dogberry, — his wonder was diminished, though his curiosity was still more inflamed, by the perusal of the next lines, which he made out with some difficulty. It seems Stanton was now in England.

About the year 1677, Stanton was in London, his mind still full of his mysterious countryman. This constant subject of his

contemplations had produced a visible change in his exterior, —
his walk was what Sallust tells us of Catiline's, — his were, too,
the *'faedi oculi.'* He said to himself every moment, 'If I could
but trace that being, I will not call him man,' — and the next
moment he said, 'and what if I could?' In this state of mind, it
is singular enough that he mixed constantly in public
amusements, but it is true. When one fierce passion is
devouring the soul, we feel more than ever the necessity of
external excitement; and our dependence on the world for
temporary relief increases in direct proportion to our contempt
of the world and all its works. He went frequently to the
theatres, *then* fashionable, when

'The fair sat panting at a courtier's play,
And not a mask went unimproved away.'

The London theatres then presented a spectacle which ought
for ever to put to silence the foolish outcry against progressive
deterioration of morals, — foolish even from the pen of Juvenal,
and still more so from the lips of a modern Puritan. Vice is
always nearly on an average: The only difference in life worth
tracing, is that of manners, and there we have manifestly the
advantage of our ancestors. Hypocrisy is said to be the homage
that vice pays to virtue, — decorum is the outward expression of
that homage; and if this be so, we must acknowledge that vice
has latterly grown very humble indeed. There was, however,
something splendid, ostentatious, and obtrusive, in the vices of
Charles the Second's reign. — A view of the theatres alone
proved it, when Stanton was in the habit of visiting them. At
the doors stood on one side the footmen of a fashionable
nobleman, (with arms concealed under their liveries), surrounding the sedan of a popular actress[1], whom they were
to carry off *vi et armis*, as she entered it at the end of the play.
At the other side waited the *glass coach* of a woman of fashion,
who waited to take Kynaston (the Adonis of the day), in his
female dress, to the park after the play was over, and exhibit

him in all the luxurious splendour of effeminate beauty, (heightened by theatrical dress), for which he was so distinguished.

Plays being then performed at four o'clock, allowed ample time for the evening drive, and the midnight assignation, when the parties met by torch-light, masked, in St James's park, and verified the title of Wycherly's play, 'Love in a Wood.' The boxes, as Stanton looked round him, were filled with females, whose naked shoulders and bosoms, well testified in the paintings of Lely, and the pages of Grammont, might save modern puritanism many a vituperative groan and affected reminiscence. They had all taken the precaution to send some male relative, on the first night of a new play, to report whether it was fit for persons of 'honour and reputation' to appear at; but in spite of this precaution, at certain passages (which occurred about every second sentence) they were compelled to spread out their fans, or play with the still cherished love-lock, which Prynne himself had not been able to write down.

The men in the boxes were composed of two distinct classes, the 'men of wit and pleasure about town,' distinguished by their Flanders lace cravats, soiled with snuff, their diamond rings, the pretended gift of a royal mistress, (*n'importe* whether the Duchess of Portsmouth or Nell Gwynne); their uncombed wigs, whose curls descended to their waists, and the loud and careless tone in which they abused Dryden, Lee, and Otway, and quoted Sedley and Rochester; — the other class were the lovers, the gentle 'squires of dames,' equally conspicuous for their white fringed gloves, their obsequious bows, and their commencing every sentence addressed to a lady, with the profane exclamation of [2] 'Oh Jesu!' or the softer, but equally unmeaning one of 'I beseech you, Madam,' or, 'Madam, I burn.'[3] One circumstance sufficiently extraordinary marked the manners of the day; females had not then found their proper level in life; they were alternately adored as goddesses, and assailed as prostitutes; and the man who, this moment, addressed his mistress in language borrowed from Orondates worshipping Cassandra, in the next accosted her with ribaldry that might put to the blush the piazzas of Covent Garden.[4]

The pit presented a more various spectacle. There were the
critics armed cap-a-pee from Aristotle and Bossu; these men
dined at twelve, dictated at a coffee-house till four, then called
to the boy to brush their shoes, and strode to the theatre,
where, till the curtain rose, they sat hushed in grim repose, and
expecting their evening prey. There were the templars, spruce,
pert, and loquacious; and here and there a sober citizen, doffing
his steeple-crowned hat, and hiding his little band under the
folds of his huge puritanic cloke, while his eyes, declined with
an expression half leering, half ejaculatory, towards a masked
female, muffled in a hood and scarf, testified what had seduced
him into these 'tents of Kedar.' There were females, too, but
all in vizard masks, which, though worn as well as aunt Dinah's
in Tristram Shandy, served to conceal them from the 'young
bubbles' they were in quest of, and from all but the orange-
women, who hailed them loudly as they passed the doors.[5] In
the galleries were the happy souls who waited for the fulfilment
of Dryden's promise in one of his prologues[6]; no matter to
them whether it were the ghost of Almanzor's mother in her
dripping shroud, or that of Laius, who, according to the stage
directions, rises in his chariot, armed with the ghosts of his
three murdered attendants behind him; — a joke that did not
escape l'Abbe le Blanc[7], in his recipe for writing an English
tragedy. Some, indeed, from time to time called out for the
'burning of the Pope;' but though

> 'Space was obedient to the boundless piece,
> Which oped in Mexico and closed in Greece,'

It was not always possible to indulge them in this laudable
amusement, as the scene of the popular plays was generally laid
in Africa or Spain; Sir Robert Howard, Elkanah Settle, and
John Dryden, all agreeing in their choice of Spanish and
Moorish subjects for their principal plays. Among this joyous
groupe were seated several women of fashion masked, enjoying
in secrecy the licentiousness which they dared not openly
patronise, and verifying Gay's characteristic description, though
it was written many years later,

'Mobbed in the gallery Laura sits secure,
And laughs at jests that turn the box demure.'

Stanton gazed on all this with the look of one who 'could not be moved to smile at any thing.' He turned to the stage, the play was Alexander, then acted as written by Lee, and the principal character was performed by Hart, whose god-like ardour in making love, is said almost to have compelled the audience to believe that they beheld the 'son of Ammon.'

There were absurdities enough to offend a classical, or even a rational spectator. There were Grecian heroes with roses in their shoes, feathers in their hats, and wigs down to their waists; and Persian princesses in stiff stays and powdered hair. But the illusion of the scene was well sustained, for the heroines were rivals in real as well as theatrical life. It was that memorable night, when, according to the history of the veteran Betterton[8], Mrs Barry, who personated Roxana, had a green-room squabble with Mrs Bowtell, the representative of Statira, about a veil, which the partiality of the property-man adjudged to the latter. Roxana suppressed her rage till the fifth act, when, stabbing Statira, she aimed the blow with such force as to pierce through her stays, and inflict a severe though not dangerous wound. Mrs Bowtell fainted, the performance was suspended, and, in the commotion which this incident caused in the house, many of the audience rose, and Stanton among them. It was at this moment that, in a seat opposite to him, he discovered the object of his search for four years, — the Englishman whom he had met in the plains of Valencia, and whom he believed the same with the subject of the extraordinary narrative he had heard there.

He was standing up. There was nothing particular or remarkable in his appearance, but the expression of his eyes could never be mistaken or forgotten. The heart of Stanton palpitated with violence, — a mist overspread his eyes, — a nameless and deadly sickness, accompanied with a creeping sensation in every pore, from which cold drops were gushing, announced the . . . .
. . . .

Before he had well recovered, a strain of music, soft, solemn, and delicious, breathed round him, audibly ascending from the ground, and increasing in sweetness and power till it seemed to fill the whole building. Under the sudden impulse of amazement and pleasure, he inquired of some around him from whence those exquisite sounds arose. But, by the manner in which he was answered, it was plain that those he addressed considered him insane; and, indeed, the remarkable change in his expression might well justify the suspicion. He then remembered that night in Spain, when the same sweet and mysterious sounds were heard only by the young bridegroom and bride, of whom the latter perished on that very night. 'And am I then to be the next victim?' thought Stanton; 'and are those celestial sounds, that seem to prepare us for heaven, only intended to announce the presence of an incarnate fiend, who mocks the devoted with "airs from heaven", while he prepares to surround them with "blasts from hell"?' It is very singular that at this moment, when his imagination had reached its highest pitch of elevation, — when the object he had pursued so long and fruitlessly, had in one moment become as it were tangible to the grasp both of mind and body, — when this spirit, with whom he had wrestled in darkness, was at last about to declare its name that Stanton began to feel a kind of disappointment at the futility of his pursuits, like Bruce at discovering the source of the Nile, or Gibbon on concluding his History. The feeling which he had dwelt on so long, that he had actually converted it into a duty, was after all mere curiosity; but what passion is more insatiable, or more capable of giving a kind of romantic grandeur to all its wanderings and eccentricities? Curiosity is in one respect like love, it always compromises between the object and the feeling; and provided the latter possesses sufficient energy, no matter how contemptible the former may be. A child might have smiled at the agitation of Stanton, caused as it was by the accidental appearance of a stranger; but no man, in the full energy of his passions, was there, but must have trembled at the horrible agony of emotion with which he felt approaching, with sudden and irresistible velocity, the crisis of his destiny.

When the play was over, he stood for some moments in

the deserted streets. It was a beautiful moonlight night, and he saw near him a figure, whose shadow, projected half across the street, (there were no flagged ways then, chains and posts were the only defense of the foot passenger), appeared to him of gigantic magnitude. He had been so long accustomed to contend with those phantoms of the the imagination, that he took a kind of stubborn delight in subduing them. He walked up to the object, and observing the shadow only was magnified, and the figure was the ordinary height of man, he approached it, and discovered the very object of his search, — the man whom he had seen for a moment in Valencia, and after a search of four years, recognized at the theatre. . . . .

. . . .

‘You were in quest of me?’ — ‘I was.’ ‘Have you any thing to inquire of me?’ — ‘Much.’ ‘Speak, then,’ — ‘This is no place.’ ‘No place! poor wretch, I am independent of time and place. Speak, if you have any thing to ask or to learn?’ — ‘I have many things to ask, but nothing to learn, I hope, from you.’ ‘You deceive yourself, but you will be undeceived when next we meet. — ‘And when shall that be?’ said Stanton, grasping his arm; ‘name your hour and place.’ ‘The hour shall be mid-day,’ answered the stranger, with a horrid and unintelligible smile; ‘and the place shall be the bare walls of a madhouse, where you shall rise rattling in your chains, and rustling from your straw, to greet me,—yet still you shall have the *curse of sanity* and of memory. My voice shall ring in your ears till then, and the glance of these eyes shall be reflected from every object animate or inaminate till you behold them again.’ — ‘It is under circumstances so horrible we are to meet again?’ said Stanton, shrinking under the full-lighted blaze of those demon eyes. ‘I never,’ said the stranger in an emphatic tone, — ‘I *never desert my friends in misfortune.* When they are plunged in the lowest abyss of human calamity, *they are sure to be visited by me.*’. . .

. . . .

The narrative, when Melmoth was again able to trace its continuation, described Stanton, some years after, plunged in a state the most deplorable.

He had been always reckoned of a singular turn of mind, and the belief of this, aggravated by his constant talk of Melmoth, his wild pursuit of him, his strange behaviour at the theatre, and his dwelling on the various particulars of their extraordinary meetings, with all the intensity of the deepest conviction, (while he never could impress them on any one's conviction but his own), suggested to some prudent people the idea that he was deranged. Their malignity probably took part with their prudence. The selfish Frenchman[9] says, we feel a pleasure even in the misfortunes of our friends – *a plus forte* in those of our enemies; and as every one is an enemy of a man of genius of course, the report of Stanton's malady was propagated with infernal and successful industry. Stanton's next relative, a needy unprincipled man, watched the report in its circulation, and saw the snares closing around his·victim. He waited on him one morning, accompanied by a person of a grave, though somewhat repulsive appearance. Stanton was as usual abstracted and restless, and after a few moments conversation, he proposed a drive a few miles out of London, which he said would revive and refresh him. Stanton objected, on account of the difficulty getting a hackney coach, (for it is singular that at this period the number of private equipages, though infinitely fewer than they are now, exceeded the number of hired ones), and proposed going by water. This, however did not suit the kinsman's views; and after pretending to send for a carriage, (which was in waiting at the end of the street), Stanton and his companions entered it, and drove about two miles out of London.

The carriage then stopped. 'Come, Cousin,' said the younger Stanton, – 'come and view a purchase I have made.' Stanton absently alighted, and followed him across a small paved court; the other person followed. 'In troth, Cousin,' said Stanton, 'your choice appears not to have been discreetly made; your house has something of a gloomy aspect. – 'Hold your content, Cousin,' replied the other; 'I shall take order that you like it better when you have been some time a dweller therein.' Some attendants of a mean appearance, and with most suspicious visages, awaited them on their entrance, and they ascended a narrow staircase, which led to a room meanly furnished. 'Wait here,' said the kinsman, to the man who accompanied them, 'till I go for company to divertise my cousin in his loneliness.' They were left alone. Stanton took no notice of his companion, but as usual seized the first book near him, and began to read. It was a volume in manuscript, — they were then much more common than now.

The first lines struck him as indicating insanity in the writer. It was a wild proposal (written apparently after the great fire of London) to rebuild it with stone, and attempting to prove, on a calculation wild, false, and yet sometimes plausible, that this could be done out of the colossal fragments of Stonehenge, which the writer proposed to remove for that purpose. Subjoined were several grotesque drawings of engines designed to remove those massive blocks, and in a corner of the page was a note, — 'I would have drawn these more accurately, but was not allowed a knife to mend my pen.'

The next was entitled, 'A modest proposal for the spreading of Christianity in foreign parts, whereby it is hoped its entertainment will become general all over the world.' — This modest proposal was, to convert the Turkish ambassadors, (who had been in London a few years before), by offering them their choice of being strangled on the spot, or becoming Christians. Of course the writer reckoned on their embracing the easier alternative, but even this was to be clogged with a heavy condition, — namely, that they must be bound before a magistrate to convert twenty mussulmans a day, on their return to Turkey. The rest of the pamphlet was reasoned very much in the conclusive style of Captain Bobadil, — these twenty will convert twenty more a piece, and these two hundred converts, converting their due number in the same time, all Turkey would be converted before the Grand Signior knew where he was. Then comes the *coup d'eclat*, — one fine morning, every minaret in Constantinople was to ring out with bells, instead of the cry of the Muezzins; and the Imaum, coming out to see what was the matter, was to be encountered by the Archbishop of Canterbury, *in pontificalibus*, performing Cathedral service in the church of St Sophia, which was to finish the business. Here an objection appeared to arise, which the ingenuity of the writer had anticipated. — 'It may be redargued,' saith he, 'by those who have more spleen than brain, that forasmuch as the Archbishop preacheth in English, he will not thereby much edify the Turkish folk, who do altogether hold in a vain gabble of their own.' But this (to use his own language) he 'evites,' by judiciously observing, that where service was performed in an unknown tongue, the devotion of the people was always observed to be much increased thereby; as, for instance, in the church of Rome, — that St Augustine, with his monks, advanced to meet King Ethelbert singing litanies, (in a language his majesty could not possibly have understood), and converted him and his whole court on the spot; — that the sybilline books

. . . .

Cum multis aliis.

Between the pages were cut most exquisitely in paper the likenesses of some of these Turkish ambassadors; the hair of the beards, in particular, was feathered with a delicacy of touch that seemed the work of fairy fingers, — but the pages ended with a complaint of the operator, that his *scissars had been taken from him*. However, he consoled himself and the reader with the assurance that he would that night catch a moon-beam as it entered through the grating, and, when he had whetted it on the iron knobs of his door, would do wonders with it. In the next page was found a melancholy proof of powerful but prostrated intellect. It contained some insane lines, ascribed to Lee the dramatic poet, commencing,

'O that my lungs could bleat like buttered pease,' &c.

There is no proof whatever that these miserable lines were really written by Lee, except that the measure is the fashionable quatrain of the period. It is singular that Stanton read on without suspicion of his own danger, quite absorbed in *the album of a mad-house*, without ever reflecting on the place where he was, and which such compositions too manifestly designated.

It was after a long interval that he looked round, and perceived that his companion was gone. Bells were unusual then. He proceeded to the door, — it was fastened. He called

aloud, — his voice was echoed in a moment by many others, but in tones so wild and discordant, that he desisted in involuntary terror. As the day advanced, and no one approached, he tried the window, and then perceived for the first time it was grated. It looked out on the narrow flagged yard, in which no human being was; and if there had, from such a being no human feeling could have been extraced.

Sickening with unspeakable horror, he sunk rather than sat down beside the miserable window, and 'wished for day.'

At midnight he started from a doze, half a swoon, half a sleep, which probably the hardness of his seat, and of the deal table on which he leaned, had not contributed to prolong.

He was in complete darkness; the horror of his situation struck him at once, and for a moment he was indeed almost qualified for an inmate of that dreadful mansion. He felt his way to the door, shook it with desperate strength, and uttered the most frightful cries, mixed with expostulations and commands. His cries were in a moment echoed by a hundred voices. In maniacs there is a peculiar malignity, accompanied by an extraordinary acuteness of some of the senses, particularly in distinguishing the voice of a stranger. The cries that he heard on every side seemed like a wild and infernal yell of joy, that their mansion of misery had obtained another tenant.

He paused, exhausted, — a quick and thundering step was heard in the passage. The door was opened, and a man of savage appearance stood at the entrance, — two more were seen indistinctly in the passage. — 'Release me, villain!' 'Stop, my fine fellow, what's all this noise for?' 'Where am I?' 'Where you ought to be.' 'Will you dare to detain me?' 'Yes, and a little more than that,' answered the ruffian, applying a loaded horse-whip to his back and shoulders, till the patient soon fell to the ground convulsed with rage and pain. 'Now you see you are where you ought to be,' repeated the ruffian, brandishing the horse-whip over him, 'and now take the advice of a friend, and make no more noise. The lads are ready for you with the darbies, and they'll clink them on in the crack of this whip, unless you prefer another touch of it first.' They then were advancing into the room as he spoke, with fetters in their hands, (strait waistcoats being then little known or used), and shewed, by their frightful countenances and gestures, no unwillingness to apply them. Their harsh rattle on the stone pavement made Stanton's blood run cold; the effect, however, was useful. He had the presence of mind to acknowledge his (supposed) miserable condition, to supplicate the forbearance of the ruthless keeper, and promise complete submission to his orders. This pacified the ruffian, and he retired.

Stanton collected all his resolution to encounter the horrible night; he saw all that was before him, and summoned himself to meet it. After much agitated deliberation, he conceived it best to continue the same appearance of submission and tranquillity, hoping that thus he might in time either propitiate the wretches in whose hands he was, or, by his apparent inoffensiveness, procure such opportunities of indulgence, as might perhaps ultimately facilitate his escape. He therefore determined to conduct himself with the utmost tranquillity, and never to let his voice be heard in the house; and he laid down several other resolutions with a degree of prudence which he already shuddered to think might be the cunning of incipient madness, or the beginning results of the horrid habits of the place.

These resolutions were put to desperate trial that very night. Just next to Stanton's apartment were lodged two most un-congenial neighbours. One of them was a puritanical weaver, who had been driven mad by a single sermon from the celebrated Hugh Peters, and was sent to the mad-house as full of election and reprobation as he could hold, — and fuller. He regularly repeated over the *five points* while day-light lasted, and imagined himself preaching in a conventicle with distinguished success; towards twilight his visions were more gloomy, and at midnight his blasphemies became horrible. In the opposite cell was lodged a loyalist tailor, who had been ruined by giving credit to the cavaliers and their ladies, — (for at this time, and much later, down to the reign of Anne, tailors were employed by females even *to make* and *fit on their stays*), — who had run mad with drink and loyalty on thé burning of the Rump, and ever since had made the cells of the madhouse echo with fragments of the ill-fated Colonel Lovelace's songs, scraps from Cowley's 'Cutter of Coleman street,' and some curious specimens from Mrs Aphra Behn's plays, where the cavaliers are denominated the *heroicks*, and Lady Lambert and Lady Desborough represented as going to meeting, their large Bibles carried before them by their pages, and falling in love with two banished cavaliers by the way. — 'Tabitha, Tabitha,' cried a voice half in exultation and half in derision; 'thou shalt go with thy hair curled, and thy breasts naked;' — and then added in an affected voice, — 'I could dance the Canaries once, spouse.' This never failed to rouse the feelings, or rather operate on the instincts of the puritanic weaver, who immediately answered, 'Colonel Harrison shall come out of the west, riding on a sky-coloured mule, which signifies instruction.'[10] 'Ye lie, ye round-head son of a b——h,' roared the cavalier tailor, 'Colonel Harrison will be damned before he ever mounts a sky-coloured mule;' and he concluded this pithy sentence with fragments of anti-Oliverian songs.

> 'And may I live to see
> Old Noll upon a tree,
> And many such as he;
> Confound him, confound him,
> Diseases all around him.'

'Ye are honest gentlemen, I can play many tunes,' squeaked a poor mad loyalist fiddler, who had been accustomed to play in the taverns to the cavalier party, and just remembered the words of a similar minstrel playing for Colonel Blunt in the committee. 'Then play me the air to 'Rebellion is breaking up house,' exclaimed the tailor, dancing wildly about his cell (as far as his chains allowed him) to an imaginary measure. The weaver could contain no longer. 'How long, Lord, how long,' he exclaimed, 'shall thine enemies insult thy sanctuary, in which I have been placed an anointed teacher? even here, where I am placed to preach to the souls in prison? — Open the flood-gates of thy power, and though thy waves and storms go over me, let

me testify in the midst of them, even as he who spreadeth forth
his hands to swim may raise one of them to warn his companion
that he is about to sink. — Sister Ruth, why does thou uncover
thy bosom to discover my frailty? — Lord, let thine arm of
power be with us as it was when thou brakest the shield, the
sword, and the battle. — when thy foot was dipped in the blood
of thine enemies, and the tongue of thy dogs was red through
the same. — Dip all thy garments in blood, and let me weave
thee fresh when thou art stained. — When shall thy saints tread
the winepress of thy wrath? Blood! blood! the saints call for
it, earth gapes to swallow it, hell thirsts for it! — Sister Ruth, I
pray thee, conceal thy bosom, and be not as the vain women of
this generation. — Oh for a day like that, a day of the Lord of
hosts, when the towers fell! — Spare me in the battle, for I am
not a mighty man of war; leave me in the rear of the host, to
curse, with the curse of Meroz, those who come not to the help
of the Lord against the mighty, — even to curse this malignant
tailor, — yea, curse him bitterly. — Lord, I am in the tents of
Kedar, my feet stumble on the dark mountains, — I fall, — I
fall!' — And the poor wretch, exhausted by his delirious
agonies, fell, and grovelled for some time in the straw. 'Oh! I
have had a grievous fall, — Sister Ruth, — Oh Sister Ruth! —
Rejoice not against me. Oh mine enemy! though I fall, I shall
rise again.' Whatever satisfaction Sister Ruth might have derived
from this assurance, if she could have heard it, was enjoyed
tenfold by the weaver, whose amorous reminiscences were in
a moment exchanged for war-like ones, borrowed from a
wretched and disarranged mass of intellectual rubbish. 'The
Lord is a man of war,' he shouted. — 'Look to Marston Moor! —
Look to the city, the proud city, full of pride and sin! — Look
to the waves of the Severn, as red with blood as the waves of
the Red Sea! — There were the hoofs broken by means of the
prancings, the prancings of the mighty ones. — Then, Lord, was
thy triumph, and the triumph of thy saints, to bind their kings
in chains, and their nobles in links of iron.' The malignant tailor
burst out in his turn: 'Thank the false Scots, and their solemn
league and covenant, and Carisbrook Castle, for that, ye crop-
eared Puritan,' he yelled. 'If it had not been for them, I would

have taken measure of the king for a velvet cloak as high as
the Tower of London, and one flirt of its folds would have
knocked the 'copper nose' into the Thames, and sent it a-
drift to Hell.' 'Ye lie, in your teeth,' echoed the weaver; 'and
I will prove it unarmed, with my shuttle against your needle,
and smite you to the earth thereafter, as David smote Goliah.
It was *the man's* (such was the indecent language in which
Charles the First was spoken of by the Puritans)—it was the
man's carnal, self-seeking, world-loving, prelatical hierarchy,
that drove the godly to seek the sweet word in season from
their own pastors, who righteously abominated the Popish
garniture of lawn-sleeves, lewd organs, and steeple houses.
Sister Ruth, tempt me not with that calf's head, it is all
streaming with blood; — drop it, I beseech thee, sister, it is
unmeet in a woman's hand, though the brethren drink of it. —
Woe be unto thee, gainsayer, dost thou not see how flames
envelope the accursed city under his Arminian and Popish
son? — London is on fire! — on fire!' he yelled; 'and the brands
are lit by the half-papist, whole-arminian, all-damned people
thereof. — Fire! — fire!' The voice in which he shrieked out the
last words was powerfully horrible, but it was like the moan of
an infant, compared to the voice which took up and re-echoed
the cry, in a tone that made the building shake. It was the voice
of a maniac, who had lost her husband, children, subsistence,
and finally her reason, in the dreadful fire of London. The cry
of fire never failed to operate with terrible punctuality on her
associations. She had been in a disturbed sleep, and now started
from it as suddenly as on that dreadful night. It was Saturday
night, too, and she was always observed to be particularly
violent on that night, — it was the terrible weekly festival of
insanity with her. She was awake, and busy in a moment escaping from the flames; and she dramatized the whole scene
with such hideous fidelity, that Stanton's resolution was far
more in danger from her than from the battle between his
neighbours *Testimony* and *Hothead*. She began exclaiming
she was suffocated by the smoke; then she sprung from her
bed, calling for a light, and appeared to be struck by the sudden
glare that burst through her casement. — 'The last day,' she

shrieked, 'The last day! The very heavens are on fire!' — 'That will not come till the Man of Sin be first destroyed,' cried the weaver; 'thou ravest of light and fire, and yet thou art in utter darkness. — I pity thee, poor mad soul, I pity thee!' The maniac never heeded him; she appeared to be scrambling up a stair-case to her children's room. She exclaimed she was scorched, singed, suffocated; her courage appeared to fail, and she retreated. 'But my children are there!' she cried in a voice of unspeakeable agony, as she seemed to make another effort; 'here I am — here I am come to save you. — Oh God! They are all blazing! — Take this arm — no, not that, it is scorched and disabled — well, any arm — take hold of my clothes — no, they are blazing too! — Well, take me all on fire as I am! — And their hair, how it hisses! — Water, one drop of water for my youngest — he is but an infant — for my youngest, and let me burn!' She paused in horrid silence, to watch the fall of a blazing rafter that was about to shatter the stair-case on which she stood. — 'The roof has fallen on my head!' she exclaimed. 'The earth is weak, and all the inhabitants thereof,' chaunted the weaver; 'I bear up the pillars of it.'

The maniac marked the destruction of the spot where she thought she stood by one desperate bound, accompanied by a wild shriek, and then calmly gazed on her infants as they rolled over the scorching fragments, and sunk into the abyss of fire below. 'There they go, — one — two — three — all!' and her voice sunk into low mutterings, and her convulsions into faint, cold shudderings, like the sobbings of a spent storm, as she imagined herself to 'stand in safety and despair,' amid the thousand houseless wretches assembled in the suburbs of London on the dreadful nights after the fire, without food, roof, or raiment, all gazing on the burning ruins of their dwellings and their property. She seemed to listen to their complaints, and even repeated some of them very affectingly, but invariably answered them with the same words, 'But I have lost all my children — *all!*' It was remarkable that when this sufferer began to rave, all the others became silent. The cry of nature hushed every other cry, — she was the only patient in the house who was not mad from politics, religion,

ebriety, or some perverted passion; and terrifying as the out-
break of her frenzy always was, Stanton used to await it as a
kind of relief from the dissonant, melancholy, and ludicrous
ravings of the others.

But the utmost efforts of his resolution began to sink under
the continued horrors of the place. The impression on his
senses began to defy the power of reason to resist them. He
could not shut out these frightful cries nightly repeated, nor the
frightful sound of the whip employed to still them. Hope began
to fail him, as he observed, that the submissive tranquillity
(which he had imagined, by obtaining increased indulgence,
might contribute to his escape, or perhaps convince the keeper
of his sanity) was interpreted by the callous ruffian, who was
acquainted only with the varieties of *madness*, as a more refined species of that cunning which he was well accustomed
to watch and baffle.

On his first discovery of his situation, he had determined to
take the utmost care of his health and intellect that the place
allowed, as the sole basis of his hope of deliverance. But as that
hope declined, he neglected the means of realizing it. He had at
first risen early, walked incessantly about his cell, and availed
himself of every opportunity of being in the open air. He took
the strictest care of his person in point of cleanliness, and with
or without appetite, regularly forced down his miserable meals;
and all these efforts were even pleasant, as long as hope
prompted them. But now he began to relax them all. He passed
half the day in his wretched bed, in which he frequently took
his meals, declined shaving or changing his linen, and, when the
sun shone into his cell, turned from it on his straw with a sigh
of heart-broken despondency. Formerly, when the air breathed
through his grating, he used to say, 'Blessed air of heaven, I
shall breathe you once more in freedom! — Reserve all your
freshness for that delicious evening when I shall inhale you,
and be as free as you myself.' Now when he felt it, he sighed
and said nothing. The twitter of the sparrows, the pattering
of rain, or the moan of the wind, sounds that he used to sit
up in his bed to catch with delight, as reminding him of nature,
were now unheeded.

He began at times to listen with sullen and horrible pleasure to the cries of his miserable companions. He became squalid, listless, torpid, and disgusting in his appearance.

It was one of those dismal nights, that, as he tossed on his loathsome bed, — more loathsome from the impossibility to quit it without feeling more 'unrest,' — he perceived the miserable light that burned in the hearth was obscured by the intervention of some dark object. He turned feebly towards the light, without curiosity, without excitement, but with a wish to diversify the monotony of his misery, by observing the slightest change made even accidentally in the dusky atmosphere of his cell. Between him and the light stood the figure of Melmoth, just as he had seen him from the first; the figure was the same, the expression of the face was the same, — cold, stony, and rigid; the eyes, with their infernal and dazzling lustre, were still the same.

Stanton's ruling passion rushed on his soul; he felt this apparition like a summons to a high and fearful encounter. He heard his heart beat audibly, and could have exclaimed with Lee's unfortunate heroine, — 'It pants as cowards do before a battle; Oh the great march has sounded!'

Melmoth approached him with that frightful calmness that mocks the terror it excites. 'My prophecy has been fulfilled; — you rise to meet me rattling from your chains, and rustling from your straw — am I not a true prophet?' Stanton was silent. 'Is not your situation very miserable?' — Still Stanton was silent; for he was beginning to believe this an illusion of madness. He thought to himself, 'How could he have gained entrance here?' — 'Would you not wish to be delivered from it?' Stanton tossed on his straw, and its rustling seemed to answer the question. 'I have the power to deliver you from it.' Melmoth spoke very slowly and very softly, and the melodious smoothness of his voice made a frightful contrast to the stony rigour of his features, and the fiend-like brilliancy of his eyes. 'Who are you, and whence come you?' said Stanton, in a tone that was meant to be interrogatory and imperative, but which, from his habits of squalid debility, was at once feeble and querulous. His intellect had become affected by the gloom of his miserable habitation, as the wretched inmate of a similar mansion, when produced before a medical examiner, was reported to be a complete Albinos. — 'His skin was bleached, his eyes turned white; he could not bear the light; and, when exposed to it, he turned away with a mixture of weakness and restlessness, more like the writhings of a sick infant than the struggles of a man.'

Such was Stanton's situation; he was enfeebled now, and the power of the enemy seemed without a possibility of opposition from either his intellect or corporeal powers . . . .

. . . .

Of all their horrible dialogue, only these words were legible in the manuscript, 'You know me now.' — 'I always knew you.' — 'That is false; you imagined you did, and that has been the cause of all the wild . . . .

. . . .

. . . .
of the . . . .
. . . . of your finally being lodged in this mansion of misery, where only I would seek, where only I can succour you.' 'You, demon!' — 'Demon! — Harsh words! — Was it a demon or a human being placed you here? — Listen to me, Stanton; nay, wrap not yourself in that miserable blanket, — that cannot shut out my words. Believe me, were you folded in thunder-clouds, you must hear *me!* Stanton, think of your misery. These bare walls — what do they present to the intellect or to the senses? — White-wash, diversified with the scrawls of charcoal or red chalk, that your happy predecessors have left for you to trace over. You have a taste for drawing, — I trust it will improve. And here's a grating, through which the sun squints on you like a step-dame, and the breeze blows, as if it meant to tantalize you with a sigh from that sweet mouth, whose kiss you must never enjoy. And where's your library, — intellectual man, — travelled man?' he repeated in a tone of bitter derision; 'where be your com-

panions, your peaked men of countries, as your favourite
Shakespeare has it? You must be content with the spider and
the rat, to crawl and scratch round your flock-bed! I have
known prisoners in the Bastile to feed them for companions, —
why don't you begin your task? I have known a spider to
descend at the tap of a finger, and a rat to come forth when the
daily meal was brought, to share it with his fellow-prisoner! —
How delightful to have vermin for your guests! Aye, and when
the feast fails them, they make a meal of their entertainer! —
You shudder — Are you, then, the first prisoner who has been
devoured alive by the vermin that infested his cell? — Delightful banquet, not 'where you eat, but where you are eaten!'
Your guests, however, will give you one token of repentance
while they feed; there will be *gnashing of teeth*, and you shall
hear it, and feel it too perchance! — And then for meals — Oh
you are daintily off! — The soup that the cat has lapped; and
(as her progeny has probably contributed to the hell-broth)
why not? — Then your hours of solitude, deliciously diversified by the yell of famine, the howl of madness, the crash of
whips, and the broken-hearted sob of those who, like you,
are supposed, or *driven* mad by the crimes of others! — Stanton,
do you imagine your reason can possibly hold out amid such
scenes? — Supposing your reason was unimpaired, your health
not destroyed, — suppose all this, which is, after all, more than
fair supposition can grant, guess the effect of the continuance
of these scenes on your senses alone. A time will come, and
soon, when, from mere habit, you will echo the scream of
every delirious wretch that harbours near you; then you will
pause, clasp your hands on your throbbing head, and listen
with horrible anxiety whether the scream proceeded from *you*
or *them*. The time will come, when, from the want of occupation, the listless and horrible vacancy of your hours, you
will feel as anxious to hear those shrieks, as you were at first
terrified to hear them, — when you will watch for the ravings
of your next neighbour, as you would for a scene on the stage.
All humanity will be extinguished in you. The ravings of these
wretches will become at once your sport and your torture.
You will watch for the sounds, to mock them with the grimaces

and bellowings of a fiend. The mind has a power of accommo-
dating itself to its situation, that you will experience in its most
frightful and deplorable efficacy. Then comes the dreadful
doubt of one's own sanity, the terrible announcer that *that*
doubt will soon become fear, and *that* fear certainty. Perhaps
(still more dreadful) the *fear* will at last become a *hope*, —
shut out from society, watched by a brutal keeper, writhing
with all the impotent agony of an incarcerated mind without
communication and without sympathy, unable to exchange
ideas but with those whose ideas are only the hideous spectres
of departed intellect, or even to hear the welcome sound of the
human voice, except to mistake it for the howl of a fiend,
and stop the ear desecrated by its intrusion, — then at last
your fear will become a more fearful hope; you will wish to
become one of them, to escape the agony of consciousness.
As those who have long leaned over a precipice, have at last
felt a desire to plunge below, to relieve the intolerable temp-
tation of their giddiness[11], you will hear them laugh amid
their wildest paroxysms; you will say, 'Doubtless those wretches
have some consolation, but I have none; my sanity is my
greatest curse in this abode of horrors. They greedily devour
their miserable meals, while I loathe mine. They sleep sometimes soundly, while my sleep is — worse than their waking.
They are revived every morning by some delicious illusion of
cunning madness, soothing them with the hope of escaping,
baffling or tormenting their keeper; my sanity precludes all such
hope. *I know I never can escape*, and the preservation of my
faculties is only an aggravation of my sufferings. I have all their
miseries, — I have none of their consolations. They laugh, — I
hear them; would I could laugh like them.' You will try, and the
very effort will be an invocation to the demon of insanity to
come and take full possession of you from that moment for
ever.

(There were other details, both of the menaces and temp-
tations employed by Melmoth, which are too horrible for in-
sertion. One of them may serve for an instance).

'You think that the intellectual power is something distinct from the vitality of the soul, or, in other words, that if
even your reason should be destroyed, (which it nearly is),

your soul might yet enjoy beatitude in the full exercise of its enlarged and exalted faculties, and all the clouds which obscured them be dispelled by the Sun of Righteousness, in whose beams you hope to bask for ever and ever. Now, without going into any metaphysical subtleties about the distinction between mind and soul, experience must teach you, that there can be no crime into which madmen would not, and do not precipitate themselves; mischief is their occupation, malice their habit, murder their sport, and blasphemy their delight. Whether a soul in this state can be in a hopeful one, it is for you to judge; but it seems to me, that with the loss of reason, (and reason cannot long be retained in this place), you lose also the hope of immortality. — Listen,' said the tempter, pausing, 'listen to the wretch who is raving near you, and whose blasphemies might make a demon start. — He was once an eminent puritanical preacher. Half the day he imagines himself in a pulpit, denouncing damnation against Papists, Arminians, and even Sublapsarians, (he being a Supra-lapsarian himself). He foams, he writhes, he gnashes his teeth; you would imagine him in the hell he was painting, and that the fire and brimstone he is so lavish of, were actually exhaling from his jaws. At night his *creed retaliates on him*; he believes himself one of the reprobates he has been all day denouncing, and curses God for the very decree he has all day been glorifying Him for.

'He, whom he has for twelve hours been vociferating "is the loveliest among ten thousand," becomes the object of demoniac hostility and execration. He grapples with the iron posts of his bed, and says he is rooting out the cross from the very foundations of Calvary; and it is remarkable, that in proportion as his morning exercises are intense, vivid and eloquent, his nightly blasphemies are outrageous and horrible. — Hark! Now he believes himself a demon; listen to his diabolical eloquence of horror!'

Stanton listened, and shuddered . . . .

. . . .

'Escape — escape for your life,' cried the tempter; 'break forth into life, liberty, and sanity. Your social happiness, your intellectual powers, your immortal interests, perhaps, depend on the choice of this moment. — There is the door, and the key is my hand. Choose — choose!' — 'And how comes the key in your hand? and what is the condition of my liberation?' said Stanton. . . . .

. . . .

The explanation occupied several pages, which, to the torture of young Melmoth, were wholly illegible. It seemed, however, to have been rejected by Stanton with the utmost rage and horror, for Melmoth at last made out, — 'Begone, monster, demon! — begone to your native place. Even this mansion of horror trembles to contain you; its walls sweat, and its floors quiver, while you tread them.' . . . .

. . . .

The conclusion of this extraordinary manuscript was in such a state, that, in fifteen mouldy and crumbling pages, Melmoth could hardly make out that number of lines. No antiquarian, unfolding with trembling hand the calcined leaves of an Herculaneum manuscript, and hoping to discover some lost lines of the Aeneis in Virgil's own autograph, or at least some unutterable abomination of Petronius or Martial, happily elucidatory of the mysteries of the Spintriae, or the orgies of the Phallic worshippers, ever pored with more luckless diligence, or shook a head of more hopeless despondency over his task. He could but just make out what tended rather to excite than assuage that feverish thirst of curiosity which was consuming his inmost soul. The manuscript told no more of Melmoth, but mentioned that Stanton was finally liberated from his confinement, — that his pursuit of Melmoth was incessant and indefatigable, — that he himself allowed it to be a species of insanity, — that while he acknowledged it to be the master-passion, he also felt it the master-torment of his life. He again visited the Continent, returned to England, — pursued, in-

quired, traced, bribed, but in vain. The being whom he had met
thrice, under circumstances so extraordinary, he was fated never
to encounter again *in his life-time.* At length, discovering that
he had been born in Ireland, he resolved to go there, — went,
and found his pursuit again fruitless, and his inquiries un-
answered. The family knew nothing of him, or at least what
they knew or imagined, they prudently refused to disclose to
a stranger, and Stanton departed unsatisfied. It is remarkable,
that he too, as appeared from many half-obliterated pages of
the manuscript, never disclosed to mortals the particulars of
their conversation in the mad-house; and the slightest allusion
to it threw him into fits of rage and gloom equally singular
and alarming. He left the manuscript, however, in the hands of
the family, possibly deeming, from their incuriosity, their
apparent indifference to their relative, or their obvious in-
acquaintance with reading of any kind, manuscript or books,
his deposit would be safe. He seems, in fact, to have acted like
men, who, in distress at sea, intrust their letters and dispatches
to a bottle sealed, and commit it to the waves. The last lines
of the manuscript that were legible, were sufficiently extra-
ordinary . . . .

. . . .

'I have sought him everywhere. — The desire of meeting him
once more, is become as a burning fire within me, — it is the
necessary condition of my existence. I have vainly sought him
at last in Ireland, of which I find he is a native. — Perhaps our
final meeting will be in . . . .

Such was the conclusion of the manuscript which Melmoth
found in his uncle's closet. When he had finished it, he sunk
down on the table near which he had been reading it, his face
hid in his folded arms, his senses reeling, his mind in a mingled
state of stupor and excitement. After a few moments, he raised
himself with an involuntary start, and saw the picture gazing at
him from its canvas. He was within ten inches of it as he sat,
and the proximity appeared increased by the strong light that

was accidentally thrown on it, and its being the only re-
presentation of a human figure in the room. Melmoth felt for a
moment as if he were about to receive an explanation from its
lips.

He gazed on it in return, — all was silent in the house, — they
were alone together. The illusion subsided at length; and as the
mind rapidly passes to opposite extremes, he remembered the
injunction of his uncle to destroy the portrait. He seized it; —
his hand shook at first, but the mouldering canvas appeared to
assist him in the effort. He tore it from the frame with a cry
half terrific, half triumphant; — it fell at his feet, and he
shuddered as it fell. He expected to hear some fearful sounds,
some unimaginable breathings of prophetic horror, follow this
act of sacrilege, for such he felt it, to tear the portrait of his
ancestor from his native walls. He paused and listened: — 'There
was no voice, nor any that answered;' — but as the wrinkled and
torn canvas fell to the floor, its undulations gave the appearance
of smiling. Melmoth felt horror indescribable at this transient
and imaginary resuscitation of the figure. He caught it up, rushed
into the next room, tore, cut, and hacked it in every direction,
and eagerly watched the fragments that burned like tinder in
the turf-fire which had been lit in his room. As Melmoth saw
the last blaze he threw himself into bed, in hope of a deep
and intense sleep. He had done what was required of him, and
felt exhausted both in mind and body; but his slumber was not
so sound as he had hoped for. The sullen light of the turf-fire,
burning but never blazing, disturbed him every moment. He
turned and turned, but still there was the same red light glaring
on, but not illuminating, the dusky furniture of the apartment.
The wind was high that night, and as the creaking door swung
on its hinges, every noise seemed like the sound of a hand
struggling with the lock, or of a foot pausing on the threshold.
But (for Melmoth never could decide) was it in a dream or not,
that he saw the figure of his ancestor appear at the door? —
hesitatingly as he saw him at first on the night of his uncle's
death, — saw him enter the room, approach his bed, and heard
him whisper, 'You have burned me, then; but those are flames
I can survive. — I am alive, — I am beside you.' Melmoth started,

sprung from his bed, — it was broad day-light. He looked round, — there was no human being in the room but himself. He felt a slight pain in the wrist of his right arm. He looked at it, it was black and blue, as from the recent gripe of a strong hand.

FOOTNOTES

1   Mrs Marshall, the original Roxana in Lee's Alexander, and the only virtuous woman then on the stage. She was carried off in the manner described, by Lord Orrery, who, finding all his solicitations repelled, had recourse to a sham marriage performed by a servant in the habit of a clergyman.

2   Vide Pope, (copying from Donne).
      'Peace, fools, or Gonson will for Papists seize you,
      If once he catch you at your Jesu, Jesu.'

3   Vide the Old Bachelor, whose Araminta, wearied by the repetition of these phrases forbids her lover to address her in any sentence commencing with them.

4   Vide any old play you may have the patience to peruse; or, *instar omnium*, read the courtly loves of Rhodophil and Melantha, Palamede and Doralice, in Dryden's Marriage a la Mode.

5   Vide Southern's Oroonoko, — I mean the comic part.

6   'A charm, a song, a murder, and a ghost.' *Prologue to Oedipus*.

7   Vide Le Blanc's Letters.

8   Vide Betterton's History of the Stage.

9   Rochefoucault.

10   Vide Cutter of Coleman street.

11   A fact, related to me by a person who was near committing suicide in a similar situation, to escape what he called 'the excruciating torture of giddiness.'

Joseph Sheridan Le Fanu

JOSEPH SHERIDAN LE FANU (1814-1873)

WITHOUT SHERIDAN LE FANU there might never have been a *Dracula* or a *Jane Eyre*. It is a bold statement but one that is justified for it was a short story 'Carmilla' which inspired Le Fanu's fellow Dubliner, Bram Stoker, to write the vampire novel which has developed into a world wide cult and the plot of another of his stories which furnished Charlotte Brontë with the idea for her *tour de force*.

When Le Fanu died in 1873 he had combined into his 59 years the professions of an editor, newspaper proprietor, poet, ballad writer, exponent of the short story and author of fifteen novels, many of which are still avidly read today and hailed as classics. Critics still acclaim him as one of the greatest writers of ghost stories in the English language.

Joseph Sheridan Le Fanu was born in Dublin on August 28, 1814, and came from a literary family. An ancestor, Peter Le Fanu, was author of a play entitled *Smock Alley Secrets*, produced in Dublin in 1778 while, on his mother's side, he was related to the prolific Sheridan family. He entered Trinity College in 1883 to train for the legal profession but, while still a student, he decided to embark on writing as a career and published his first tale of the macabre in the *Dublin University Magazine* at the age of 23. This tale was entitled 'The Ghost and the Bone Setter' and showed his skill at Gothic horror which, combined with matchless brevity, gave a biting realism to the story.

Dublin University Magazine was, in those days, a 'popular magazine' and had no connection with the university. Le Fanu was to be its editor from 1869-1872. The magazine became Le Fanu's major outlet for his many stories. In the late 1830's Charlotte Brontë wrote Le Fanu a letter of appreciation about his work. What is interesting is that Le Fanu's short tale 'A Chapter in the History of a Tyrone Family' is almost identical with the plot of Charlotte Brontë's *Jane Eyre*. Le Fanu's story appeared in the *Dublin University Magazine* in October, 1839, while *Jane Eyre* was published eight years later in 1847.

Thackeray had written to Charlotte to point out that the plot of the book was familiar but he did not connect it with Le Fanu.

This is not to accuse Charlotte of plagiarism. When she replied to Thackeray, she was certain her plot was 'original', forgetting the story she had read in a magazine some years before. That is how things happen with writers. One can never be sure that the superb plot they have conceived is entirely original or a mixture of half forgotten tales that they have encountered before.

By 1839 Le Fanu had devoted himself to journalism and had bought three Dublin newspapers which he merged into one — the *Dublin Evening Mail*.

He published his first novel in 1847. It was a tale of the Williamite wars entitled *Torlogh O'Brien* and it was immediately acclaimed by critics as one of the best Irish historical novels. A lapse of nearly twenty years was to take place before his next book which has remained his masterpiece — *Uncle Silas* (1864). The book is a most sinister psychological suspense tale and since its first publication has hardly been out of print. The same year also saw the publication of his first full blooded supernatural novel — *Wylder's Hand*.

But during the 1840's and 1850's Le Fanu had written comparatively little fiction and had been working hard on editing his newspaper, the *Dublin Evening Mail*. The change in his life occurred when, in 1858, his wife died and he virtually shut himself off from life. Indeed, he became known in Dublin as the 'invisible prince' for he was rarely seen in public.

On such occasions his tall, muffled figure was seen silently stealing into some old and out of the way bookshop with

requests for ancient books on demonology and witchcraft.
He wrote mostly at night aided by cups of strong tea. In fact,
in his chilling tale 'Green Tea' he says: 'I believe that everyone
who sets about writing in earnest does his work on something —
tea, coffee or tobacco.'

His years shut away from outside life were his most prolific
as a writer. His subsequent twelve books were published in a
ten year period and that same period saw the publication
of his greatest short stories. His best known collection (which
has hardly ever been out of print since 1872) was *In A Glass
Darkly*. This collection contains such gems as 'Carmilla' and
'Green Tea'. 'Carmilla' is a tale of vampires and was the inspiration for Stoker's *Dracula*. In fact, one chapter of *Dracula*
so closely resembled 'Carmilla' that Stoker's publisher, Constable, advised him to delete it from the·novel. This he did
but it was later posthumously published in a collection of
short stories as 'Dracula's Guest'.

In 1970 Hammer Films, following their success with *Dracula*
and other vampire films, used 'Carmilla' as the basis for a new
film starring Peter Cushing and which they entitled 'The Vampire Lovers'. Fontana Books immediately issued an anthology
of Le Fanu's short stories under the same title retitling 'Carmilla' to fall in line with the film.

Another classic was 'Green Tea'. The distinguished writer and
critic V.S. Pritchett has listed 'among the best half-dozen
ghost stories in the English language'. The critic Harry Ludlam
(one of Bram Stoker's biographers) has also stated: 'As a tale
of the haunted innocent "Green Tea" has never been equalled'.

'The Familiar', which I have chosen here is another classic,
a story which had a profound effect on such writers as M.R.
James and H.P. Lovecraft.

Towards the end of his life Le Fanu was haunted by strange
recurrent nightmares, which assisted him in describing scenes
of terror such as those in his powerful novel *The House by the
Churchyard* (1863). The action takes place in Chapelizod and
an early chapter gives a really horrifying and masterly description of the haunting of an old house by the ghost of a hand.
The chapter was so electrifying that it has been anthologised

as a short story under the title 'Narrative of the Ghost of a Hand. (*The Vampire Lovers*, Fontana, 1970).

Le Fanu died at his home at No. 18 (now No. 70) Merrion Square, Dublin, on February 7, 1873. The heart disease from which he had begun to suffer in the declining years following his wife's death finally claimed him. An obituary notice in the *Dublin University Magazine* described him as 'a man who thought deeply, especially on religious subjects. To those who knew him he was very dear; they admired him for his learning, his sparkling wit and pleasant manner.'

Today, over one hundred years after his death, he is still also admired for his craftmanship. Even some of his very early work is still in demand such as his experiments in macabre entitled 'Ghost Stories of Chapelizod' which were published in the *Dublin University Magazine* of 1851. They were out of print for many years but in 1973 were issued by Mercier Press of Cork as *Irish Ghost Stories of Sheridan Le Fanu* selected and introduced by Patrick F. Byrne. No anthology of ghost stories seems complete without a contribution from Le Fanu. He was undoubtedly one of the great masters of the literary macabre who created some of the most enduring and horrifying tales in the fantasy field.

THE FAMILIAR
Joseph Sheridan le Fanu

PROLOGUE

 UT OF ABOUT TWO HUNDRED and thirty cases of similar type studied by Dr. Martin Hesselius, I select the following, which I call 'The Familiar'.

To this MS. Dr. Hesselius has, after his wont, attached some sheets of letter-paper, on which are written, in his hand nearly as compact as print, his own remarks upon the case. He says —

'In point of conscience, no more unexceptionable narrator, than the venerable Irish Clergyman who has given me this paper, on Mr. Barton's case, could have been chosen. The statement is, however, medically imperfect. The report of an intelligent physician, who had marked its progress, and attended the patient, from its earlier stages to its close, would have supplied what is wanting to enable me to pronounce with confidence. I should have been acquainted with Mr. Barton's probable hereditary predispositions; I should have known, possibly, by very early indications, something of a remote origin of the disease than can now be ascertained.

'In a rough way, we may reduce all similar cases to three distinct classes. They are founded on the primary distinction between the subjective and the objective. Of those whose senses are alleged to be subject to supernatural impressions — some are simply visionaries, and propagate the illusions of which they complain, from diseased brain or nerves. Others are, unquestionably, infested by, as we term them, spiritual agencies, exterior to themselves. Others, again, owe their sufferings to a mixed condition. The interior sense, it is true, is opened; but it has been and continues open by the action of disease. This form of disease may, in one sense, be compared to the loss of the scarf-skin, and a consequent exposure of surfaces for whose excessive sensitiveness, nature has provided a muffling. The loss of this covering is attended by an habitual impassibility, by influences against which we were intended to be guarded. But in the case of the brain, and the nerves immediately connected with its functions and its sensuous impressions, the cerebral circulation undergoes periodically that vibratory disturbance, which, I believe, I have satisfactorily examined and demonstrated, in my MS. Essay, A. 17. This vibratory disturbance differs, as I there prove, essentially from the congestive disturbance, the phenomena of which are examined in A. 19. It is, when excessive, invariably accompanied by *illusions*.

'Had I seen Mr. Barton, and examined him upon the points, in his case, which need elucidation, I should have without difficulty referred those phenomena to their proper disease. My diagnosis is now, necessarily, conjectural.'

Thus writes Dr. Hesselius; and adds a great deal which is of interest only to a scientific physician.

The Narrative of the Rev. Thomas Herbert, which furnishes all that is known of the case, will be found in the chapters that follow.

1 FOOTSTEPS

I was a young man at the time, and intimately acquainted with some of the actors in this strange tale; the impression which its incidents made on me, therefore, were deep and lasting. I shall now endeavour, with precision, to relate them all, combining, of course, in the narrative, whatever I have learned from various sources, tending, however imperfectly, to illuminate the darkness which involves its progress and termination.

Somewhere about the year 1794, the younger brother of a certain baronet, whom I shall call Sir James Barton, returned to Dublin. He had served in the navy with some distinction, having commanded one of His Majesty's frigates during the greater part of the American war. Captain Barton was apparently some two or three-and-forty years of age. He was an intelligent and agreeable companion when he pleased it, though generally reserved, and occasionally even moody.

In society, however, he deported himself as a man of the world, and a gentleman. He had not contracted any of the noisy brusqueness sometimes acquired at sea; on the contrary his manners were remarkably easy, quiet, and even polished. He was in person about the middle size, and somewhat strongly formed — his countenance was marked with the lines of thought, and on the whole wore an expression of gravity and melancholy; being, however, as I have said, a man of perfect breeding, as well as of good family, and in affluent circumstances, he had, of course, ready access to the best society of Dublin, without the necessity of any other credentials.

In his personal habits Mr. Barton was unexpensive. He occupied lodgings in one of the *then* fashionable streets in the south side of the town — kept but one horse and one servant — and though a reputed free-thinker, yet lived an orderly and moral life — indulging neither in gaming, drinking, nor any other vicious pursuit — living very much to himself, without forming intimacies, or choosing any companions, and appearing to mix in gay society rather for the sake of its bustle and distraction, than for any opportunities it offered of interchanging thought or feeling with its votaries.

Barton was, therefore, pronounced a saving, prudent, unsocial sort of fellow, who bid fair to maintain his celibacy alike against stratagem and assault, and was likely to live to a good old age, die rich and leave his money to a hospital.

It was now apparent, however, that the nature of Mr. Barton's plans had been totally misconceived. A young lady, whom I shall call Miss Montague, was at this time introduced into the gay world by her aunt, the Dowager Lady L——. Miss

Montague was decidedly pretty and accomplished, and having some natural cleverness, and a great deal of gaiety, became for a while a reigning toast.

Her popularity, however, gained her, for a time, nothing more than that unsubstantial admiration which, however pleasant as an incense to vanity, is by no means necessarily antecedent to matrimony — for, unhappily for the young lady in question, it was an understood thing, that beyond her personal attractions, she had no kind of earthly provision. Such being the state of affairs, it will readily be believed that no little surprise was consequent upon the appearance of Captain Barton as the avowed lover of the penniless Miss Montague.

His suit prospered, as might have been expected, and in a short time it was communicated by old Lady L —— to each of her hundred and fifty particular friends in succession, that Captain Barton had actually tendered proposals of marriage, with her approbation, to her niece, Miss Montague, who had, moreover, accepted the offer of his hand, conditionally upon the consent of her father, who was then upon his homeward voyage from India, and expected in two or three weeks at the furthest.

About this consent there could be no doubt — the delay, therefore, was one merely of form — they were looked upon as absolutely engaged, and Lady L ——, with a rigour of old-fashioned decorum with which her niece would, no doubt, gladly have dispensed, withdrew her thenceforward from all further participation in the gaieties of the town.

Captain Barton was a constant visitor, as well as a frequent guest at the house, and was permitted all the privileges of intimacy which a betrothed suitor is usually accorded. Such was the relation of parties, when the mysterious circumstances which darken this narrative first begun to unfold themselves.

Lady L —— resided in a handsome mansion at the north side of Dublin, and Captain Barton's lodgings, as we have already said, were situated at the south. The distance intervening was considerable, and it was Captain Barton's habit generally to walk home without an attendant, as often as he passed the evening with the old lady and her fair charge.

His shortest way in such nocturnal walks, lay, for a considerable space, through a line of street which had as yet merely been laid out, and little more than the foundation of the houses constructed.

One night shortly after his engagement with Miss Montague had commenced, he happened to remain unusually late, in company with her and Lady L ——. The conversation had turned upon the evidences of revelation, which he had disputed with the callous scepticism of a confirmed infidel. What were called 'French principles', had in those days found their way a good deal into fashionable society, especially that portion of it which professed allegiance to Whiggism, and neither the old lady nor her charge were so perfectly free from the taint, as to look upon Mr. Barton's views as any serious objection to the proposed union.

The discussion had degenerated into one upon the supernatural and the marvellous, in which he had pursued precisely the same line of argument and ridicule. In all this, it is but truth to state, Captain Barton was guilty of no affectation — the doctrines upon which he insisted, were, in reality, but too truly the basis of his own fixed belief, if so it might be called; and perhaps not the least strange of the many strange circumstances connected with my narrative, was the fact that the subject of the fearful influences I am about to describe, was himself, from the deliberate conviction of years, an utter disbeliever in what are usually termed preternatural agencies.

It was considerably past midnight when Mr. Barton took his leave, and set out upon his solitary walk homeward. He had now reached the lonely road, with its unfinished dwarf walls tracing the foundations of the projected row of houses on either side — the moon was shining mistily, and its imperfect light made the road he trod but additionally dreary — that utter silence which has in it something indefinably exciting, reigned there, and made the sound of his steps, which alone broke it, unnaturally loud and distinct.

He had proceeded thus some way, when he, on a sudden, heard other footfalls, pattering at a measured pace, and, as it seemed, about two-score steps behind him.

The suspicion of being dogged is at all times unpleasant: it is, however, especially so in a spot so lonely: and this suspicion became so strong in the mind of Captain Barton, that he abruptly turned about to confront his pursuer, but, though there was quite sufficient moonlight to disclose any object upon the road he had traversed, no form of any kind was visible there.

The steps he had heard could not have been the reverberation of his own, for he stamped his foot upon the ground, and walked briskly up and down, in the vain attempt to awake an echo; though by no means a fanciful person, therefore, he was at last fain to charge the sounds upon his imagination, and treat them as an illusion. Thus satisfying himself, he resumed his walk, and before he had proceeded a dozen paces, the mysterious footfall was again audible from behind, and this time, as if with the special design of showing that the sounds were not the responses of an echo — the steps sometimes slackened nearly to a halt, and sometimes hurried for six of eight strides to a run, and again abated to a walk.

Captain Barton, as before, turned suddenly round, and with the same result — no object was visible above the deserted level of the road. He walked back over the same ground, determined that, whatever might have been the cause of the sounds which had so disconcerted him, it should not escape his search — the endeavour, however, was unrewarded.

In spite of all his scepticism, he felt something like a superstitious fear stealing fast upon him, and with these unwonted and uncomfortable sensations, he once more turned and pursued his way. There was no repetition of these haunting sounds, until he had reached the point where he had last stopped to retrace his steps — here they were resumed — and with sudden starts of running, which threatened to bring the unseen pursuer up to the alarmed pedestrian.

Captain Barton arrested his course as formerly — the unaccountable nature of the occurance filled him with vague and disagreeable sensations — and yielding to the excitement that was gaining upon him, he shouted sternly, 'Who goes there?' The sound of one's own voice, thus exerted, in utter solitude, and followed by total silence, has in it something unpleasantly dismaying, and he felt a degree of nervousness which, perhaps, from no cause had he ever known before.

To the very end of this solitary street the steps pursued him — and it required a strong effort of stubborn pride on his part, to resist the impulse that prompted him every moment to run for safety at the top of his speed. It was not until he had reached his lodging, and sat by his own fireside, that he felt sufficiently reassured to rearrange and reconsider in his own mind the occurrences which had so discomposed him. So little a matter, after all, is sufficient to upset the pride of scepticism and vindicate the old simple laws of nature within us.

2 THE WATCHER

Mr. Barton was next morning sitting at a late breakfast, reflecting upon the incidents of the previous night, with more of inquisitiveness than awe, so speedily do gloomy impressions upon the fancy disappear under the cheerful influence of day, when a letter just delivered by the postman was placed upon the table before him.

There was nothing remarkable in the address of this missive, except that it was written in a hand which he did not know — perhaps it was disguised — for the tall narrow characters were sloped backward; and with the self-inflicted suspense which we often see practised in such cases, he puzzled over the inscription for a full minute before he broke the seal. When he did so, he read the following words, written in the same hand:

Mr. Barton, late captain of the *Dolphin*, is warned of DANGER. He will do wisely to avoid —— Street — [here the locality of his last night's adventure was named] — if he walks there as usual he will meet with something unlucky — let him take warning, once for all, for he has reason to dread
                                                    'THE WATCHER.'

Captain Barton read and re-read this strange effusion; in every light and in every direction he turned it over and over; he examined the paper on which it was written, and scrutinised the handwriting once more. Defeated here, he turned to the seal; it was nothing but a patch of wax, upon which the accidental impression of a thumb was imperfectly visible.

There was not the slightest mark, or clue of any kind, to lead him to even a guess as to its possible origin. The writer's object seemed a friendly one, and yet he subscribed himself as one whom he had 'reason to dread'. Altogether the letter, its author, and its real purpose were to him an inexplicable puzzle, and one, moreover, unpleasantly suggestive, in his mind, of other associations connected with his last night's adventure.

In obedience to some feeling — perhaps of pride — Mr. Barton did not communicate, even to his intended bride, the occurrences which I have just detailed. Trifling as they might appear, they had in reality most disagreeably affected his imagination, and he cared not to disclose, even to the young lady in question, what she might possibly look upon as evidences of weakness. The letter might very well be but a hoax, and the mysterious footfall but a delusion or a trick. But although he affected to treat the whole affair as unworthy of a thought, it yet haunted him pertinaciously, tormenting him with perplexing doubts, and depressing him with undefined apprehensions. Certain it is, that for a considerable time afterwards he carefully avoided the street indicated in the letter as the scene of danger.

It was not until about a week after the receipt of the letter which I have transcribed, that anything further occurred to remind Captain Barton of its contents, or to counteract the gradual disappearance from his mind of the disagreeable impression then received.

He was returning one night, after the interval I have stated, from the theatre, which was then situated in Crow Street, and having there seen Miss Montague and Lady L —— into their carriage, he loitered for some time with two or three acquaintances.

With these, however, he parted close to the college, and pursued his way alone. It was now fully one o'clock, and the streets were quite deserted. During the whole of his walk with the companions from whom he had just parted, he had been at times painfully aware of the sound of steps, as it seemed, dogging them on their way.

Once or twice he had looked back, in the uneasy anticipation that he was again about to experience the same mysterious annoyances which had so disconcerted him a week before, and earnestly hoping that he might *see* some form to account naturally for the sounds. But the street was deserted — no one was visible.

Proceeding now quite alone upon his homeward way, he grew really nervous and uncomfortable, as he became sensible, with increased distinctness, of the well-known and now absolutely dreaded sounds.

By the side of the dead wall which bounded the college park, the sounds followed, recommencing almost simultaneously with his own steps. The same unequal pace — sometimes slow, sometimes for a score yards or so, quickened almost to a run — was audible from behind him. Again and again he turned; quickly and stealthily he glanced over his shoulder — almost at every half-dozen steps; but no one was visible.

The irritation of this intangible and unseen pursuit became gradually all but intolerable; and when at last he reached his home, his nerves were strung to such a pitch of excitement that he could not rest, and did not attempt even to lie down until after the daylight had broken.

He was awakened by a knock at his chamber door, and his servant entering, handed him several letters which had just been received by the penny post. One among them instantly arrested his attention — a single glance at the direction aroused him thoroughly. He at once recognised its character, and read as follows.

You may as well think, Captain Barton, to escape from your own shadow as from me; do what you may, I will see you as often as I please, and you shall see me, for I do not want to hide myself, as you fancy. Do not let it trouble your rest, Captain Barton; for, with a *good conscience*, what need you fear from the eye of

'THE WATCHER'

It is scarcely necessary to dwell upon the feelings that accompanied a perusal of this strange communication. Captain Barton was observed to be unusually absent and out of spirits for several days afterwards! but no one divined the cause.

Whatever he might think as to the phantom steps which followed him, there could be no possible illusion about the letters he had received; and, to say the least, their immediate sequence upon the mysterious sounds which had haunted him, was an odd coincidence.

The whole circumstance was, in his own mind, vaguely and instinctively connected with certain passages in his past life, which, of all others, he hated to remember.

It happened, however, that in addition to his own approaching nuptials, Captain Barton had just then — fortunately, perhaps, for himself — some business of an engrossing kind connected with the adjustment of a large and long-litigated claim upon certain properties.

The hurry and excitement of business had its natural effect in gradually dispelling the gloom which had for a time occasionally oppressed him, and in a little while his spirits had entirely recovered their accustomed tone.

During all this time, however, he was, now and then, dismayed by indistinct and half-heard repetitions of the same annoyance, and that in lonely places, in the daytime as well as after nightfall. These renewals of the strange impressions from which he had suffered so much, were, however, desultory and faint, insomuch that often he really could not, to his own satisfaction, distinguish between them and the mere suggestions of an excited imagination.

One evening he walked down to the House of Commons with a Member, an acquaintance of his and mine. This was one of the few occasions upon which I have been in company with Captain Barton. As we walked down together, I observed that he became absent and silent, and to a degree that seemed to argue the pressure of some urgent and absorbing anxiety.

I afterwards learned that during the whole of our walk, he had heard the well-known footsteps tracking him as we proceeded.

This, however, was the last time he suffered from this phase of the persecution, of which he was already the anxious victim. A new and a very different one was about to be presented.

3 AN ADVERTISEMENT

Of the new series of impressions which were afterwards gradually to work out his destiny, I that evening witnessed the first; and but for its relation to the train of events which followed, the incident would scarcely have been now remembered by me.

As we were walking in at the passage from College Green, a man, of whom I remember only that he was short in stature, looked like a foreigner, and wore a kind of fur travelling-cap, walked very rapidly, and as if under fierce excitement, directly towards us, muttering to himself, fast and vehemently the while.

This odd-looking person walked straight towards Barton, who was foremost of the three, and halted, regarding him for a moment or two with a look of maniacal menace and fury; and then turning about as abruptly, he walked before us at the same agitated pace, and disappeared at a side passage. I do distinctly remember being a good deal shocked at the countenance and bearing of this man, which indeed irresistibly impressed me with an undefined sense of danger, such as I have never felt before or since from the presence of anything human; but these sensations were, on my part, far from amounting to anything so disconcerting as to flurry or excite me — I had seen only a singularly evil countenance, agitated, as it seemed, with the excitement of madness.

I was absolutely astonished, however, at the effect of this apparition upon Captain Barton. I knew him to be a man of proud courage and coolness in real danger — a circumstance which made his conduct upon this occasion the more conspicuously odd. He recoiled a step or two as the stranger advanced, and clutched my arm in silence, with what seemed to be a spasm of agony or terror! and then, as the figure disappeared, shoving me roughly back, he followed it for a few paces, stopped in great disorder, and sat down upon a form. I never beheld a countenance more ghastly and haggard.

'For God's sake, Barton, what is the matter?' said ——, our companion, really alarmed at his appearance. 'You're not hurt, are you? — or unwell? What is it?'

'What did he say? — I did not hear it — what was it?' asked Barton, wholly disregarding the question.

'Nonsense,' said ——, greatly surprised; 'who cares what the fellow said. You are unwell, Barton — decidedly unwell; let me call a coach.'

'Unwell! No — not unwell,' he said evidently making an effort to recover his self-possession; 'but, to say the truth, I am fatigued — a little over-worked — and perhaps over-anxious. You know I have been in Chancery, and the winding-up of a suit is always a nervous affair. I have felt uncomfortable all this evening; but I am better now. Come, come — shall we go on?'

'No, no. Take my advice Barton, and go home; you really do need rest; you are looking quite ill. I really do insist on your allowing me to see you home,' replied his friend.

I seconded ——'s advice, the more readily as it was obvious that Barton was not himself disinclined to be persuaded. He left us, decling our offered escort. I was not sufficiently intimate with —— to discuss the scene we had both just witnessed. I was, however, convinced from his manner in the few commonplace comments and regrets we exchanged, that he was just as little satisfied as I with the extempore plea of illness with which he had accounted for the strange exhibition, and that we were both agreed in suspecting some lurking mystery in the matter.

I called next day at Barton's lodgings, to inquire for him, and learned from the servant that he had not left his room since his return the night before; but that he was not seriously indisposed, and hoped to be out in a few days. That evening he sent for Dr. R——, then in a large and fashionable practice in Dublin, and their interview was, it is said, and odd one.

He entered into a detail of his own symptoms in an abstracted and desultory way, which seemed to argue a strange want of interest in his own cure, and, at all events, made it manifest that there was some topic engaging his mind of more engrossing importance than his present ailment. He complained of occasional palpitations and headache.

Dr. R —— asked him, among other questions, whether there was any irritating circumstance or anxiety then occupying his thoughts. This he denied quickly and almost peevishly; and the physician thereupon declared his opinion that there was nothing amiss except some slight derangement of the digestion, for which he accordingly wrote a prescription, and was about to withdraw, when Mr. Barton, with the air of a man who recollects a topic which had nearly escaped him, recalled him.

'I beg your pardon, doctor, but I really almost forgot; will you permit me to ask you two or three medical questions — rather odd ones, perhaps, but as a wager depends upon their solution, you will, I hope, excuse my unreasonableness?'

The physician readily undertook to satisfy the inquirer.

Barton seemed to have some difficulty about opening the proposed interrogatories, for he was silent for a minute, then walked to his book-case, and returned as he had gone; at last he sat down, and said ——

'You'll think them very childish questions, but I can't recover my wager without a decision; so I must put them. I want to know the first about lock-jaw. If a man actually has that complaint, and appears to have died of it — so much so, that a physician of average skill pronounces him actually dead — may he, after all, recover?'

The physician smiled, and shook his head.

'But — but a blunder may be made,' resumed Barton. 'Suppose an ignorant pretender to medical skill; may *he* be so deceived by any stage of the complaint, as to mistake what is only a part of the progress of the disease, for death itself?'

'No one who had ever seen death,' answered he, 'could mistake it in a case of lock-jaw.'

Barton mused for a few minutes. 'I am going to ask you a question, perhaps still more childish; but first, tell me, are the regulations of foreign hospitals, such as that of, let us say, Naples, very lax and bungling. May not all kinds of blunders and slips occur in their entries of names, and so forth?'

Dr. R —— professed his incompetence to answer that query.

'Well, then, doctor, here is the last of my questions. You will, probably, laugh at it; but it must out nevertheless. Is there any

disease, in all the range of human maladies, which would
have the effect of perceptibly contracting the stature, and the
whole frame — causing the man to shrink in all his proportions,
and yet to preserve his exact resemblance to himself in every
particular — with the one exception, his height and bulk; *any*
disease, mark — no matter how rare — how little believed in,
generally — which could possibly result in producing such an
effect?'

The physician replied with a smile, and a very decided nega-
tive.

'Tell me, then,' said Barton, abruptly, 'if a man be in reason-
able fear of assault from a lunatic who is at large, can he not
procure a warrant for his arrest and detention?'

'Really, that is more a lawyer's question than one in my
way,' replied Dr. R——; 'but I believe, on applying to a magistrate, such a course would be directed.'

The physician then took his leave; but, just as he reached the
hall door, remembered that he had left his cane upstairs, and
returned. His reappearance was awkward, for a piece of paper,
which he recognised as his own prescription, was slowly burning upon the fire, and Barton sitting close by with an expression
of settled gloom and dismay.

Dr. R—— had too much tact to observe what presented itself; but he had seen quite enough to assure him that the mind,
and not the body, of Captain Barton was in reality the seat of
suffering.

A few days afterwards, the following advertisement appeared
in the Dublin newspapers:

'If Sylvester Yelland, formerly a foremast man on board
His Majesty's frigate *Dolphin*, or his nearest of kin, will apply
to Mr. Hubert Smith, attorney, at his office, Dame Street,
he or they may hear of something greatly to his or their
advantage. Admission may be had at any hour up to twelve
o'clock at night, should parties desire to avoid observation;
and the strictest secrecy, as to all communications intended
to be confidential, shall be honourably observed.'

The *Dolphin*, as I have mentioned, was the vessel which
Captain Barton had commanded; and this circumstance, connected with the extraordinary exertions made by the circulation
of handbills, etc., as well as by repeated advertisements, to
secure for this strange notice the utmost possible publicity,
suggested to Dr. R—— the idea that Captain Barton's extreme
uneasiness was somehow connected with the individual to
whom the advertisement was addressed, and he himself the
author of it.

This, however, it is needless to add, was no more than a
conjecture. No information, whatsoever, as to the real purpose
of the advertisement was divulged by the agent, nor yet any
hint as to who his employer might be.

4 HE TALKS WITH A CLERGYMAN

Mr. Barton, although he had latterly begun to earn for himself
the character of an hypochondriac, was yet very far from deserving it. Though by no means lively, he had yet, naturally,
what are termed 'even spirits', and was not subject to undue
depressions.

He soon, therefore, began to return to his former habits; and
one of the earliest symptons of this healthier tone of spirits was
his appearing at a grand dinner of the Freemasons, of which
worthy fraternity he was himself a brother. Barton, who had
been at first gloomy and abstracted, drank much more freely
than was his wont – possibly with the purpose of dispelling his
own secret anxieties – and under the influence of good wine
and pleasant company, became gradually (unlike himself)
talkative, and even noisy.

It was under this unwonted excitement that he left his
company at about half past ten o'clock; and as conviviality is
a strong incentive to gallantry, it occurred to him to proceed
forthwith to Lady L——'s, and pass the remainder of the
evening with her and his destined bride.

Accordingly, he was soon at —— Street, and chatting gaily
with the ladies. It is not to be supposed that Captain Barton
had exceeded the limits which propriety prescribes to good
fellowship – he had merely taken enough wine to raise his

spirits, without, however, in the least degree unsteadying his mind, or affecting his manners.

With this undue elevation of spirits had supervened an entire oblivion or contempt of those undefined apprehensions which had for so long weighted upon his mind, and to a certain extent estranged him from society; but as the night wore away, and his artificial gaiety began to flag, these painful feelings gradually intruded themselves again, and he grew abstracted and anxious as heretofore.

He took his leave at length, with an upleasant foreboding of some coming mischief, and with a mind haunted with a thousand mysterious apprehensions, such as, even while he acutely felt their pressure, he, nevertheless, inwardly strove, or affected to contemn.

It was this proud defiance of what he regarded as his own weakness, which prompted him upon the present occasion to that course which brought the adventure I am now about to relate.

Mr. Barton might have easily called a coach, but he was conscious that his strong inclination to do so proceeded from no cause other than what he desperately persisted in representing to himself to be his own superstitious tremors.

He might also have returned home by a *route* different from that against which he had been warned by his mysterious correspondent; but for the same reason he dismissed this idea also, and with a dogged and half desperate resolution to force matters to a crisis of some kind, if there were any reality in the causes of his former suffering, and if not, satisfactorily to bring their delusiveness to the proof, he determined to follow precisely the course which he had trodden upon the night so painfully memorable in his own mind as that on which his strange persecution commenced. Though, sooth to say, the pilot who for the first time steers his vessel under the muzzles of a hostile battery, never felt his resolution more serverely tasked than did Captain Barton, as he breathlessly pursued this solitary path — a path which, spite of every effort of scepticism and reason, he felt to be infested by some (as respected *him*) malignant being.

He pursued his way steadily and rapidly, scarcely breathing from intensity of suspense; he, however, was troubled by no renewal of the dreaded footsteps, and was beginning to feel a return of confidence, as more than three-fourths of the way being accomplished with impunity, he approached the long line of twinkling oil lamps which indicated the frequented streets.

This feeling of self-congratulation was, however, but momentary. The report of a musket at some hundred yards behind him, and the whistle of a bullet close to his head, disagreeably and startling dispelled it. His first impulse was to retrace his steps in pursuit of the assassin; but the road on either side was, as we have said, embarrassed by the foundations of a street, beyond which extended waste fields, full of rubbish and neglected lime- and brick-kilns, and all now as utterly silent as though no sound had ever disturbed their dark and unsightly solitude. The futility of, single-handed, attempting, under such circumstances, a search for the murderer, was apparent, especially as no sound, either of retreating steps or any other kind, was audible to direct his pursuit.

With the tumultuous sensations of one whose life has just been exposed to a murderous attempt, and whose escape has been the narrowest possible, Captain Barton turned again; and without, however, quickening his pace actually to a run, hurriedly pursued his way.

He had turned, as I have said, after a pause of a few seconds, and had just commenced his rapid retreat, when on a sudden he met the well-remembered little man in the fur cap. The encounter was but momentary. The figure was walking at the same exaggerated pace, and with the same strange air of menace as before; and as it passed him, he thought he heard it say, in a furious whisper, 'Still alive — still alive!'

The state of Mr. Barton's spirits began now to work a corresponding alteration in his health and looks, and to such a degree that it was impossible that the change should escape general remark.

For some reason, known but to himself, he took no steps whatsoever to bring the attempt upon his life, which he had so narrowly escaped, under the notice of the authorities; on the contrary, he kept it jealously to himself; and it was not for many weeks after the occurrence that he mentioned it, and then in strict confidence, to a gentleman, whom the torments of his mind at last compelled him to consult.

Spite of his blue devils, however, poor Barton, having no satisfactory reason to render to the public for any undue remissness in the attentions exacted by the relation existing between him and Miss Montague, was obliged to exert himself, and present to the world a confident and cheerful bearing.

The true source of his sufferings, and every circumstance connected with them he guarded with a reserve so jealous, that it seemed dictated by at least a suspicion that the origin of his strange persecution was known to himself, and that it was of a nature which, upon his own account, he could not or dared not disclose.

The mind thus turned in upon itself, and constantly occupied with a haunting, anxiety which it dared not reveal or confide to any human breast, became daily more excited, and, of course, more vividly impressible, by a system of attack which operated through the nervous system; and in this state he was destined to sustain, with increasing frequency, the stealthy visitations of that apparition which from the first had seemed to possess so terrible a hold upon his imagination.

It was about this time that Captain Barton called upon the then celebrated preacher, Dr.——, with whom he had a slight acquaintance, and an extraordinary conversation ensued.

The divine was seated in his chambers in college, surrounded with works upon his favourite pursuit, and deep in theology when Barton was announced.

There was something at once embarrassed and excited in his manner, which, along with his wan and haggard countenance, impressed the student with the unpleasant consciousness that his visitor must have recently suffered terribly indeed, to account for an alteration so striking — almost shocking.

After the usual interchange of polite greeting, and a few commonplace remarks, Captain Barton, who obviously perceived the surprise which his visit had excited, and which Dr. —— was unable wholly to conceal, interrupted a brief pause by remarking —

'This is a strange call, Dr. ——, perhaps scarcely warranted by an acqauaintance so slight as mine with you. I should not under ordinary circumstances have ventured to disturb you; but my visit is neither an idle nor impertinent intrusion. I am sure you will not so account it, when I tell you how afflicted I am.'

Dr. —— interrupted him with assurances such as good breeding suggested, and Barton resumed:

'I am come to task your patience by asking your advice. When I say your patience, I might, indeed, say more; I might have said your humanity — your compassion; for I have been and am a great sufferer.'

'My dear sir,' replied the churchman, 'it will, indeed, afford me infinite gratification if I can give you comfort in any distress of mind! but — you know ——'

'I know what you would say,' resumed Barton, quickly; 'I am an unbeliever, and, therefore, incapable of deriving help from relgion; but don't take that for granted. At least you must not assume that, however unsettled my convictions may be, I do not feel a deep — a very deep — interest in the subject. Circumstances have lately forced it upon my attention, is such a way as to compel me to review the whole question in a more candid and teachable spirit, I believe, than I ever studied it in before.'

'Your difficulties, I take it for granted, refer to the evidences of revelation,' suggested the clergyman.

'Why — no — not altogether; in fact, I am ashamed to say I have not considered even my objections sufficiently to state them connectedly; but — but there is one subject on which I feel a peculiar interest.'

He paused again, and Dr. —— pressed him to proceed.

'The fact is' said Barton, 'whatever may be my uncertainty as to the authenticity of what we are taught to call revelation, of one fact I am deeply and horribly convinced, that there does exist beyond this a spiritual world — a system whose workings are generally in mercy hidden from us — a system which may be, and which is sometimes, partially and terribly revealed. I am sure — I *know*,' continued Barton, with increasing excitement, 'that there is a God — a dreadful God — and that retribution

follows guilt, in ways the most mysterious and stupendous — by
agencies the most inexplicable and terrific; — there is a spiritual
system — great God, how I have been convinced! — a system
malignant, and implacable, and omnipotent, under whose persecutions I am, and have been, suffering the torments of the
damned! — yes, sir — yes — the fires and frenzy of hell!'

As Barton spoke, his agitation became so vehement that the
Divine was shocked, and even alarmed. The wild and excited
rapidity with which he spoke, and, above all, the indefinable
horror that stamped his features, afforded a contrast to his
ordinary cool and unimpassioned self-possession striking and
painful in the last degree.

5 MR. BARTON STATES HIS CASE

'My dear sir,' said Dr. ——, after a brief pause, 'I fear you have
been very unhappy, indeed; but I venture to predict that the
depression under which you labour will be found to originate in
purely physical causes, and that with a change of air, and the
aid of a few tonics, your spirits will return, and the tone of
your mind be once more cheerful and tranquil as heretofore.
There was, after all, more truth than we are quite willing to
admit in the classic theories which assigned the undue pre-
dominance of any one affection of the mind, to the undue
action or torpidity of one or other of our bodily organs. Believe
me, that a little attention to diet, exercise, and the other essen-
tials of health, under competent direction, will make you as
much yourself as you can wish.'

'Dr ——,' said Barton, with something like a shudder, 'I
cannot delude myself with such a hope. I have no hope to cling
to but one, and that is, that by some other spiritual agency
more potent than that which tortures me, *it* may be combated,
and I delivered. If this may not be, I am lost — now and for ever
lost.'

'But, Mr. Barton, you must remember,' urged his companion,
'that others have suffered as you have done, and ——'

'No, no, no,' interrupted he, with irritability — 'no, sir, I am
not a credulous — far from a superstitious man. I have been,
perhaps, too much the reverse — too sceptical, too slow of

belief; but unless I were one whom no amount of evidence could convince unless I were to contemn the repeated, the *perpetual* evidence of my own senses, I am now — now at last constrained to believe — I have no escape from the conviction — the overwhelming certainty — that I am haunted and dogged, go where I may, by — by a DEMON!'

There was a preternatural energy of horror in Barton's face, as, with its damp and death-like lineaments turned towards his companion, he thus delivered himself.

'God help you, my poor friend,' said Dr. ——, much shocked. 'God help you; for, indeed, you *are* a sufferer, however your sufferings may have been caused.'

'Ay, ay, God help me,' echoed Barton, sternly; 'but *will* He help me — will He help me?'

'Pray to Him — pray in an humble and trusting spirit,' said he.

'Pray, pray,' echoed he again; 'I can't pray — I could as easily move a mountain by an effort of my will. I have not belief enough to pray; there is something within me that will not pray. You prescribe impossibilities — literal impossibilities.'

'You will not find it so, if you will but try,' said Dr. ——.

'Try! I *have* tried, and the attempt only fills me with confusion: and, sometimes, terror: I have tried in vain, and more than in vain. The awful, unutterable idea of eternity and infinity oppresses and maddens my brain whenever my mind approaches the contemplation of the Creator: I recoil from the effort scared. I tell you, Dr. ——, if I am to be saved, it must be by other means. The idea of an eternal Creator is to me intolerable — my mind cannot support it.'

'Say, then, my dear sir,' urged he, 'say how you would have me serve you — what you would learn of me — what I can do or say to relieve you.'

'Listen to me first,' replied Captain Barton, with a subdued air, and an effort to suppress his excitement, 'listen to me while I detail the circumstances of the persecution under which my life has become all but intolerable — a persecution which has made me fear *death* and the world beyond the grave as much as I have grown to hate existence.'

The Familiar 1794.

Jeanette A. Dunne Dec 78

Barton then proceeded to relate the circumstances which I have already detailed, and then continued:

'This has now become habitual — an accustomed thing. I do not mean the actual seeing him in the flesh — thank God, that at least is not permitted daily. Thank God, from the ineffable horrors of that visitation I have been mercifully allowed intervals of repose, though none of security; but from the consciousness that a malignant spirit is following and watching me wherever I go I have never, for a single instant, a temporary respite. I am pursued with blasphemies, cries of despair, and appalling hatred. I hear those dreadful sounds called after me as I turn the corners of the streets; they come in the night-time, while I sit in my chamber alone; they haunt me everywhere, charging me with hideous crimes, and — great God! — threatening me with coming vengeance and eternal misery. Hush! do you hear *that*?' he cried, with a horrible smile of triumph; 'there — there, will that convince you?'

The clergyman felt a chill of horror steal over him, while during the wail of a sudden gust of wind, he heard, or fancied he heard, the half-articulate sounds of rage and derision mingling in the sough.

'Well, what do you think of *that*?' at length Barton cried, drawing a long breath through his teeth.

'I heard the wind,' said Dr. ——. 'What should I think of it — what is there remarkable about it?'

'The prince of the powers of the air,' muttered Barton, with a shudder.

'Tut, tut! my dear sir,' said the student, with an effort to reassure himself; for though it was broad daylight, there was nevertheless something disagreeably contagious in the nervous excitement under which his visitor so miserably suffered. 'You must not give way to those wild fancies; you must resist these impulses of the imagination.'

'Ay, ay; "resist the devil and he will flee from thee",' said Barton, in the same tone; 'but *how* resist him? ay, there it is — there is the rub. What — *what* am I to do? what *can* I do?

'My dear sir, this *is* fancy,' said the man of folios; 'you are your own tormentor.'

'No, no, sir — fancy has no part in it,' answered Barton, somewhat sternly. 'Fancy! was it that made *you*, as well as me, hear, but this moment, those accents of hell? Fancy, indeed! No, no.'

'But you have seen this person frequently,' said the ecclesiastic; 'why have you not accosted or secured him? Is it not a little precipitate, to say no more, to assume, as you have done, the existence of preternatural agency; when, after all, everything may be easily accountable, if only proper means were taken to sift the matter.'

'There are circumstances connected with this — this *appearance*,' said Barton, 'which it is needless to disclose, but which to *me* are proofs of its horrible nature. I know that the being that follows me is not human — I say I *know* this; I could prove it to your own conviction.' He paused for a minute, and then added, 'And as to accosting it, I dare not, I could not; when I see it I am powerless; I stand in the gaze of death, in the triumphant presence of infernal power and malignity. My strength, and faculties, and memory, all forsake me. O God, I fear, sir, you know not what you speak of. Mercy, mercy; heaven have pity on me!'

He leaned his elbow on the table, and passed his hand across his eyes, as if to exclude some image of horror, muttering the last words of the sentence he had just concluded, again and again.

'Dr. ——,' he said, abruptly raising himself, and looking full upon the clergyman with an imploring eye, 'I know you will do for me whatever may be done. You know now fully the circumstances and the nature of my affliction. I tell you I cannot help myself; I cannot hope to escape. I am utterly passive. I conjure you, then, to weigh my case well, and if anything may be done for me by vicarious suplication — by the intercession of the good — or by any aid or influence whatsoever, I implore of you, I adjure you in the name of the Most High, give me the benefit of that influence — deliver me from the body of this death. Strive for me, pity me; I know you will; you cannot refuse this; it is the purpose and object of my visit. Send me away with some hope — however little — some faint hope of ultimate deliverance, and I will nerve myself to endure, from hour to hour, the hideous dream into which my existence has been transformed.'

Dr. —— assured him that all he could do was to pray earnestly for him, and that so much he would not fail to do. They parted with a hurried and melancholy valediction. Barton hasened to the carriage that awaited him at the door, drew down the blinds, and drove away, while Dr. —— returned to his chamber, to ruminate at leisure upon the strange interview which had just interrupted his studies.

6 SEEN AGAIN

It was not to be expected that Captain Barton's changed and eccentric habits should long escape remark and discussion. Various were the theories suggested to account for it. Some attributed the alteration to the pressure of secret pecuniary embarrassments; others to a repugnance to fulfil an engagement into which he was presumed to have too precipitately entered; and others, again, to the supposed incipiency of mental disease, which latter, indeed, was the most plausible, as well as the most generally received, of the hypotheses circulated in the gossip of the day.

From the very commencement of this change, at first so gradual in its advances, Miss Montague had of course been aware of it. The intimacy involved in their peculiar relation, as well as the near interest which it inspired afforded, in her case, a like opportunity and motive for the successful exercise of that keen and penetrating observation peculiar to her sex.

His visits became, at length, so interrupted, and his manner, while they lasted, so abstracted, strange, and agitated, that Lady L——, after hinting her anxiety and her suspicions more than once, at length distinctly stated her anxiety, and pressed for an explanation.

The explanation was given, and although its nature at first relieved the worst solicitudes of the old lady and her niece, yet the circumstances which attended it, and the really dreadful consequences which it obviously indicated, as regarded the spirits, and indeed the reason of the now wretched man, who

made the strange declaration, were enough, upon little reflection, to fill their minds with perturbation and alarm.

General Montague, the young lady's father, at length arrived.
He had himself slightly known Barton, some ten or twelve years
previously, and being aware of his fortune and connections, was
disposed to regard him as an unexceptionable and indeed a
most desirable match for his daughter. He laughed at the story
of Barton's supernatural visitations, and lost no time in calling
upon his intended son-in-law.

'My dear Barton,' he continued, gaily, after a little conversation, 'my sister tells me that you are a victim to blue devils, in
quite a new and original shape.'

Barton changed countenance, and sighed profoundly.

'Come, come; I protest this will never do,' contiued the
General; 'you are more like a man on his way to the gallows
than to the altar. These devils have made quite a saint out of
you.'

Barton made an effort to change the conversation.

'No, no, it won't do,' said his visitor laughing; 'I am resolved
to say what I have to say upon this magnificent mock mystery
of yours. You must not be angry, but really it is too bad to see
you at your time of life, absolutely frightened into good be-
havour, like a naughty child by a bugaboo, and as far as I can
learn, a very contemptible one. Seriously, I have been a good
deal annoyed at what they tell me; but at the same time thoroughly convinced that there is nothing in the matter that may
not be cleared up, with a little attention and management,
within a week at furthest.

'Ah, General, you do not know ——,' he began.

'Yes, but I do know quite enough to warrant my confidence,'
interrupted the soldier, 'don't I know that all your annoyance
proceeds from the occasional appearance of a certain little man
in a cap and greatcoat, with a red vest and a bad face, who
follows you about, and pops upon you at corners of lanes, and
throws you into ague fits. Now, my dear fellow, I'll make it my
business to *catch* this mischievous little mountebank, and either
beat him to a jelly with my own hands, or have him whipped
through the town, at the cart's tail, before a month passes.'

'If *you* knew what *I* knew,' said Barton, with gloomy agitation, 'you would speak very differently. Don't imagine that I am so weak as to assume, without proof the most overwhelming, the conclusion to which I have been forced — the proofs are here, locked up here.' As he spoke he tapped upon his breast, and with an anxious sigh continued to walk up and down the room.

'Well, well, Barton,' said his visitor, 'I'll wager a rump and a dozen I collar the ghost, and convince even you before many days are over.'

He was running on in the same strain when he was suddenly arrested, and not a little shocked, by observing Barton, who had approached the window, stagger slowly back, like one who had received a stunning blow; his arm extended towards the street — his face and his very lips white as ashes — while he muttered, 'There — by heaven! — there — there!'

General Montague started mechanically to his feet, and from the window of the drawing-room, saw a figure corresponding, as well as his hurry would permit him to discern, with the description of the person whose appearance so persistently disturbed the repose of his friend.

The figure was just turning from the rails of the area upon which it had been leaning, and, without waiting to see more, the old gentleman snatched his cane and hat, and rushed down the stairs and into the street, in the furious hope of securing the person, and punishing the audacity of the mysterious stranger.

He looked round him, but in vain, for any trace of the person he had himself distinctly seen. He ran breathlessly to the nearest corner, expecting to see from thence the retiring figure, but no such form was visible. Back and forward, from crossing to crossing, he ran, at fault, and it was not until the curious gaze and laughing countenances of the passers-by reminded him of the absurdity of his pursuit, that he checked his hurried pace, lowered his walking cane from the menacing altitude which he had mechanically given it, adjusted his hat, and walked composedly back again inwardly vexed and flurried. He found Barton pale and trembling in every joint; they both remained silent, though under emotions very different. At last Barton whispered, 'You saw it?'

'*It* — him — some one — you mean — to be sure I did,' replied Montague, testily. 'But where is the good or the harm of seeing him? The fellow runs like a lamplighter. I wanted to *catch* him, but he had stolen away before I could reach the hall door. However, it is no great matter; next time, I dare say, I'll do better; and, egad, if I once come within reach of him, I'll introduce his shoulders to the weight of my cane.'

Notwithstanding General Montague's undertakings and exhortations, however, Barton continued to suffer from the seflsame unexplained cause; go how, when, or where he would, he was still constantly dogged or confronted by the being who had established over him so horrible an influence.

Nowhere and at no time was he secure against the odious appearance which haunted him with such diabolic perseverance.

His depression, misery, and excitement became more settled and alarming every day, and the mental agonies that ceaselessly preyed upon him, began at last so sensibly to affect his health, that Lady L—— and General Montague succeeded, without, indeed, much difficulty, in persuading him to try a short tour on the Continent, in the hope that an entire change of scene would, at all events, have the effect of breaking through the influences of local association, which the more sceptical of his friends assumed to be by no means inoperative in suggesting and perpetuating what they conceived to be a mere form of nervous illusion.

General Montague indeed was persuaded that the figure which haunted his intended son-in-law was by no means the creation of his imagination, but, on the contrary, a substantial form of flesh and blood, animated by a resolution, perhaps with some murderous object in perspective, to watch and follow the unfortunate gentleman.

Even this hypothesis was not a very pleasant one; yet it was plain that if Barton could ever be convinced that there was nothing preternatural in the phenomenon which he had hitherto regarded in that light, the affair would lose all its terrors in his eyes, and wholly cease to exercise upon his health and spirits the baleful influence which it had hitherto done. He therefore reasoned, that if the annoyance were actually escaped by mere locomotion and change of scene, it obviously could not have originated in any supernatural agency.

7 FLIGHT

Yielding to their persuasions, Barton left Dublin for England, accompanied by General Montague. They posted rapidly to London, and thence to Dover, whence they took the packet with a fair wind for Calais. The General's confidence in the result of the expedition on Barton's spirits had risen day by day, since their departure from the shores of Ireland; for to the inexpressible relief and delight of the latter, he had not since then, so much as even once fancied a repetition of those impressions which had, when at home, drawn him gradually down to the very depths of despair.

This exemption from what he had begun to regard as the inevitable condition of his existence, and the sense of security which began to pervade his mind, were inexpressibly delightful; and in the exultation of what he considered his deliverance, he indulged in a thousand happy anticipations for a future into which so lately he had hardly dared to look; and, in short, both he and his companion secretly congratulated themselves upon the termination of that persecution which had been to its immediate victim a source of such unspeakable agony.

It was a beautiful day, and a crowd of idlers stood upon the jetty to receive the packet, and enjoy the bustle of the new arrivals. Montague walked a few paces in advance of his friend, and as he made his way through the crowd, a little man touched his arm, and said to him, in a broad provincial *patois*;

'Monsieur is walking too fast; he will lose his sick comrade in the throng, for, by my faith the poor gentleman seems to be fainting.'

Mongague turned quickly, and observed that Barton did indeed look deadly pale. He hastened to his side.

'My dear fellow, are you ill?' he asked anxiously.

The question was unheeded, and twice repeated, ere Barton stammered:

'I saw him — by ——, I saw him!'

'*Him*! — the wretch — who — where now? — where is he?' cried Montague, looking around him.

'I saw him — but he is gone,' repeated Barton faintly.

'But where — where? For God's sake speak,' urged Montague, vehemently.

'It is but this moment — *here*,' said he.

'But what did he look like — what had he on — what did he wear — quick, quick,' urged his excited companion, ready to dart among the crowd and collar the delinquent on the spot.

'He touched your arm — he spoke to you — he pointed to me. God be merciful to me, there is no escape,' said Barton, in the low, subdued tones of despair.

Montague had already bustled away in all the flurry of mingled hope and rage; but though the singular *personnel* of the stranger who had accosted him was vividly impressed upon his recollection, he failed to discover among the crowd even the slightest resemblance to him.

After a fruitless search, in which he enlisted the services of several of the bystanders, who aided all the more zealously, as they believed he had been robbed, he at length, out of breath and baffled, gave over the attempt.

'Ah, my friend, it won't do,' said Barton, with the faint voice and bewildered, ghastly look of one who had been stunned by some mortal shock; 'there is no use in contending; whatever it is, the dreadful association between me and it is now established — I shall never escape — never!'

'Nonsense, nonsense, my dear Barton; don't talk so,' said Montague, with something at once of irritation and dismay; 'you must not, I say; we'll jockey the scoundrel yet; never mind, I say — never mind.'

It was, however, but labour lost to endeavour henceforward to inspire Barton with one ray of hope; he became desponding.

This intangible, and, as it seemed, utterly inadequate influence was fast destroying his energies of intellect, character and health. His first object was now to return to Ireland, there, as he believed, and now almost hoped, speedily to die.

To Ireland accordingly he came, and one of the first faces he saw upon the shore, was again that of his implacable and dreaded attendant. Barton seemed at last to have lost not only all enjoyment and every hope in existence, but all independence of will besides. He now submitted himself passively to the management of the friends most nearly interested in his welfare.

With the apathy of entire despair, he implicitly assented to whatever measures they suggested and advised; and as a last resource, it was determined to remove him to a house of Lady L——'s, in the neighbourhood of Clontarf, where, with the advice of his medical attendant, who persisted in his opinion that the whole train of consequences resulted merely from some nervous derangement, it was resolved that he was to confine himself strictly to the house, and make use only of those apartments which commanded a view of an enclosed yard, the gates of which were to be kept jealously locked.

Those precautions would certainly secure him against the casual appearance of any living form, that his excited imagination might possibly confound with the spectre which, as it was contended, his fancy recognised in every figure that bore even a distant or general resemblance to the peculiarities with which his fancy had at first invested it.

A month or six weeks' absolute seclusion under these conditions, it was hoped might, by interrupting the series of these terrible impressions, gradually dispel the predisposing apprehensions, and the associations which had confirmed the supposed disease, and rendered recovery hopeless.

Cheerful society and that of his friends was to be constantly supplied, and on the whole, very sanguine expectations were indulged in, that under the treatment thus detailed, the obstinate hypochondria of the patient might at length give way.

Accompanied, therefore, by Lady L——, General Montague and his daughter — his own affianced bride — poor Barton — himself never daring to cherish a hope of his ultimate emancipation from the horrors under which his life was literally wasting away — took possession of the apartments, whose situations protected him against the intrusions, from which he shrank with such unutterable terror.

After a little time, a steady persistence in this system began to manifest its results, in a very marked though gradual improvement, alike in the health and spirits of the invalid. Not, indeed that anything at all approaching complete recovery was yet discernible. On the contrary, to those who had not seen him since the commencement of his strange sufferings, such an alteration would have been apparent as might well have shocked them.

The improvement, however, such as it was, was welcomed with gratitude and delight, especially by the young lady, whom her attachment to him, as well as her now singularly painful position consequent on his protracted illness, rendered an object scarcely one degree less to be commiserated than himself.

A week passed — a fortnight — a month — and yet there had been no recurrence of the hated visitation. The treatment had, so far forth, been followed by complete success. The chain of associations was broken. The constant pressure upon the over-tasked spirits had been removed, and, under these comparatively favourable circumstances, the sense of social community with the world about him and something of human interest, if not of enjoyment, began to reanimate him.

It was about this time that Lady L—— who, like most old ladies of the day, was deep in family receipts, and a great pretender to medical science, dispatched her own maid to the kitchen garden, with a list of herbs, which were there to be carefully culled, and brought back to her housekeeper for the purpose stated. The handmaiden, however, returned with her task scarce half completed, and a good deal flurried and alarmed. Her mode of accounting for her precipitate retreat and evident agitation was odd, and, to the old lady, startling.

8 SOFTENED

It appeared that she had repaired to the kitchen garden, pursuant to her mistress's directions, and had there begun to make the specified selection among the rank and neglected herbs which crowded one corner of the enclosure, and while engaged in this pleasant labour, she carelessly sang a fragment of an old song, as she said, 'to keep herself company'. She was, however, interrupted by an ill-natured laugh; and, looking up, she saw through the old thorn hedge, which surrounded the garden, a singularly ill-looking little man, whose countenance wore the stamp of menace and malignity, standing close to her, at the other side of the hawthorn screen.

She described herself as utterly unable to move or speak, while he charged her with a message for Captain Barton; the substance of which she distinctly remembered to have been to the effect, that he, Captain Barton, must come abroad as usual, and show himself to his friends, out of doors, or else prepare for a visit in his own chamber.

On concluding this brief message, the stranger had, with a threatening air, got down into the outer ditch, and, seizing the hawthorn stems in his hands, seemed on the point of climbing through the fence — a feat which might have been accomplished without much difficulty.

Without, of course, awaiting this result, the girl — throwing down her treasures of thyme and rosemary — had turned and run, with the swiftness of terror, to the house. Lady L—— commanded her, on pain of instant dismissal, to observe an absolute silence respecting all that passed of the incident which related to Captain Barton; and, at the same time, directed instant search to be made by her men, in the garden and the fields adjacent. This measure, however, was as usual, unsuccessful, and, filled with undefinable misgivings, Lady L—— communicated the incident to her brother. The story, however, until long afterwards, went no farther, and of course, it was jealously guarded from Barton, who continued to amend though slowly.

Barton now began to walk occasionally in the courtyard which I have mentioned, and which being enclosed by a high wall, commanded no view beyond its own extent. Here he, therefore, considered himself perfectly secure: and, but for a careless violation of orders by one of the grooms, he might have enjoyed, at least for some time longer, his much-prized immunity. Opening upon the public road, this yard was entered by a wooden gate, with a wicket in it, and was further defended an iron gate upon the outside. Strict orders had been given to keep both carefully locked; but, spite of these, it had happened that one day, as Barton was slowly pacing this narrow enclosure, in his accustomed walk, and reaching the farther extremity, was turning to retrace his steps, he saw the boarded wicket ajar, and the face of his tormentor immovably looking at him through the iron bars. For a few seconds he stood riveted to the earth — breathless and bloodless — in the fascination of that dreaded gaze, and then fell helplessly insensible upon the pavement.

There he was found a few minutes afterwards, and conveyed to his room — the apartment which he was never afterwards to leave alive. Henceforward a marked and unaccountable change was observable in the tone of his mind. Captain Barton was now no longer the excited and despairing man he had been before; a strange alteration had passed upon him — an unearthly tranquility reigned in his mind — it was the anticipated stillness of the grave.

'Montague, my friend, this struggle is nearly ended now,' he said tranquilly, but with a look of fixed and fearful awe. 'I have, at last, some comfort from that world of spirits, from which my punishment has come. I now know that my sufferings will soon be over.'

Montague pressed him to speak on.

'Yes,' said he, in a softened voice, 'my punishment is nearly ended. From sorrow, perhaps. I shall never, in time or eternity, escape; but my *agony* is almost over. Comfort has been revealed to me, and what remains of my allotted struggle I will bear with submission — even with hope.'

'I am glad to hear you speak so tranquilly, my dear Barton,' said Montague; 'peace and cheer of mind are all you need to make you what you were.'

'No, no — I never can be that,' said he mournfully. 'I am no longer fit for life. I am soon to die. I am to see *him* but once again, and then all is ended.'

'He said so, then?' suggested Montague.

'*He?* — No, no: good tidings could scarcely come through him; and these were good and welcome; and they came so solemnly and sweetly — with unutterable love and melancholy, such as I could not — without saying more than is needful, or fitting, of other long past scenes and persons — fully explain to you.' As Barton said this he shed tears.

'Come, come,' said Montague, mistaking the source of his emotions, 'you must not give way. What is it, after all, but a pack of dreams and nonsense; or, at worst, the practices of a scheming rascal that enjoys his power of playing upon your nerves, and loves to exert it — a sneaking vagabond that owes you a grudge, and pays it off this way, not daring to try a more manly one.'

'A grudge, indeed, he owes me — you say rightly,' said Barton, with a sudden shudder; 'a grudge as you call it. Oh, my God! when the justice of Heaven permits the Evil one to carry out a scheme of vengeance — when its execution is committed to the lost and terrible victim of sin, who owes his own ruin to the man, the very man, whom he is commissioned to pursue — then, indeed, the torments and terrors of hell are anticipated on earth. But heaven has dealt mercifully with me — hope has opened to me at last; and if death could come without the dreadful sight I am doomed to see, I would gladly close my eyes this moment upon the world. But though death is welcome, I shrink with an agony you cannot understand — an actual frenzy of terror — from the last encounter with that — that DEMON, who has drawn me thus to the verge of the chasm and who is himself to plunge me down. I am to see him again — once more — but under circumstances unutterably more terrific than ever.'

As Barton thus spoke, he trembled so violently that Montague was really alarmed at the extremity of his sudden agitation, and hastened to lead him back to the topic which had before seemed to exert so tranquillising an effect upon his mind.

'It was not a dream,' he said, after a time; 'I was in a different state — I felt differently and strangely; and yet it was all as real, as clear, and vivid, as what I now see and hear — it was a reality.'

'And what *did* you see and hear?' urged his companion.

'When I wakened from the swoon I fell into on seeing *him*,' said Barton, continuing as if he had not heard the question, 'it was slowly, very slowly — I was lying by the margin of a broad lake,with misty hills all round, and a soft, melancholy, rose-coloured light illuminated it all. It was unusually sad and lonely, and yet more beautiful than any earthly scene. My head was leaning on the lap of a girl, and she was singing a song, that told, I know not how — whether by words or harmonies — of all my life — all that is past, and all that is still to come; and with the song the old feelings that I thought had perished within me came back, and tears flowed from my eyes — partly for the song and its mysterious beauty, and partly for the unearthly sweetness of her voice; and yet I knew the voice — oh! how well; and I was spellbound as I listened and looked at the solitary scene, without stirring, almost without breathing — and, alas! alas! without turning my eyes towards the face that I knew was near me, so sweetly powerful was the enchantment that held me. And so, slowly, the song and scene grew fainter, and fainter, to my sense, till all was dark and still again. And then I awoke to this world, as you saw, comforted, for I knew that I was forgiven much.' Barton wept again long and bitterly.

From this time, as we have said, the prevailing tone of his mind was one of profound and tranquil melancholy. This, however, was not without its interruptions. He was thoroughly impressed with the conviction that he was to experience another and a final visitation, transcending in horror all he had before experienced. From this anticipated and unkown agony, he often shrank in such paroxysms of abject terror and dis-traction, as filled the whole household with dismay and super-stitious panic. Even those among them who affected to discredit the theory of preternatural agency, were often in their secret souls visited during the silence of night with qualms and appre-hensions, which they would not have readily confessed; and none of them attempted to dissuade Barton from the resolution on which he now systematically acted, of shutting himself up in his own apartment. The window-blinds of this room were kept jealously down; and his own man was seldom out of his presence, day or night, his bed being placed in the same chamber.

This man was an attached and respectable servant; and his duties, in addition to those ordinarily imposed upon valets, but which Barton's independent habits generally dispensed with, were to attend carefully to the simple precautions by means of which his master hoped to exclude the dreaded intrusion of the 'Watcher'. And, in addition to attending to those arrangements, which amounted merely to guarding against the possibility of his master's being, through any unscreened window or open door, exposed to the dreaded influence, the valet was never to suffer him to be alone — total solitude, even for a minute, had become to him now almost as intolerable as the idea of going abroad into the public ways — it was an instinctive anticipation of what was coming.

9 REQUIESCAT

It is needless to say, that under these circumstances, no steps were taken towards the fulfilment of that engagement into which he had entered. There was quite disparity enough in point of years, and indeed of habits, between the young lady and Captain Barton, to have precluded anything like very vehement or romantic attachment on her part. Though grieved and anxious, therefore, she was very far from being heart-broken.

Miss Montague, however, devoted much of her time to the patient but fruitless attempt to cheer the unhappy invalid. She read for him and conversed with him; but it was apparent that whatever exertions he made, the endeavour to escape from the one everwaking fear that preyed upon him, was utterly and miserably unavailing.

Young ladies are much given to the cultivation of pets; and among those who shared the favour of Miss Montague was a fine old owl, which the gardener, who caught him napping among the ivy of ruined stable, had dutifully presented to that young lady.

The caprice which regulates such preferences was manifested in the extravagant favour with which this grim and ill-favoured bird was at once distinguished by his mistress; and, trifling as this whimsical circumstance may seem, I am forced to mention it, inasmuch as it is connected, oddly enough, with the concluding scene of the story.

Barton, far from sharing in this liking for the new favourite, regarded it from the first with an antipathy as violent as it was utterly unaccountable. Its very vicinity was unsupportable to him. He seemed to hate and dread it with a vehemence absolutely laughable, and which, to those who have never witnessed the exhibition of antipathies of this kind, would seem all but incredible.

With these words of preliminary explanation, I shall proceed to state the particulars of the last scene in this strange series of incidents. It was almost two o'clcok one winter's night, and Barton was, as usual at that hour, in his bed; the servant we have mentioned occupied a smaller bed in the same room, and a light burning. The man was on a sudden aroused by his master, who said:

'I can't get it out of my head that that accursed bird has got out somehow, and is lurking in some corner of the room. I have been dreaming about him. Get up, Smith, and look about; search for him. Such hateful dreams!'

The servant rose, and examined the chamber, and while engaged in so doing, he heard the well-known sound, more like a long-drawn gasp than a hiss, with which these birds from their secret haunts affright the quiet of the night.

This ghostly indication of its proximity — for the sound proceeded from the passage upon which Barton's chamber door opened — determined the search of the servant, who, opening the door, proceeded a step or two forward for the purpose of driving the bird away. He had, however, hardly entered the lobby, when the door behind him slowly swung to under the impulse, as it seemed, of some gentle current of air; but as immediately over the door there was a kind of window, intended in the day time to aid in lighting the passage, and through which at present the rays of the candle were issuing the valet could see quite enough for his purpose.

As he advanced he heard his master — who, lying in a well-curtained bed, had not, as it seemed, perceived his exit from the room — call him by name, and direct him to place the candle on the table by his bed. The servant, who was now some way in the long passage, and not liking to raise his voice for the purpose of replying, lest he should startle the sleeping inmates of the house, began to walk hurriedly and softly back again, when, to his amazement, he heard a voice in the interior of the chamber answering calmly, and actually saw, through the window which overtopped the door, that the light was slowly shifting, as if carried across the room in answer to his master's call. Palsied by a feeling akin to terror, yet not unmingled with curiosity, he stood breathless and listening at the threshold, unable to summon resolution to push open the door and enter. Then came a rustling of the curtains, and a sound like that of one who in a low voice hushes a child to rest, in the midst of which he heard Barton say, in a tone of stifled horror — 'Oh, God — oh, my God!' and repeat the same exclamation several times. Then ensued a silence, which again was broken by the same strange soothing sound; and at last there burst forth, in one swelling peal, a yell of agony so appalling and hideous, that, under some impulse of ungovernable horror, the man rushed to the door, and with his whole strength strove to force it open. Whether it was that, in his agitation, he had himself but imperfectly turned the handle, or that the door was really secured from the inside, he failed to effect an entrance; and as he tugged and pushed, yell after yell rang louder and wilder through the chamber, accompanied all the while by the same hushed sounds. Actually freezing with terror, and scarce knowing what he did, the man turned and ran down the passage, wringing his hands in the extremity of horror and irresolution. At the stair-head he was encounterd by General Montague, scared and eager, and just as they met the fearful sounds had ceased.

'What is it? Who — where is your master?' said Montague, with the incoherence of extreme agitation. 'Has anything — for God's sake is anything wrong?'

'Lord have mercy on us, it's all over,' said the man, staring wildly towards his master's chamber. 'He's dead, sir, I'm sure he's dead.'

Without waiting for inquiry or explanation, Montague closely followed the servant, hurried to the chamber door, turned the handle, and pushed it open. As the door yielded to his pressure, the ill-omened bird of which the servant had been in search, uttering its spectral warning, started suddenly from the far side of the bed, and flying through the doorway close over their heads, and extinguishing, in his passage, the candle which Montague carried, crashed through the skylight that overlooked the lobby, and sailed away into the darkness of the outer space.

'There it is, God bless us,' whispered the man after a breathless pause.

'Curse that bird,' mutterd the General, startled by the suddenness of the apparition, and unable to conceal his discomposure.

'The candle is moved,' said the man, after another breathless pause, pointing to the candle that still burned in the room; 'see, they put it by the bed.'

'Draw the curtains, fellow, and don't stand gaping there,' whispered Montague, sternly.

The man hesitated.

'Hold this, then,' said Montague, impatiently thrusting the candlestick into the servant's hand, and himself advancing to the bedside, he drew the curtains apart. The light of the candle, which was still burning at the bedside, fell upon a figure huddled together, and half upright, at the head of the bed. It seemed as though it had slunk back as far as the solid panelling would allow, and the hands were still clutched in the bedclothes.

'Barton, Barton, *Barton*!' cried the General, with a strange mixture of awe and vehemence. He took the candle, and held it so that it shone full upon the face. The features were fixed, stern, and white; the jaw was fallen; and the sightless eyes still open, gazed vacantly forward towards the front of the bed. 'God Almighty! he's dead,' muttered the General, as he looked upon this fearful spectacle. They both continued to gaze upon it in silence for a minute or more. 'And cold, too,' whispered Montague, withdrawing his hand from that of the dead man.

'And see, see — may I never have life, sir,' added the man, another pause, with a shudder, 'but there was something else on the bed with him. Look there — look there — see that, sir.'

As the man thus spoke he pointed to a deep indenture as if caused by a heavy pressure, near the foot of the bed.

Montague was silent.

'Come, sir, come away, for God's sake,' whispered the man, drawing close up to him, and holding fast by his arm, while he glanced fearfully round; 'what good can be done here now — come away, for God's sake!'

At this moment they heard the steps of more than one approaching, and Montague, hastily desiring the servant to arrest their progress, endeavouring to loose the rigid grip with which the fingers of the dead man were clutched in the bed-clothes, and drew, as well as he was able, the awful figure into a reclining posture; then closing the curtains carefully upon it, he hastened himself to meet those persons that were approaching.

It is needless to follow the personages so slightly connected with this narrative, into the events of their after life; it is enough to say, that no clue to the solution of these mysterious occurrences was ever after discovered; and so long an interval having now passed since the event which I have just described concluded this strange history, it is scarcely to be expected that time can throw any new lights upon its dark and inexplicable outline. Until the secrets of the earth shall be no longer hidden, therefore, these transactions must remain shrouded in their original obscurity.

The only occurrence in Captain Barton's former life to which reference was ever made, as having any possible connection with the sufferings with which his existence closed, and which he himself seemed to regard as working out a retribution for some grievous sin of his past life, was a circumstance which not for several years after his death was brought to light. The nature of this disclosure was painful to his relatives, and discreditable to his memory.

It appeared that some six years before Captain Barton's final return to Dublin, he had formed, in the town of Plymouth, a guilty attachment, the object of which was the daughter of one of the ship's crew under his command. The father had visited the frailty of his unhappy child with extreme harshness, and even brutality, and it was said that she had died heart-broken. Presuming upon Barton's implication of her guilt, this man had conducted himself towards him with marked insolence, and Barton retaliated this, and what he resented with still more exasperated bitterness — his treatment of the unfortunate girl — by a systematic exercise of those terrible and arbitrary severities which the regulations of the navy placed at the command of those who are responsible for its discipline. The man had at length made his escape, while the vessel was in port at Naples, but died as it was said, in an hospital in that town, of the wounds inflicted in one of his recent and sanguinary punishments.

Whether these circumstances in reality bear, or not, upon the occurrences of Barton's after-life, it is, of course, impossible to say. It seems, however, more than probable that they were at least in, in his own mind, closely associated with them. But however the truth may be, as to the origin and motives of this mysterious persecution, there can be no doubt that, with respect to the agencies by which it was accomplished, absolute and impenetrable mystery is like to prevail until the day of doom.

FITZ-JAMES O'BRIEN (1828-1862)

THOUGH HIS OUTPUT WAS SMALL the quality of Fitz-James O'Brien's work is so remarkable that its influence is still visible among fantasy writers of today. The critic Sam Moskowitz has written: 'Any serious student of American letters asked to name the half dozen writers of the nineteenth century who exerted the greatest influence upon the development of the American short story would be most unlikely to omit Fitz-James O'Brien'.

O'Brien was born in Limerick on December 31, 1828, where his father was a successful lawyer. He went to Trinity College, Dublin, to complete his education and while still a student was writing stories, verse and articles for Irish magazines. When he left Trinity he found he had inherited the sum of £8,500, a considerable fortune in those days, and he decided to go to England and earn his living as a writer. He arrived in London about 1850 and found life easier as a gentleman of leisure. Within two years he had squandered his fortune. His stay in London culminated with an unsuccessful attempt to run away with the wife of an English army officer and O'Brien was forced to flee the country.

By December, 1852, he had arrived in the United States and began a precarious living as a writer. A play, *A Gentleman from Ireland*, was presented to critical acclaim and soon his stories were much in demand in such American journals as *Atlantic*

FITZ-JAMES O'BRIEN

From a drawing by Sol Eytinge, J

Monthly, Scribner's and *Harper's.*

O'Brien lived a Bohemian life, never married and remained careless over money. He formed a group of aspiring young writers over whom he played literary God. But his literary career was cut tragically short after ten years. On Friday, April 12, 1861, soldiers of the Confederate States of America, the southern states which had seceded from the union, fired on the Union-held Fort Sumter. O'Brien, along with thousands of Irish immigrants, enlisted in the Union Army's Irish Brigade. He was commissioned as a lieutenant and wounded in one of the earliest skirmishes of the bloody American Civil War. In an operation, part of his left arm and shoulder bone were removed but the wound became infected.

He died on April 6, 1862, at the age of thirty-three.

Perhaps his best known story is *The Diamond Lens* which, when it appeared in *Atlantic Monthly*, January, 1858, became the literary sensation of the year. The story is about a young microbiologist who kills a close friend to obtain a diamond from which he can make a special lens. Analysing a drop of water he sees, in that tiny cosmos, a humanlike female creature named Animula with whom he falls hopelessly in love. But the drop of water gradually evaporates and helplessly the young scientist witnesses the death of his beloved. He is shattered by the experience and becomes a beggar.

O'Brien wrote his best work between 1855 and 1860. His mastery of the standard ghost story was displayed in his 'The Pot of Tulips' (1855) in which a man returns from the grave to reveal where he has hidden his wealth. Interestingly enough, the story is strongly reminiscent of J. Sheridan Le Fanu.

Two gems were published in the following year, 1856: 'A Terrible Night', in which a man kills his best friend as a result of a fear induced nightmare, and 'The Dragon Fang Possessed by the Conjurer Piou-Lu'.

But it was the year 1858 that saw the publication of his greatest works, including *The Diamond Lens*. In that year 'The Gold Ingot' appeared telling how an old scientist works to turn base metals into gold. One day he thinks he has succeeded when he finds a gold ingot on his work bench. He dies of a stroke when he learns that his daughter, to make him happy, has saved her money and secretly purchased the ingot.

More directly horrific was 'Jubal the Ringer' which is a forceful tale of a bell ringer who employs a flock of bats to loosen the plaster securing the stones of his belfry, then utilises the acoustical vibrations of the bells to send the stones crashing into the church to kill the woman he loves, who is marrying another, in the marriage procession. 'From Hand to Mouth', originally serialised in *The New York Picayune*, was more of a surrealistic fantasy which has disembodied eyes, ears, hands and mouths as its terrifying ingredients. The story, strangely enough, was never finished by O'Brien and the editor, Frank H. Bellew, had to write the final instalment himself. Sam Moskowitz writes: 'Despite its faults, the writing of *From Hand to Mouth* is sheer delight and the light handling of surrealistic nightmarish imagination compares favourably with Lewis Carroll'. Another story which appeared that year was 'The Lost Room', a nightmarish tale of a man who leaves his room on an errand and returns to find it filled with strangers and strange furniture. Unable to prove it is his room, he is ejected. He tries to find the room again but there is only a blank wall.

'What Was It? A Mystery' appeared in the March issue of *Harper's New Monthly Magazine* also in that same year of 1858. It is a masterpiece of horror-fantasy dealing with an invisible creature. Similar in plot are Guy de Maupassant's 'The Horla' and Ambrose Bierce's 'The Damned Thing' both of which were written after O'Brien and were undoubtedly influenced by him.

For this collection, I have chosen 'The Wondersmith' which also appeared in 1858 in the *Atlantic Monthly's* October issue. When Anthony Boucher, as editor of *The Magazine of Fantasy and Science Fiction* chose to reprint the story in December, 1950, he wrote that: 'The Wondersmith is a fine example of the completeness of Fitz-James O'Brien's thinking; in it are expressed practically every phase of the idea of robots: the evil conception of the mechanical as a slave; the use of the robot to war on unsuspecting mankind, the final turning of the android against its creator . . . almost the whole body of writing on robots is here in matrix in this story written nearly 100 years ago'. The critic Gilbert Seldes thought there was 'nothing in the story of Frankenstien's monster and nothing in the crushing fury of Capek's robots (which) gives the same sense of horror as the description of the bloodthirsty, stabbing, galvanised manikins of this story'.

Sam Moskowitz has already pointed out that 'The Wondersmith' was the genesis for A. Merritt's classic horror fantasy *Burn Witch Burn!*

There are three other stories of O'Brien's which deserve special mention. 'Mother of Pearl' (1860) in which a mother kills her child and attempts to kill her husband while under the influence of drugs, an excellent reworking of his theme of 'A Terrible Night'. 'The Child Who Loved a Grave' which appeared in *Harper's New Monthly Magazine* in April, 1861, concerns the unhappy child of drunken and bickering parents who forms an attachment for the grave of a child, a spot where he finds solitude and peace. The last story worthy of mention was, in fact, the last O'Brien story to appear in print. It was published two years after his death in the May, 1864, issue of *Harper's New Monthly Magazine*, and entitled 'How I Overcame My Gravity'. It was an important piece of science fiction in that it suggested the gyroscopic principle as a possible anti-gravity method and theorised that a weightless object hurled hard enough into space might travel away from the earth forever.

The first collected volume of his works was edited by William Winter and published by James R. Osgood and Co. of Boston in 1881 under the title of *The Poems and Stories of Fitz-James O'Brien*. As suggested by the title the book was preoccupied with O'Brien's poetry rather than his stories. The second collection of his work, however, remedied this and was produced under *The Diamond Lens and Other Stories* by Charles Scribner and Sons, New York.

O'Brien justly deserves his title as a master of the macabre and, indeed, that of the most distinguished short story writer in the genre after Edgar Allan Poe.

THE WONDERSMITH
Fitz-James O'Brien

1 GOLOSH STREET AND ITS PEOPLE

 SMALL LANE, the name of which I have for-gotten, or do not choose to remember, slants suddenly off from Chatham Street (before that headlong thoroughfare rushes into the Park). and retreats suddenly down towards the East River, as if it were disgusted with the smell of old clothes, and had determined to wash itself clean. This excellent intention it has, however, evidently contributed towards the making of that imaginary pavement mentioned in the old adage; for it is still emphatically a dirty street. It has never been able to shake of the Hebraic taint of filth which it inherits from the ancestral thorougfare. It is slushy and greasy, as if it were twin brother of the Roman Ghetto.

I like a dirty slum; not because I am naturally unclean — I have not a drop of Neapolitan blood in my veins — but be-cause I generally find a certain sediment of philosophy pre-cipitated in its gutters. A clean street is terribly prosaic. There is not food for thought in carefully swept pavements, barren kennels, and vulgarly spotless houses. But when I go down a street which has been left so long to itself that it has acquired a distinct outward character, I find plenty to think about.

The scraps of sodden letters lying in the ash-barrel have their meaning: desperate appeals, perhaps, from Tom, the baker's assistant, to Amelia, the daughter of the dry-goods retailer, who is always selling at a sacrifice in consequence of the late fire. That may be Tom himself who is now passing me in a white apron, and I look up at the windows of the house (which does not, however, give any signs of a recent conflagration) and almost hope to see Amelia wave a white pocket-handker-chief.

The bit of orange-peel lying on the sidewalk inspires thought. Who will fall over it? who but the industrious mother of six children, the youngest of which is only nine months old, all of whom are dependent on her exertions for support? I see her slip and tumble. I see the pale face convulsed with agony, and the vain struggle to get up; the pitying crowd closing her off from all air; the anxious young doctor who happened to be passing by; the manipulation of the broken limb, the shake of the head, the moan of the victim, the litter borne on men's shoulders. the gates of the New York hospital unclosing, the subscription taken up on the spot.

There is some food for speculation in that three-year-old, tattered child, masked with dirt, who is throwing a brick at another three-year-old, tattered child, masked with dirt. It is not difficult to perceive that he is destined to lurk, as it were, through life. His bad, flat face — or, at least, what can be seen of it — does not look as if it were made for the light of day. The mire in which he wallows now is but a type of the moral mire in which he will wallow hereafter. The feeble little hand lifted at this instant to smite his companion, half in earnest, half in jest, will be raised against his fellow-beings for ever-more.

Golosh Street — as I will call this nameless lane before alluded to — is an interesting locality. All the oddities of trade seemed to have found their way thither and made an eccentric mercantile settlement. There is a bird-shop at one corner wainscoted with little cages containing linnets, wax-wings, canaries, black-birds, Mino-birds, with a hundred other varieties, known only to naturalists. Immediately opposite is an establishement where they sell nothing but ornaments made out of the tinted leaves of autumn, varnished and gummed into various forms. Further down is a second-hand book-stall which looks like a sentry-box mangled out flat, and which is remarkable for not containing a complete set of any work. There is a small chink between two ordinary-sized houses, in which a little Frenchman makes and sells artificial eyes, specimens of which, ranged on a black velvet cushion, stare at you unwinkingly through the window as you pass, until you shudder and hurry on, thinking how awful the world would be if everyone went about without eyelids. There are junk-shops in Golosh Street that seem to have got hold of all the old nails in the ark and all the old brass of Corinth. Madame Filomel, the fortune-teller, lives at No. 12 Golosh Street, second story front, pull the bell on the left-hand side. Next door to Madame is the shop of Herr Hippe, commonly called the Wondersmith.

Herr Hippe's shop is the largest in Golosh Street, and to all appearance is furnished with the smallest stock. Beyond a few packing-cases, a turner's lathe, and shelf laden with dissected maps of Europe, the interior of the shop is entirely unfurnished. The window, which is lofty and wide, but much begrimed with dirt, contains the only pleasant object in the place. This is a beautiful little miniature theater — that is to say, the orchestra and stage. It is fitted with charmingly painted scenery and all the appliances for scenic changes. There are tiny traps, and delicately constructed "lifts," and real foot-lights fed with burning fluid, and in the orchestra sits a diminuitve conductor before his desk, surrounded by musical manikins, all provided with the smallest of violon-cellos, flutes, oboes, drums, and such like.

There are characters also on the stage. A Templar in a white cloak is dragging a fainting female form to the parapet of a ruined bridge, while behind a great black rock on the left one can see a man concealed, who, kneeling, levels an arquebuse at the knight's heart. But the orchestra is silent; the conductor never beats the time, the musicians never play a note; the Templar never drags his victim an inch nearer to the bridge; the masked avenger takes an eternal aim with his weapon.

This repose appears unnatural; for so admirably are the figures executed that they seem replete with life. One is almost led to believe, in looking on them, that they are resting beneath some spell which hinders their motion. One expects every moment to hear the loud explosion of the arquebuse — to see the blue smoke curling, the Templar falling — to hear the orchestra playing the requiem of the guilty.

Few people knew what Herr Hippe's business or trade really was. That he worked at something was evident; else why the shop? Some people inclined to the belief that he was an inventor, or mechanician. His workshop was in the rear of the store, and into that sanctuary no one but himself had admission. He arrived in Golosh Street eight or ten years ago, and one fine morning the neighbours, taking down their shutters, observed that No. 13 had got a tenant. A tall, thin, sallow-faced man stood on a ladder outside the shop entrance, nailing up a large board, on which "Herr Hippe, Wondersmith," was painted in black letters on a yellow ground. The little theater stood in the window, where it stood ever after, and Herr Hippe was established.

But what was a Wondersmith? people asked each other. No one could reply. Madame Filomel was consulted; but she looked grave, and said that it was none of her business. Mr. Pippel, the bird-fancier, who was a German, and ought to know best, thought it was the English for some singular Teutonic profession; but his replies were so vague that Golosh Street was as unsatisfied as ever. Solon, the little humpback, who kept the odd-volume book-stall at the lowest corner, could throw no light upon it. And at length people had to come to the conclusion that Herr Hippe was either a coiner or a magician, and opinions were divided.

2 A BOTTLEFUL OF SOULS

It was a dull December evening. There was little trade doing in Golosh Street, and the shutters were up at most of the shops. Hippe's store had been closed at least an hour, and the Mino-birds and Bohemian wax-wings at Mr. Pippel's had their heads tucked under their wings in their first sleep.

Herr Hippe sat in his parlor, which was lit by a pleasant wood-fire. There were no candles in the room, and the flickering blaze played fantastic tricks on the pale gray walls. It seemed the festival of shadows. Processions of shapes, obscure and indistinct, passed across the leaden-hued panels and vanished in the dusk corners. Every fresh blaze flung up by the wayward logs created new images. Now it was a funeral throng, with the bowed figures of mourners, the shrouded coffin, the plumes that waved like extinguished torches; now a knightly cavalcade with flags and lances, and weird horses, that rushed silently along until they met the angle of the room, when they pranced through the wall and vanished.

On a table close to where Herr Hippe sat was placed a large square box of some dark wood, while over it was spread a casing of steel, so elaborately wrought in an open arabesque pattern that it seemed like a shining blue lace which was lightly stretched over its surface.

Herr Hippe lay luxuriously in his armchair, looking meditatively into the fire. He was tall and thin, and his skin was of a dull saffron hue. Long, straight hair, sharply cut, regular features, a long, thin mustache, that curled like a dark asp around his mouth, the expression of which was so bitter and cruel that it seemed to distill the venom of the ideal serpent, and a bony, muscular form, were the prominent characteristics of the Wondersmith.

The profound silence that reigned in the chamber was broken by a peculiar scratching at the panel of the door, like that which at the French courts was formerly substituted for the ordinary knock, when it was necessary to demand admission to the royal apartments. Herr Hippe started, raised his head, which vibrated on his long neck like the head of a cobra when about to strike, and after a moment's silence uttered a strange guttural sound. The door unclosed, and a squat, broad-shouldered woman, with large, wild, oriental eyes,- entered softly.

"Ah! Filomel, you are come!" said the Wondersmith, sinking back in his chair. "Where are the rest of them?"

"They will be here presently," answered Madame Filomel,

seating herself in an armchair much too narrow for a person of her proportions, and over the sides of which she bulged like a pudding.

"Have you brought the souls?" asked the Wondersmith.

"They are here," said the fortune-teller, drawing a large pot-bellied black bottle from under her cloak. "Ah! I have had such trouble with them!"

"Are they of the right brand — wild, tearing, dark, devilish fellows? We want no essence of milk and honey, you know. None but souls bitter as hemlock or scorching as lightening will suit our purpose."

"You will see, you will see, Grand Duke of Egypt! They are ethereal demons, every one of them. They are the pick of a thousand births. Do you think that I, old midwife that I am, don't know the squall of the demon child from that of the angel child, the very moment they are delivered? Ask a musician how he knows, even in the dark, a note struck by Thalberg from one struck by Liszt!"

"I long to test them," cried Wondersmith, rubbing his hands joyfully. "I long to see how little devils will behave when I give them their shapes. Ah! it will be proud day for us when we let them loose upon the cursed Christian children! Through the length and breadth of the land they will go; wherever our wandering people set foot, and wherever they are, the children of the Christians shall die. Then we, the despised Bohemians, the gipsies, as they call us, will be once more lords of the earth, as we were in the days when the accursed things called cities did not exist, and men lived in the free woods and hunted the game of the forest. Toys indeed! Ay, ay, we will give the little dears toys! toys that all day will sleep calmly in their boxes, seemingly stiff and wooden and without life — but at night, when the souls enter them will arise and surround the cots of the sleeping children, and pierce their hearts with their keen envenomed blades! Toys indeed! Oh, yes, I will sell them toys!"

And the Wondersmith laughed horribly, while the snaky mustache on his upper lip writhed as if it had truly a serpent's power and could sting.

"Have you got your first batch, Herr Hippe?" asked Madame Filomel. "Are they all ready?"

"Oh ay! they are ready," answered the Wondersmith with gusto, opening, as he spoke, the box covered with the blue steel lacework; "they are here."

The box contained a quantity of exquisitely carved wooden manikins of both sexes, painted with great dexterity so as to present a miniature resemblance to nature. They were, in fact, nothing more than admirable specimens of those toys which children delight in placing in various positions on the table — in regiments, or sitting at meals, or grouped under the stiff green trees which always accompany them in the boxes in which they are sold at the toyshops.

The peculiarity, however, about the manikins of Herr Hippe was not alone the artistic truth with which the limbs and the features were gifted; but on the countenance of each little puppet the carver's art had wrought an expression of wickedness that was appalling. Every tiny face had its special stamp of ferocity. The lips were thin and brimful of malice; the small black bead-like eyes glittered with the fire of a universal hate. There was not one of the manikins, male or female, that did not hold in his or her hand some miniature weapon. The little men, scowling like demons, clasped in their wooden fingers swords delicate as a housewife's needle. The women, whose countenances expressed treachery and cruelty, clutched infinitesimal daggers, with which they seemed about to take some terrible vengeance.

"Good!" said Madame Filomel, taking one of the manikins out of the box and examining it attentively; "you work well, Duke Balthazar! These little ones are of the right stamp; they look as if they had mischief in them. Ah! here come our brothers."

At this moment the same scratching that preceded the entrance of Madame Filomel was heard at the door, and Herr Hippe replied with a hoarse, guttural cry. The next moment two men entered. The first was a small man with very brilliant eyes. He was wrapt in a long shabby cloak, and wore a strange nondescript species of cap on his head, such a cap as one sees only in the low billiard-rooms in Paris. His companion was tall, long-limbed, and slender; and his dress, although of the ordinary cut, either from the disposition of colors or from the careless, graceful attitudes of the wearer, assumed a certain air of picturesqueness. Both the men possessed the same marked oriental type of countenance which distinguished the Wondersmith and Madame Filomel. True gipsies they seemed, who would not have been out of place telling fortunes, or stealing chickens in the green lanes of England, or wandering with their wild music and their sleight-of-hand tricks through Bohemian villages.

"Welcome, brothers!" said the Wondersmith; "you are in time. Sister Filomel has brought the souls, and we are about to test them. Monsieur Kerplonne, take off your cloak. Brother Oaksmith, take a chair. I promise you some amusement this evening; so make yourselves comfortable. Here is something to aid you."

And while the Frenchman Kerplonne and his tall companion, Oaksmith, were obeying Hippe's invitation, he reached over to a little closet let into the wall, and took thence a squat bottle and some glasses, which he placed on the table.

"Drink, brothers!" he said: "it is not Christian blood, but good stout wine of Oporto. It goes right to the heart, and warms one like the sunshine of the south."

"It is good," said Kerplonne, smacking his lips with enthusiasm.

"Why don't you keep brandy? Hang wine!" cried Oaksmith, after having swallowd two bumpers in rapid succession.

"Bah! Brandy has been the ruin of our race. It has made us sots and thieves. It shall never cross my threshold," cried the Wondersmith, with a somber indignation.

"A little of it is not bad, though, Duke," said the fortuneteller. "It consoles us for our misfortunes; it gives us the crowns we once wore; it restores to us the power we once wielded; it carries us back, as if by magic, to that land of the sun from which fate has driven us; it darkens the memory of all the evils that we have for centuries suffered!"

"It is a devil; may it be cursed!" cried Herr Hippe, passionately, "It is a demon that stole from me my son, the finest youth in all Courland. Yes! my son, the son of the Waywode Balthazar, Grand Duke of Lower Egypt, died raving in a gutter, with an empty brandy-bottle in his hands. Were it not that the plant is a sacred one to our race, I would curse the grape and the vine that bore it."

This outburst was delivered with such energy that the three gipsies kept silence. Oaksmith helped himself to another glass of port, and the fortune-teller rocked to and fro in her chair, too much overawed by the Wondersmith's vehemence of manner to reply. The little Frenchman, Kerplonne, took no part in the discussion, but seemed lost in admiration of the manikins, which he took from the box in which they lay, handling them with the greatest care.

After the silence had lasted for about a minute, Herr Hippe broke it with the sudden question, "How does your eye get on, Kerplonne?"

"Excellently, Duke. It is finished. I have it here." And the little Frenchman put his hand into his breeches pocket and pulled out a large artificial human eye. Its great size was the only thing in this eye that would lead anyone to suspect its artificiality. It was at least twice the size of life; but there was a fearful speculative light in its iris, which seemed to expand and contract like the eye of a living being, that rendered it a horrible staring paradox. It looked like the naked eye of the Cyclops, torn from his forehead, and still burning with wrath and the desire for vengeance.

The little Frenchman laughed pleasantly as he held the eye in his hand, and gazed down on that huge, dark pupil, that stared back at him, it seemed, with an air of defiance and mistrust.

"It is a devil of an eye," said the little man, wiping the enameled surface with an old silk pocket-handkerchief; "it reads like a demon. My niece — the unhappy one — has a wretch of a lover, and I have a long time feared that she would run away with him. I could not read her correspondence, for she kept her writing-desk closely locked. But I asked her yesterday to keep this eye in some very safe place for me. She put it, as I knew she would, into her desk, and by its aid I read every one of her letters. She was to run away next Monday, the ungrateful! but she will find herself disappointed."

And the little man laughed heartily at the success of his stratagem, and polished and fondled the great eye until that optic seemed to grow sore with rubbing.

"And you have been at work too, I see, Herr Hippe. Your manikins are excellent. But where are the souls?"

"In that bottle," answered the Wondersmith, pointing to the pot-bellied black bottle that Madame Filomel had brought with her. "Yes, Monsieur Kerplonne," he continued, "my manikins are well made. I invoked the aid of Abigor, the demon of soldiery, and he inspired me. The little fellows will be famous assassins when they are animated. We will try them tonight."

"Good!" cried Kerplonne, rubbing his hands joyously. "It is close upon New Year's day. We will fabricate millions of the little murderers by New Year's eve, and sell them in large quantities; and when the households are all asleep, and the Christian children are waiting for Santa Claus to come, the small ones will troop from their boxes, and the Christian children will die. It is famous! Health to Abigor!"

"Let us try them at once," said Oaksmith. "Is your daughter, Zonela, in bed, Herr Hippe? Are we secure from intrusion?"

"No one is stirring about the house," replied the Wondersmith, gloomily.

Filomel leaned over to Oaksmith, and said in an undertone, "Why do you mention his daughter? You know he does not like to have her spoken about."

"I will take care that we are not disturbed," said Kerplonne, rising. "I will put my eye outside the door, to watch."

He went to the door and placed his great eye upon the floor with tender care. As he did so, a dark form, unseen by him or his second vision, glided along the passage noiselessly, and was lost in the darkness.

"Now for it!" exclaimed Madame Filomel, taking up her fat black bottle. "Herr Hippe, prepare your manikins!"

The Wondersmith took the little dolls out, one by one, and set them upon the table. Such an array of villainous countenances was never seen. An army of Italian bravoes, seen through the wrong end of a telescope, or a band of prisoners at the galleys in Lilliput, will give some faint idea of the appearance they presented. While Madame Filomel uncorked the black bottle, Herr Hippe covered the dolls with a species of linen tent, which he took also from the box. This done, the fortune-teller held the mouth of the bottle to the door of the tent, gathering the loose cloth closely round the glass neck. Immediately tiny noises were heard inside the tent. Madame Filomel removed the bottle, and the Wondersmith lifted the covering in which he had enveloped his little people.

A wonderful transformation had taken place. Wooden and inflexible no longer, the crowd of manikins were now in full motion. The bead-like eyes turned, glittering, on all sides; the thin, wicked lips quivered with bad passions; the tiny hands sheathed and unsheathed the little swords and daggers. Episodes, common to life, were taking place in every direction. Here two martial manikins paid court to a pretty, sly-faced female, who smiled on each alternately, but gave her hand to be kissed to a third manikin, an ugly little scoundrel, who crouched behind her. There a pair of friendly dolls walked arm in arm, apparently on the best terms, while, all the time, one was watching his opportunity to stab the other in the back.

"I think they'll do," said the Wondersmith, chuckling as he watched these various incidents. "Treacherous, cruel, blood-thirsty. All goes marvelously well. But stay! I will put the grand test to them."

So saying, he drew a gold dollar from his pocket, and let it fall on the table, in the very midst of the throng of manikins. It had hardly touched the table when there was a pause on all sides. Every head was turned towards the dollar. Then about twenty of the little creatures rushed towards the glittering coin. One, fleeter than the rest, leaped upon it and drew his sword. The entire crowd of little people had now gathered round this new center of attraction. Men and women struggled and shoved to get nearer to the piece of gold. Hardly had the first Lilliputian mounted upon the treasure, when a hundred blades flashed back a defiant answer to his, and a dozen men, sword in hand, leaped upon the yellow platform and drove him off at the sword's point. Then commenced a general battle. The miniature faces were convulsed with rage and avarice. Each furious doll tried to plunge dagger or sword into his or her neighbor, and the women seemed possessed by a thousand devils.

"They will break themselves into atoms," cried Filomel, as she watched with eagerness this savage *mêlée*. "You had better gather them up, Herr Hippe. I will exhaust my bottle and suck all the souls back from them."

"Oh, they are perfect devils! they are magnificent little demons!" cried the Frenchman, with enthusiasm. "Hippe, you are a wonderful man. Brother Oaksmith, you have no such man as Hippe among your English gipsies."

"Not exactly," answered Oaksmith, rather sullenly, "not exactly. But we have men there who can make a twelve-year-old horse look like a four-year-old — and who can take you and Herr Hippe up with one hand, and throw you over their shoulders."

"The good God forbid!" said the little Frenchman. "I do not love such play. It is incommodious."

While Oaksmith and Kerplonne were talking, the Wonder-smith had placed the linen tent over the struggling dolls, and Madame Filomel, who had been performing some mysterious manipulations with her black bottle, put the mouth once more to the door of the tent. In an instant the confused murmur within ceased. Madame Filomel corked the bottle quickly. The Wondersmith withdrew the tent, and, lo! the furious dolls were once more wooden-jointed and inflexible; and the old sinister look was again frozen on their faces.

"They must have blood, though," said Herr Hippe, as he gathered them up and put them into their box. "Mr. Pippel, the bird-fancier, is asleep. I have a key that opens his door. We will let them loose among the birds; it will be rare fun."

"Magnificent!" cried Kerplonne. "Let us go on the instant. But first let me gather up my eye."

The Frenchman pocketed his eye, after having given it a polish with the silk handkerchief; Herr Hippe extinguished the lamp; Oaksmith took a last bumper of port; and the four gipsies departed for Mr. Pippel's, carrying the box of mani-kins with them.

3 SOLON

The shadow that glided along the corridor, at the moment that Monsieur Kerplonne deposited his sentinel eye outside the door of the Wondersmith's apartment, sped swiftly through the passage and ascended the stairs to the attic. Here the shadow stopped at the entrance to one of the chambers and knocked at the door. There was no reply.

"Zonéla, are you asleep?" said the shadow, softly.

"Oh, Solon, is it you?" replied a sweet low voice from with-in. "I thought it was Herr Hippe. Come in."

The shadow opened the door and entered. There were neither candles nor lamp in the room; but through the projecting win-down, which was open, there came the faint gleams of the star-light, by which one could distinguish a female figure seated on a low stool in the middle of the floor.

"Has he left you without light again, Zonéla?" asked the shadow, closing the door of the apartment. "I have brought my little lantern with me, though."

"Thank you, Solon," answered she called Zonéla; "you are a good fellow. He never gives me any light of an evening, but bids me go to bed. I like to sit sometimes and look at the moon and the stars — the stars more than all; for they seem all the time to look right back into my face, very sadly, as if they would say, 'We see you, and pity you, and would help you, if we could.' But it is so mournful to be always looking at such myriads of melancholy eyes! and I long so to read those nice books that you lend me, Solon!"

By this time the shadow had lit the lantern and was a shadow no longer. A large head, covered with a profusion of long blond hair, which was cut after that fashion known as *aux enfants d'Edouard*; a beautiful pale face, lit with wide, blue, dreamy eyes; long arms and slender hands, attenuated legs, and — an enormous hump; — such was Solon, the shadow. As soon as the humpback had lit the lamp, Zonéla arose from the low stool on which she had been seated, and took Solon's hand affectionately in hers.

Zonéla was surely not of gipsy blood. That rich auburn hair, that looked almost black in the lamplight, that pale, transparent skin, tinged with an under-glow of warm rich blood, the hazel eyes, large and soft as those of a fawn, were never begotten of a Zingaro. Zonéla was seemingly about sixteen; her figure although somewhat thin and angular, was full of the unconscious grace of youth. She was dressed in an old cotton print, which had been once of an exceedingly boisterous pattern, but was now a mere suggestion of former splendour; while round her head was twisted, in fantastic fashion, a silk handkerchief of green ground spotted with bright crimson. This strange head-dress gave her an elfish appearance.

"I have been out all day with the organ, and I am so tired, Solon! — not sleepy, but weary, I mean. Poor Furbelow was sleepy, though, and he's gone to bed."

"I'm weary, too, Zonéla; not weary as you are, though, for I sit in my little book-stall all day long, and do not drag round an organ and a monkey and play old tunes for pennies — but weary of myself, of life, of the load that I carry on my shoulders;" and, as he said this, the poor humpback glanced sideways, as if to call attention to his deformed person.

"Well, but you ought not to be melancholy amidst your books, Solon. Gracious! If I could only sit in the sun and read as you do, now happy I should be! But it's very tiresome to trudge round all day with that nasty organ, and look up at the houses, and know that you are annoying the people inside; and then the boys play such bad tricks on poor Furbelow, throwing him hot pennies to pick up, and burning his poor little hands; and oh! sometimes, Solon, the men in the street make me so afraid — they speak to me and look at me so oddly! — I'd a great deal rather sit in your book-stall and read."

"I have nothing but odd volumes in my stall," answered the humpback. "Perhaps that's right, though; for, after all, I'm nothing but an odd volume myself."

"Come, don't be melancholy, Solon. Sit down and tell me a story. I'll bring Furbelow to listen."

So saying, she went to a dusky corner of the cheerless attic room, and returned with a little Brazilian monkey in her arms — a poor, mild, drowsy thing, that looked as if it had cried itself to sleep. She sat down on her little stool, with Furbelow in her lap, and nodded her head to Solon, as much as to say, "Go on; we are attentive."

"You want a story, do you?" said the humpback, with a mournful smile. "Well, I'll tell you one. Only what will your father say, if he catches me here?"

"Herr Hippe is not my father," cried Zonéla, indignantly. "He's a gipsy, and I know I'm stolen; and I'd run away from him, if I only knew where to run to. If I were his child, do you think that he would treat me as he does? make me trudge round the city all day long, with a barrel-organ and a monkey — though I love poor, dear little Furbelow — and keep me up in a garret, and give me ever so little to eat? I know I'm not his child, for he hates me."

"Listen to my story, Zonéla, and we'll talk of that afterwards. Let me sit at your feet;" and, having coiled himself up at the little maiden's feet, he commenced:

"There once lived in a great city, just like this city of New York, a poor little hunchback. He kept a second-hand book-stall, where he made barely enough money to keep body and soul together. He was very sad at times, because he knew scarce anyone, and those that he did know did not love him. He had passed a sickly, secluded youth. The children of his neighbourhood would not play with him, for he was not made like them; and the people in the streets stared at him with pity, or scoffed at him when he went by. Ah! Zonéla, how his poor heart was wrung with bitterness when he beheld the procession of shapely men and fine women that every day passed him by in the thoroughfares of the great city! How he repined and cursed his fate as the torrent of fleet-footed firemen dashed past him to the toll of the bells, magnificent in their over-flowing vitality and strength! But there was one consolation left him — one drop of honey in the jar of gall, so sweet that it ameliorated all the bitterness of life. God had given him a deformed body, but his mind was straight and healthy. So the poor hunchback shut himself into the world of books, and was, if not happy, at least contented. He kept company with courteous paladins, and romantic heroes, and beautiful women; and this society was of such excellent breeding that it never so much as once noticed his poor crooked back or his lame walk.

"The love of books grew upon him with his years. He was remarked for his studious habits; and when, one day, the obscure people that he called father and mother — parents only in name — died, a compassionate book-vender gave him enough stock in trade to set up a little stall of his own. Here, in his book-stall, he sat in the sun all day, waiting for the customers that seldom came, and reading the fine deeds of the people of the ancient time, or the beautiful thoughts of the poets that had warmed millions of hearts before that hour, and still glowed for him with undiminished fire.

"One day, when he was reading some book, that, small as it was, was big enough to shut the whole world out from him, he heard some music in the street. Looking up from his book, he saw a little girl, with large eyes, playing an organ, while a monkey begged for alms from a crowd of idlers who had nothing in their pockets but their hands. The girl was playing, but she was also weeping. The merry notes of the polka were ground out to a silent accompaniment of tears. She looked very sad, this organ-girl, and her monkey seemed to have caught the infection, for his large brown eyes were moist, as if he also wept.

"The poor hunchback was struck with pity, and called the little girl over to give her a penny — not, dear Zonéla, because he wished to bestow alms, but because he wanted to speak with her. She came, and they talked together. She came the next day — for it turned out that they were neighbours — and the next, and, in short, every day. They became friends. They were both lonely and afflicted, with this difference, that she was beautiful, and he — was a hunchback."

"Why, Solon," cried Zonéla, "that's the very way you and I met!"

"It was then," continued Solon, with a faint smile, "that
life seemed to have its music. A great harmony seemed to the
poor cripple to fill the world. The carts that took the flour-
barrels from the wharves to the store-houses seemed to emit
joyous melodies from their wheels. The hum of the great
business streets sounded like grand symphonies of triumph.
As one who has been traveling through a barren country
without much heed feels with singular force the sterility of the
lands he has passed through when he reaches the fertile plains
that lie at the end of his journey, so the humpback, after his
vision had been freshened with this blooming flower, remembered for the first time the misery of the life that he had led.
But he did not allow himself to dwell upon the past. The
present was so delightful that it occupied all his thoughts.
Zonéla, he was in love with the organ-girl."

"Oh, that's so nice!" said Zonéla, innocently − pinching
poor Furbelow, as she spoke, in order to dispel a very evident
snooze that was creeping over him. "It's going to be a love-
story."

"Ah! but, Zonéla, he did not know whether she loved him in
return. You forget that he was deformed."

"But," answered the girl bravely, "he was good."

A light like the flash of an aurora illuminated Solon's face
for an instant. He put out his hand suddenly, as if to take
Zonéla's and press it to his heart; but an unaccountable timidity
seemed to arrest the impulse, and he only stroked Furbelow's
head − upon which that individual opened one large brown eye
to the extent of the eighth of an inch, and, seeing that it was
only Solon, instantly closed it again, and resumed his dream of
a city where there were no organs and all the copper coin of
the realm was iced.

"He hoped and feared," continued Solon, in a low, mournful voice; "but at times he was very miserable, because he did
not think it possible that so much happiness was reserved for
him as the love of this beautiful, innocent girl. At night, when
he was in bed, and all the world was dreaming, he lay awake
looking up at the old books against the walls, thinking how he
could bring about the charming of her heart.

"One night, when he was thinking of this, with his eyes fixed upon the moldy backs of the odd volumes that lay on their shelves, and looked back at him wistfully, as if they would say, 'We also are like you, and wait to be completed,' it seemed as if he heard a rustle of leaves. Then one by one, the books came down from their places to the floor, as if shifted by invisible hands, opened their worm-eaten covers, and from between the pages of each the hunchback saw issue forth a curious throng of little people that danced here and there through the apartment. Each one of these little creatures was shaped so as to bear resemblance to some one of the letters of the alphabet. One tall, long-legged fellow seemed like the letter A; a burly fellow, with a big head and a paunch, was the model of B; another leering little chap might have passed for a Q; and so on through the whole. These fairies — for fairies they were — climbed upon the hunchback's bed, and clustered thick as bees upon his pillow.

" 'Come!' they cried to him, 'we will lead you into fairyland.'

"So saying, they seized his hand, and he suddenly found himself in a beautiful country, where the light did not come from sun or moon or stars, but floated round and over and in everything like the atmosphere. On all sides he heard mysterious melodies sung by strangely musical voices. None of the features of the landscape was definite; yet when he looked on the vague harmonies of color that melted one into another before his sight he was filled with a sense of inexplicable beauty. On every side of him fluttered radiant bodies, which darted to and fro through the illumined space. They were not birds, yet they flew like birds; and as each one crossed the path of his vision he felt a strange delight flash through his brain, and straightway an interior voice seemed to sing beneath the vaulted dome of his temples a verse containing some beautiful thought. The little fairies were all this time dancing and fluttering around him, perching on his head, on his shoulders, or balancing themselves on his finger-tips.

" 'Where am I?,' he asked, at last, of his friends, the fairies.

" 'Ah, Solon!' he heard them whisper, in tones that sounded

like the distant tinkling of silver bells, 'this land is nameless; but those whom we lead hither, who tread its soil, and breathe its air, and gaze on its floating sparks of light, are poets for evermore.'

"Having said this, they vanished, and with them the beautiful indefinite land, and the flashing lights, and the illumined air; and the hunchback found himself again in bed, with the moonlight quivering on the floor, and the dusty books on their shelves, grim and moldy as ever."

"You have betrayed yourself. You called yourself Solon," cried Zonéla. "Was it a dream?"

"I do not know," answered Solon; "but since that night I have been a poet."

"A poet?" screamed the little organ girl — "a real poet, who makes verses which everyone reads and everyone talks of?"

"The people call me a poet," answered Solon, with a sad smile. "They do not know me by the name of Solon, for I write under an assumed title; but they praise me, and repeat my songs. But Zonéla, I can't sing this load off my back, can I?"

"Oh, bother the hump!" said Zonéla, jumping up suddenly. "You're a poet, and that's enough, isn't it? I'm so glad you're a poet, Solon! You must repeat all your best things to me, won't you?"

Solon nodded assent.

"You don't ask me," he said, "who was the little girl that the hunchback loved."

Zonéla's flace flushed crimson. She turned suddenly away, and ran into a dark corner of the room. In a moment she returned with an old hand-organ in her arms.

"Play, Solon, play!" she cried. "I am so glad that I want to dance. Furbelow, come and dance in honour of Solon the Poet."

It was her confession. Solon's eyes flamed, as if his brain had suddenly ignited. He said nothing; but a triumphant smile broke over his countenance. Zonéla, the twilight of whose cheeks was still rosy with the setting blush, caught the lazy Furbelow by his little paws; Solon turned the crank of the organ, which wheezed out as merry a polka as its asthma would allow, and the girl and the monkey commenced their fantastic dance. They had taken but a few steps when the door suddenly opened, and the tall figure of the Wondersmith appeared on the threshold. His face was convulsed with rage, and the black snake that quivered on his upper lip seemed to rear itself as if about to spring upon the hunchback.

4 THE MANIKINS AND THE MINOS

The Four gipsies left Herr Hippe's house cautiously, and directed their steps towards Mr. Pippel's bird-shop. Golosh Street was asleep. Nothing was stirring in that tenebrous slum, save a dog that savagely gnawed a bone which lay on a dust-heap, tantalizing him with the flavor of food without its substance. As the gipsies moved stealthily along in the darkness they had a sinister and murderous air that would not have failed to attract the attention of the policeman of the quarter, if that worthy had not at the moment been comfortably ensconced in the neighboring "Rainbow" bar-room, listening to the improvisations of that talented vocalist, Mr. Harrison, who was making impromptu verses on every possible subject, to the accompaniment of a cithern which was played by a sad little Italian in a large cloak, to whom the host of the "Rainbow" gave so many toddies and a dollar for his nightly performance.

Mr. Pippel's shop was but a short distance from the Wondersmith's house, A few moments, therefore, brought the gipsy party to the door, when, by the aid of a key which Herr Hippe produced, they silently slipped into the entry. Here the Wondersmith took a dark-lantern from under his cloak, removed the cap that shrouded the light, and led the way into the shop, which was separated from the entry only by a glass door, that yielded, like the outer one, to a key which Hippe took from his pocket. The four gipsies now entered the shop and closed the door behind them.

It was a little world of birds. On every side, whether in large or small cages, one beheld balls of various-colored feathers standing on one leg and breathing peacefully. Love-birds, nestling shoulder to shoulder, with their heads tucked under their wings and all their feathers puffed out, so that they looked like gloves of malachite; English bull-finches, with ashen-colored backs, in which their black heads were buried, and corselets of a rosy down; Java sparrows, fat and sleek and cleanly; troupials, so glossy and splendid in plumage that they looked as if they were dressed in the celebrated armor of the Black Prince, which was jet, richly damascened with gold; a cock of the rock, gleaming, a ball of tawny fire, like a setting sun; the campanero of Brazil, white as snow, with his dilatable tolling-tube hanging from his head, placid and silent;— these, with a humbler crowd of linnets, canaries, robins, mocking-birds, and phoebes, slumbered calmly in their little cages, that were hung so thickly on the wall as not to leave an inch of if visible.

"Splendid little morsels, all of them!" excalimed Monseiur Kerplonne. "Ah, we are going to have a rare beating!"

"So Pippel does not sleep in his shop," said the English gipsy, Oaksmith.

"No. The fellow lives somewhere up one of the avenues," answered Madame Filomel. "He came, the other evening, to consult me about his fortune. I did not tell him," she added with a laugh, "that he was going to have so distinguished a sporting party on his premises."

"Come," said the Wondersmith, producing the box of manikins, "get ready with souls, Madame Filomel. I am impatient to see my little men letting out lives for the first time." Just at the moment that the Wondersmith uttered this sentence, the four gipsies were startled by a hoarse voice issuing from a corner of the room, and propounding in the most guttural tones the intemperate query of "What'll you take?" This sottish invitation had scarce been given, when a second extremely thick voice replied from an opposite corner, in accents so rough that they seemed to issue from a throat torn and furrowed by the liquid lava of many bar-rooms, "Brandy and water."

"Holla! who's here?" muttered Herr Hippe, flashing the light of his lantern round the shop.

Oaksmith turned up his coat-cuffs, as if to be ready for a fight; Madame Filomel glided, or rather rolled, towards the door, while Kerplonne put his hand into his pocket, as if to assure himself that his supernumerary optic was all right.

The Wondersmith. (GOLOSH ST.)

Jeanette Dunne Dec. 78.

"What'll you take?" croaked the voice in the corner, once more.

"Brandy and water," rapidly replied the second voice in the other corner. And then, as if by a concerted movement, a series of bibular invitations and acceptances were rolled backwards and forwards with a volubility of utterance that threw Patter versus Clatter into the shade.

"What the devil can it be?" muttered the Wondersmith, flashing his lantern here and there. "Ah! it is those Minos."

So saying, he stopped under one of the wicker cages that hung high up on the wall, and raised the lantern above his head, so as to throw the light upon that particular cage. The hospitable individual who had been extending all those hoarse invitations to partake of intoxicating beverages was an inhabitant of the cage. It was a large Mino-bird, who now stood perched on his cross-bar, with his yellowish-orange bill sloped slightly over his shoulder, and his white eye cocked knowingly upon the Wondersmith. The respondent voice in the other corner came from another Mino-bird, who sat in the dusk in a similar cage, also attentively watching the Wondersmith. These Mino-birds have a singular aptitude for acquiring phrases.

"What'll you take?" repeated the Mino, cocking his other eye upon Herr Hippe.

"*Mon Dieu!* what a bird!" exclaimed the little Frenchman. "He is, in truth, polite."

"I don't know what I'll take," said Hippe, as if replying to the Mino-bird; "but I know what you'll get, old fellow! Filomel, open the cage-doors, and give me the bottle."

Filomel opened, one after another, the doors of the numberless little cages, thereby arousing from slumber their feathered occupants, who opened their beaks, and stretched their claws, and stared with great surprise at the lantern and the midnight visitors.

By this time the Wondersmith had performed the mysterious manipulations with the bottle, and the manikins were once more in full motion, swarming out of their box, sword and dagger in hand, with their little black eyes glittering fiercely, and their white teeth shining. The little creatures seemed to scent their prey. The gipsies stood in the center of the shop, watching the proceedings eagerly, while the Lilliputians made in a body towards the wall and commenced climbing from cage to cage. Then was heard a tremendous fluttering of wings, and faint, desparing "quirks" echoed on all sides. In almost every cage there was a fierce manikin thrusting his sword or dagger vigorously into the body of some unhappy bird. It recalled the antique legend of the battles of the Pigmies and the Cranes. The poor love-birds lay with their emerald feathers dabbled in their heart's blood, shoulder to shoulder in death as in life. Canaries gasped at the bottom of their cages, while the water in their little glass fountains ran red. The bullfinches wore an unnatural crimson on their breasts. The mocking-bird lay on his back, kicking spasmodically, in the last agonies, with a tiny sword-thrust cleaving his melodious throat in twain, so that from the instrument which used to gush with wondrous music only scarlet drops of blood now trickled.

The manikins were ruthless. Their faces were ten times wickeder than ever, as they roamed from cage to cage, slaughtering with a fury that seemed entirely unappeasable. Presently the feather rustlings became fewer and fainter, and the little pipings of despair died away; and in every cage lay a poor murdered minstrel, with the song that abode within him for ever quenched — in every cage but two, and those two were high up on the wall; and in each glared a pair of wild, white eyes; and an orange beak, tough as steel, pointed threateningly down. With the needles which they grasped as swords all wet and warm with blood, and their bead-like eyes flashing in the light of the lantern, the Lilliputian assassins swarmed up the cages in two separate bodies, until they reached the wickets of the habitations in which the Minos abode.

Mino saw them coming — had listened attentively to the many death-struggles of his comrades, and had, in fact, smelt a rat. Accordingly he was ready for the manikins. There he stood at the barbican of his castle, with a formidable beak couched like a lance. The manikins made a gallant charge. "What'll you take?" was rattled out by the Mino, in a deep bass, as with one plunge of his sharp bill he scattered the ranks of the enemy, and sent three of them flying to the floor, where they lay with broken limbs. But the manikins were brave automata, and again they closed and charge the gallant Mino. Again the wicked white eyes of the bird gleamed, and again the orange bill dealt destruction.

Everything seemed to be going on swimmingly for Mino, when he found himself attacked in the rear by two treacherous manikins, who had stolen upon him from behind, through the lattice-work of the cage. Quick as lightening the Mino turned to repel his assault, but all too late; two slender, quivering threads of steel crossed in his poor body, and he staggered into a corner of the cage. His white eyes closed, then opened; a shiver passed over his body, beginning at his shoulder-tips and dying off in the extreme tips of the wings; he gasped as if for air, and then, with a convulsive shudder, which ruffled all his feathers, croaked out feebly his little speech. "What'll you take?" Instantly from the opposite corner came the old response still feebler than the question — a mere gurgle, as it were, of "Brandy and water." Then all was silent. The Mino-birds were dead.

"They spill blood like Christians," said the Wondersmith, gazing fondly on the manikins. "They will be famous assassins."

5 TIED UP

Herr Hippe stood in the doorway, scowling. His eyes seemed to scorch the poor hunchback, whose form, physically inferior, crouched before that baneful, blazing glance, while its head, mentally brave, reared itself as if to redeem the cowardice of the frame to which it belonged. So the attitude of the serpent: the body pliant, yielding, supple; but the crest thrown aloft, erect, and threatening. As for Zonéla, she was frozen in the attitude of motion — a dancing mymph in colored marble; agility stunned; elasticity petrified.

Furbelow, astonished at this sudden change, and catching, with all the mysterious rapidity of instinct peculiar to the lower animals, at the enigmatical character of the situation, turned his pleading, melancholy eyes from one to another of the motionless three, as if begging that his humble intellect (pardon me, naturalists, for the use of this word "intellect" in the matter of a monkey) should be enlightened as speedily as possible. Not receiving the desired information, he, after the manner of trained animals, returned to his muttons; in other words, he conceived that this unusual entrance, and consequent dramatic tableau, meant "shop." He therefore dropped Zonéla's hand, and pattered on his velvety feet over towards the grim figure of the Wondersmith, holding out his poor little paw for the customary copper. He had but one idea drilled into him — soulless creature that he was — and that was alms. But I have seen creatures that professed to have souls, and that would have been indignant if you had denied them immortality, who took to the soliciting of alms as naturally as if beggary had been the original sin, and was regularly born with them, and never baptized out of them. I will give these Bandits of the Order of Charity this credit, however, that they knew the best highways and the richest founts of benevolance — unlike to Furbelow, who, unreasoning and undiscriminating, begged from the first peson that was near. Furbelow, owing to this intellectual inferiority to the before-mentioned Alsatians, frequently got more kicks than coppers, and the present supplication which he indulged in towards the Wondersmith was a terrible confirmation of the rule. The reply to the extended pleading paw was what might be called a double-barreled kick — kick to be represented by the power of two when the foot touched the object, multiplied by four when the entire leg formed an angle of forty-five degrees with the spinal column. The long, nervous leg of the Wondersmith caught the little creature in the centre of the body, doubled up his brown, hairy form, till he looked like a fur driving-glove, and sent him whizzing across the room into a far corner, where he dropped senseless and flaccid.

This vengeance which Herr Hippe executed upon Furbelow seemed to have operated as a sort of escape-valve, and he found voice. He hissed out the question, "Who are you?" to the hunchback; and in listening to that essence of sibilation it really seemed as if it proceeded from the serpent that curled upon his upper lip.

"Who are you? Deformed dog, who are you? What do you

here?"

"My name is Solon," answered the fearless head of the hunchback, while the frail, cowardly body shivered and trembled inch by inch into a corner.

"So you come to visit my daughter in the night-time, when I am away?" continued the Wondersmith, with a sneering tone that dropped from his snake-wreathed mouth like poison. "You are a brave and gallant lover, are you not? Where did you win that Order of the Curse of God that decorates your shoulders? The women turn their heads and look after you in the street, when you pass, do they not? lost in admiration of that symmetrical figure, those graceful limbs, that neck pliant as the stem that moors the lotus! Elegant, conquering, Christian cripple, what do you here in my daughter's room?"

Can you imagine Jove, limitless in power and wrath, hurling from his vast grasp mountain after mountain upon the struggling Enceladus — and picture the Titan sinking, sinking deeper and deeper into the earth, crushed and dying, with nothing visible through the superincombent masses of Pelion and Ossa but a gigantic head and two flaming eyes, that, despite the death which is creeping through each vein, still flash back defiance to the divine enemy? Well, Solon and Herr Hippe presented such a picture, seen through the wrong end of a telescope — reduced in proportion, but alike in action. Solon's feeble body seemed to sink into utter annihilation beneath the horrible taunts that his enemy hurled at him, while the large, brave brow and unconquered eyes still sent forth a magnetic resistance.

Suddenly the poor hunchback felt his arm grasped. A thrill seemed to run through his entire body. A warm atmosphere, invigorating and full of delicous odor, surrounded him. It appeared as if invisible bandages were twisted all about his limbs, giving him a strange strength. His sinking legs straightened. His powerless arms were braced. Astonished, he glanced round for an instant, and beheld Zonéla, with a world of love burning in her large lambent eyes, wreathing her round white arms about his humped shoulders. Then the poet knew the great sustaining power of love. Solon reared himself boldly.

"Sneer at my poor form," he cried in strong, vibrating tones, flinging out one long arm and one thin finger at the Wondersmith, as if he would have impaled him like a beetle. "Humiliate me if you can. I care not. You are a wretch, and I am honest and pure. This girl is not your daughter. You are like one of those demons in the fairy-tales that held beauty and purity locked in infernal spells. I do not fear you, Herr Hippe. There are stories abroad about you in the neighborhood, and when you pass people say that they feel evil and blight covering over their threshold. You persecute this girl. You are her tyrant. You hate her. I am a cripple. Providence has cast this lump upon my shoulders. But that is nothing. The camel, that is the salvation of the children of the desert, has been given his hump in order that he might bear his human burden better. This girl, who is homeless as the Arab, is my appointed load in life, and please God, I will carry her on this back, hunched though it may be. I have come to see her because I love her — because she loves me. You have no claim on her; so I will take her from you."

Quick as lightening the Wondersmith had stridden a few paces, and grasped the poor cripple, who was yet quivering with the departing thunder of his passion. He seized him in his bony, muscular grasp, as he would have seized a puppet, and held him at arm's legnth, gasping and powerless; while Zonéla, pale, breathless, entreating, sank half kneeling on the floor.

"Your skeleton will be interesting to science when you are dead, Mr. Solon," hissed the Wondersmith. "But before I have the pleasure of reducing you to an anatomy, which I will assuredly do, I wish to compliment you on your power of penetration, or sources of information; for I know not if you have derived your knowledge from your own mental research or the efforts of others. You are perfectly correct in your statement that this charming young person, who day after day parades the streets with a barrel-organ and a monkey — the last unhappily indisposed at present — listening to the degrading jokes of ribald boys and depraved men — you are quite correct, sir, in stating that she is not my daughter. On the contrary, she is the daughter of an Hungarian nobleman who had the misfortune to incur my displeasure.

"I had a son, crooked spawn of a Christian! — a son, not like you, cankered, gnarled stump of life that you are — but a youth tall and fair and noble in aspect, as became a child of one whose lineage makes Pharaoh modern — a youth whose foot in the dance was as swift and beautiful to look at as the golden sandals of the sun when he dances upon the sea in summer. This youth was virtuous and good; and being of a good race, and dwelling in a country where his rank, gipsy as he was, was recognized, he mixed with the proudest of the land.

"One day he fell in with this accursed Hungarian, a fierce drinker of that devil's blood called brandy. My child until that hour had avoided this bane of our race. Generous wine he drank, because the soul of the sun, our ancestor, palpitated in its purple waves. But brandy, which is fallen and accursed wine, as devils are fallen and accursed angels, had never crossed his lips, until in an evil hour he was seduced by this Christian hog, and from that day forth his life was one fiery debauch, which set only in the black waves of death. I vowed vengeance on the destroyer of my child, and I kept my word. I have destroyed *his* child — not compassed her death, but blighted her life, steeped her in misery and poverty, and now, thanks to the thousand devils, I have discovered a new torture for her heart. She thought to solace her life with a love-episode! Sweet little epicure that she was! She shall have her little crooked lover, shan't she! Oh, yes! She shall have him, cold and stark and livid, with that great, black, heavy hunch, which no back, however broad, can bear, Death, sitting between his shoulders!"

There was something so awful and demoniac in this entire speech and the manner in which it was delivered, that it petrified Zonéla into a mere inanimate figure, whose eyes seemed unalterably fixed on the fierce, cruel face of the Wondersmith. As for Solon, he was paralyzed in the grasp of his foe. He heard, but could not reply. His large eyes, dilated with horror to far beyond their ordinary size, expressed unutterable agony.

The last sentence had hardly been hissed out by the gipsy when he took from his pocket a long, thin coil of whip-cord, which he entangled in a complicated mesh around the cripple's body. It was not the ordinary binding of a prisoner. The slender lash passed and repassed in a thousand intricate folds over the powerless limbs of the poor hunchback. When the operation was completed, he looked as if he had been sewed from head to foot in some singularly ingenious species of network.

"Now, my pretty lop-sided little lover," laughed Herr Hippe, flinging Solon over his shoulder as a fisherman might fling a netful of fish, "we will proceed to put you into your little cage until your little coffin is quite ready. Meanwhile we will lock up your darling beggar-girl to mourn over your untimely end."

So saying, he stepped from the room with his captive, and securely locked the door behind him.

When he had disappeared, the frozen Zonéla thawed, and with a shriek of anguish flung herself on the inanimate body of Furbelow.

6 THE POISONING OF THE SWORDS

It was New Year's eve, and 11 o'clock at night. All over this great land, and in every great city in the land, curly heads were lying on white pillows, dreaming of the coming of the generous Santa Claus. Innumerable stockings hung by countless bedsides. Visions of beautiful toys, passing in splendid pageantry through myriads of dimly lit dormitories, made millions of little hearts palpitate in sleep. Ah! what heavenly toys those were that the children of this soil beheld, that mystic night, in their dreams! Painted cars with orchestral wheels, making music more delicious than the roll of planets. Agile men, of cylindrical figure, who sprang unexpectedly out of meek-looking boxes, with a supernatural fierceness in their crimson cheeks and fur-whiskers. Herds of marvelous sheep, with fleeces as impossible as the one that Jason sailed after; animals entirely indifferent to grass and water and "rot" and "ticks." Horses spotted with an astounding regularity, and furnished with the most ingenious methods of locomotion. Slender foreigners, attired in painfully short tunics, whose existence passed in continually turning heels over head down a steep flight of steps, at the bottom of which they lay in an exhausted condition with dislocated limbs, until they were restored to their former elevation, when they went at it again as if nothing had happened. Stately swans, that seemed to have a touch of the ostrich in them; for they swam continually after a piece of iron which was held before them, as if consumed with a ferruginous hunger. Whole farmyards of roosters, whose tails curled the wrong way — a slight defect, that was, however, amply atoned for by the size and brilliancy of their scarlet combs, which, it would appear, Providence had intended for pen-wipers. Pears, that, when applied to youthful lips, gave forth sweet and inspiring sounds. Regiments of soldiers, that performed neat but limited evolutions on cross-jointed contractile battlefields, All these things, idealized, transfigured, and illuminated by the powers and atmosphere and colored lamps of dreamland, did the millions of dear sleeping children behold, the night of the New Year's eve of which I speak.

It was on this night, when Time was preparing to shed his skin, and come out young and golden and glossy as ever — when, in the vast chambers of the universe, silent and infallible preparations were making for the wonderful birth of the coming year — when mystic dews were secreted for his baptism, and mystic instruments were tuned in space to welcome him — it was at this solemn hour that the Wondersmith and his three companions sat in close conclave in the little parlor before mentioned.

There was a fire roaring in the gate. On a table, nearly in the center of the room, stood a huge decanter of port wine, that glowed in the blaze which lit the chamber like a flask of crimson fire. On every side, piled in heaps, inanimate, but scowling with the same old wondrous scowl, lay myriads of the manikins, all clutching in their wooden hands their tiny weapons. The Wondersmith held in one hand a small silver bowl filled with a green, glutinous substance, which he was delicately applying, with the aid of a camel's-hair brush, to the tips of tiny swords and daggers. A horrible smile wandered over his sallow face — a smile as unwholesome in appearance as the sickly light that plays above reeking graveyards.

"Let us drink great drafts, brothers," he cried, leaving off his strange anointment for a while, to lift a great glass, filled with sparkling liquor, to his lips. "Let us drink to our approaching triumph. Let us drink to the great poison, Macousha. Subtle seed of Death — swift hurricane that sweeps away Life — fast hammer that crushes brain and heart and artery with its resistless weight — I drink to it."

"It is a noble decoction, Duke Balthazar," said the old fortune-teller and mid-wife, Madame Filomel, nodding in her chair as she swallowed her wine in great gulps. "Where did you obtain it?"

"It is made," said the Wondersmith, swallowing another great draft of wine ere he replied, "in the wild woods of Guiana, in silence and in mystery. But one tribe of Indians, the Macoushi Indians, know the secret. It is simmered over fires built of strange woods, and the maker of it dies in the making. The place, for a mile around the spot where it is fabricated, is shunned as accursed. Devils hover over the pot in which it stews; and the birds of the air, scenting the smallest breath of its vapors from far away, drop to earth with paralyzed wings, cold and dead."

"It kills, then, fast?" asked Kerplonne, the artificial-eye maker — his own eyes gleaming, under the influence of the wine, with a sinister luster, as if they had been fresh from the factory, and were yet untarnished by use.

"Kills?" echoed the Wondersmith, derisively; "it is swifter than thunder-bolts, stronger than lightning. But you shall see it proved before we let forth our army on the city accursed. You shall see a wretch die, as if smitten by a falling fragment of the sun."

"What? Do you mean Solon?" asked Oaksmith and the fortune-teller together.

"Ah, you mean the young man who makes the commerce with books?" echoed Kerplonne. "It is well. His agonies will instruct us."

"Yes! Solon," answered Hippe, with a savage accent. "I hate him, and he shall die this horrid death. Ah! how the little fellows will leap upon him, when I bring him in, bound and helpless, and give their beautiful wicked souls to them! How they will pierce him in ten thousand spots with their poisoned weapons, until his skin turns blue and violet and crimson, and his form swells with the venom — until his hump is lost in shapeless flesh! He hears what I say, every word of it. He is in the closet next door, and is listening. How comfortable he feels! How the sweat of terror rolls on his brow! How he tries to loosen his bonds, and curses all earth and heaven when he finds that he cannot! Ho! Ho! Handsome lover of Zonéla, will she kiss you when you are livid and swollen? Brothers, let us drink again — drink always. Here, Oaksmith, take these brushes — and you, Filomel — and finish the anointing of these swords. This wine is grand. This poison is grand. It is fine to have good wine to drink, and good poison to kill with; is it not?" — and, with flushed face and rolling eyes, the Wondersmith continued to drink and use his brush alternately.

The others hastened to follow his example. It was a horrible scene: those four wicked faces; those myriads of tiny faces, just as wicked; the certain unearthly air that pervaded the apartment; the red, unwholesome glare cast by the fire; the wild and reckless way in which the weird company drank the red-illumined wine.

The anointing of the swords went on rapidly, and the wine went as rapidly down the throats of the four poisoners. Their faces grew more and more inflamed each instant; their eyes shone like rolling fireballs; their hair was moist and disheveled. The old fortune-teller rocked to and fro in her chair, like those legless plaster figures that sway upon convex loaded bottoms. All four began to mutter incoherent sentences, and babble unintelligible wickedness. Still the anointing of the swords went on.

"I see the faces of millions of young corpses," babbled Herr Hippe, gazing, with swimming eyes, into the silver bowl that contained the Macousha poison, "all young, all Christians — and the little fellows dancing, dancing, and stabbing, stabbing. Filomel, Filomel, I say!"

"Well, Grand Duke," snored the old woman, giving a violent lurch.

"Where's the bottle of souls?"

"In my right hand pocket, Herr Hippe;" and she felt, so as to assure herself that it was there. She half drew out the black bottle, before described in this narrative, and let it slide again into her pocket — let it slide again, but it did not completely regain its former place. Caught by some accident, it hung half out, swaying over the edge of the pocket — as the fat midwife rolled backwards and forwards in her drunken efforts at equilibrium.

"All right," said Herr Hippe, "perfectly right! Let's drink."

He reached out his hand for his glass, and, with a dull sigh, dropped on the table, in the instantaneous slumber of intoxication. Oaksmith soon fell back in his chair, breathing, heavily. Kerplonne followed. And the heavy, stertorous breathing of Filomel told that she slumbered also; but still her chair retained its rocking motion, and still the bottle of souls balanced itself on the edge of her pocket.

7 LET LOOSE

Sure enough, Solon heard every word of the fiendish talk of the Wondersmith. For how many days he had been shut up, bound in the terrible net, in that dark closet, he did not know; but now he felt that his last hour was come. His little strength was completely worn out in efforts to disentangle himself. Once a day a door opened, and Herr Hippe placed a crust of bread and a cup of water within his reach. On this meager fare he had subsisted. It was a hard life; but, bad as it was, it was better than the horrible death that menaced him. His brain reeled with terror at the prospect of it. Then, where was Zonéla? Why did she not come to his rescue? But she was, perhaps, dead. The darkness, too, appalled him. A faint light, when the moon was bright, came at night through a chink far up in the wall; and the only other hole in the chamber was an aperture through which, at some former time, a stove-pipe had been passed. Even if he were free, there would have been small hope of escape; but, laced as it were in a network of steel, what was to be done? He groaned and writhed upon the floor, and tore at the boards with his hands, which were free from the wrists down. All else was as solidly laced up as an Indian papoose. Nothing but pride kept him from shrieking aloud, when, on the night of New Year's eve, he heard the fiendish Hippe recite the program of his murder.

While he was thus wailing and gnashing his teeth in darkness and torture, he heard a faint noise above his head. Then something seemed to leap from the ceiling and alight softly on the floor. He shuddered with terror. Was it some new torture of the Wondersmith's invention? The next moment he felt some small animal crawling over his body, and a soft, silky paw was pushed timidly across his face. His heart leaped with joy.

"It is Furbelow!" he cried. "Zonéla has sent him. He came through the stove-pipe hole."

It was Furbelow, indeed, restored to life by Zonéla's care, and who had come down a narrow tube, that no human being could have threaded, to console the poor captive. The monkey nestled closely into the hunchback's bosom, and, as he did so, Solon felt something cold and hard hanging from his neck. He touched it. It was sharp. By the dim light that struggled through the apperture high up in the wall, he discovered a knife, suspended by a bit of cord. Ah! how the blood came rushing through the veins that crossed over and through his heart, when life and liberty came to him in this bit of rusty steel! With his manacled hands he loosened the heaven-sent weapon; a few cuts were rapidly made in the cunning network of cord that enveloped his limbs, and in a few seconds he was free! — cramped and faint with hunger, but free! — free to move, to use the limbs that God had given him for his preservation — free to fight — to die fighting, perhaps — but still to die free. He ran to the door. The bolt was a weak one, for the Wondersmith had calculated more surely on his prison of cords than any jail of stone — and more; and with a few efforts the door opened. He went cautiously out into the darkness, with Furbelow perched on his shoulder, pressing his cold muzzle against his cheek. He had made but a few steps when a trembling hand was put into his, and in another moment Zonéla's palpitating heart was pressed against his own. One long kiss, an embrace, a few whispered words, and the hunchback and the girl stole softly towards the door of the chamber in which the four gipsies slept. All seemed still; nothing but the hard breathing of the sleepers and the monotonous rocking of Madame Filomel's chair broke the silence. Solon stooped down and put his eye to the keyhole, through which a red bar of light streamed into the entry. As he did so, his foot crushed some brittle substance that lay outisde the door; at the same moment a howl of agony was heard to issue from the room within. Solon started; nor did he know that at that instant he had crushed into dust Monsieur Kerplonne's supernumerary eye, and the owner, though wrapt in a drunken sleep, felt the pang quiver through his brain. While Solon peeped through the keyhole, all in the room was motionless. He had not gazed, however, for many seconds, when the chair of the fortune-teller gave a sudden lurch, and the black bottle already hanging half out of her wide pocket, slipped entirely from its resting-place, and, falling heavily to the ground, shivered into fragments.

Then took place an astonishing spectacle. The myriads of armed dolls, that lay in piles about the room, became suddenly imbued with motion. They stood up straight, their tiny limbs moved, their black eyes flashed with wicked purposes, their thread-like swords gleamed as they waved them to and fro. The villainous souls imprisoned in the bottle began to work within them. Like the Lilliputians, when they found the giant Gulliver asleep, they scaled in swarms the burly sides of the four sleeping gipsies. At every step they took, they drove their thin swords and quivering daggers into the flesh of the drunken authors of their being. To stab and kill was their mission, amd they stabbed and killed with incredible fury. They clustered on the Wondersmith's sallow cheeks and sinewy throat, piercing every portion with their diminutive poisoned blades. Filomel's fat carcass was alive with them. They blackened the spare body of Monsier Kerplonne. They covered Oaksmith's huge form like a cluster of insects.

Overcome completely with the fumes of wine, these tiny wounds did not for a few moments awaken the sleeping victims. But the swift and deadly poison Macousha with which the weapons had been so fiendishly anointed, began to work. Herr

Hippe, stung into sudden life, leaped to his feet, with a dwarf army clinging to his clothes and his hands — always stabbing, stabbing, stabbing. For an instant, a look of stupid bewilderment clouded his face; then the horrible truth burst upon him. He gave a shriek like that which a horse utters when he finds himself fettered and surrounded by fire — a shriek that curdled the air for miles and miles.

"Oaksmith! Kerplonne! Filomel! Awake! awake! We are lost! The souls have got loose! We are dead! poisoned! O accursed ones! O demons, ye are slaying me! Ah! fiends of hell!"

Aroused by these frightful howls, the three gipsies sprang also to their feet, to find themselves stung to death by the manikins. They raved, they shrieked, they swore. They staggered round the chamber. Blinded in the eyes by the ever-stabbing weapons — with the poison already burning in their veins like red-hot lead — their forms swelling and discoloring visibly every moment — their howls and attitudes and furious gestures made the scene look like a chamber in hell.

Maddened beyond endurance, the Wondersmith, half blinded and choking with the venom that had congested all the blood-vessels of his body, seized dozens of the manikins and dashed them into the fire, trampling them down with his feet.

"Ye shall die too, if I die," he cried, with a roar like that of a tiger. "Ye shall burn, if I burn. I gave ye life — I give ye death. Down! — down! — burn! flame! Fiends that ye are, to slay us! Help me, brothers! Before we die, let us have our revenge!"

On this, the other gipsies, themselves maddened by approaching death, began hurling manikins, by handfuls into the fire. The little creatures, being wooden of body, quickly caught the flames, and an awful struggle for life took place in miniature in the grate. Some of them escaped from between the bars and ran about the room, blazing, writhing in agony, and igniting the curtains and other draperies that hung around. Others fought and stabbed one another in the very core of the fire, like combating salamanders. Meantime, the motions of the gipsies grew more languid and slow, and their curses were uttered in choked guttural tones. The faces of all four were spotted with red and green and violet, like so many egg-plants. Their bodies were swollen to a frightful size, and at last they dropped on the floor, like over-ripe fruit shaken from the boughs by the winds of autumn.

The chamber was now a sheet of fire. The flames roared round and round, as if seeking for escape, licking every projecting cornice and sill with greedy tongues, as the serpent licks his prey before he swallows it. A hot, putrid breath came through the keyhole, and smote Solon and Zonéla like a wind of death. They clasped each other's hands with a moan of terror, and fled from the house.

The next morning, when the young year was just unclosing its eyes, and the happy children all over the great city were peeping from their beds into the myriads of stockings hanging near by, the blue skies of heaven shone through a black network of stone and charred rafters. These were all that remained of the habitation of Herr Hippe, the Wondersmith.

Bram Stoker
1906

BRAM STOKER (1847-1912)

FEW AUTHORS HAVE HAD THE STUNNING world impact that Bram Stoker has had and yet remained so obscure. Mention his name to the general public and few people will recognise it. Mention the name of his creation — *Dracula* — and you will achieve a very different response.

Dracula! A name known throughout the world. A name that has held generations frozen to their seats as they have followed the intrepid Victorian heroes in their mission to destroy the king of vampires, the evil count who leaves his grave at night to prey upon the blood of the living.

Since Constable first published the novel in 1897 the book has never been out of print. No one can even begin to guess at its sales in the English language, let alone in its numerous foreign language editions. In the world of the cinema scarcely a year goes by without some new Dracula film bursting its gory way onto the screen; youngsters huddle over Dracula comics and the spin-offs are almost too numerous to mention . . . take Dracula sweets for example!

The Romanian Government, in whose territory the forbidding peaks of Transylvania lie and in which area is the home of the count, make £5 million a year out of tourism to the area. Tourists from all over the world flock to Sighisoara on special 'Dracula tours' to see where lived Vlad Dracula, ruler of Wallachia from 1452-62, whose ferocity and blood thirstiness earned him the title of 'wampyr' and inspired Stoker's immortal character. The Romanians are currently hastening the completion of a 146 bedroom hotel called Hotel Dracula.

Such is the popularity of Bram Stoker's creation.

Yet of Bram Stoker, whose fertile imagination gave birth to a world legend, little is heard. Only the faithful members of the British Dracula Society and the American Count Dracula Society hold his memory dear, along with *aficionados* of the horror fantasy genre. Stoker's creation has, for the past eighty years, completely overshadowed his other works. He was the author of eighteen books, six of which were of the Gothic Fantasy type, four were collections of short stories — mostly in the same mould —, four were romantic tales and four were works of non-fiction.

Stoker was born on November 8, 1847, at No. 15 The Crescent, Clontarf, just north of Dublin Bay. His father, Abraham Stoker, was a clerk in the civil service attached to the Secretary for Ireland's office. His mother, who came from Sligo, was a determined social reformer who preached 'women's liberation' to a shocked Victorian society. Abraham Junior, known simply as Bram, was the third son in a family of four boys and two girls.

Bram graduated from Trinity College in 1876 with honours in science and joined the civil service. His main interest, however, was the theatre. He felt that the Irish newspapers were not doing a good job with their theatrical criticism, so Stoker convinced the editor of the *Dublin Evening Mail* (Sheridan Le Fanu's newspaper) to take him on as part time, unpaid, theatre critic. He was soon moving in Dubin's chic literary and theatrical circles, becoming friendly with such people as Sir William and Lady Wilde, whose son Oscar had just entered Trinity College.

Still working full time in the civil service, Stoker helped to launch a new newspaper, *The Irish Echo*, with himself as part-time editor. It was a hard period, for the *Echo* was an evening newspaper which lasted four months before it folded up. As well as two jobs, Stoker was still writing theatrical criticism for the *Evening Mail* and managed to write his first story — a four part cliff hanger 'The Chain of Destiny' which appeared in the *Shamrock Magazine*.

Stoker had by now struck up two important friendships. One was with the famous actor Henry Irving and the other, a penfriendship, was with Walt Whitman, the then controversial American poet. Stoker defended Whitman's *Leaves of Grass* from the violent attacks of the literary establishment of the day.

In his job in the civil service Stoker received promotion to Inspector of the Irish Petty Sessions. His first visits to the courts revealed that clerks had no basic rule book to guide them on the sentences to be given for various offences. Stoker set to work to correct this and in 1879 *The Duties of Clerks of the Petty Sessions* in Ireland became his first published work. By the time it was published, however, he had left the civil service. In 1878 he had married a Miss Florence Anne Lemon and accepted a job offered him by Henry Irving, who had just bought the Lyceum Theatre in London. The job was that of manager for Irving's company. Stoker and his wife moved from Dublin to Cheyne Walk, Chelsea, London, where his friends and neighbours included Gabriel Dante Rosetti, James McNeil Whistler, George Eliot, Oscar Wilde and W.S. Gilbert.

Stoker was successful in his new job and accompanied Irving on tours of America where he cemented his friendship with Whitman and became a friend of Theodore Roosevelt who, he noted at the time, must surely one day become president. Another essay in writing, his impressions of America, was published in 1886 by Sampson Low as *A Glimpse of America*. How Stoker found time to write is a mystery; he led such an active life in the theatre. Yet in 1882 Sampson Low published his first work of fiction in book form. It was a collection of short stories entitled *Under the Sunset*. The title story was based on an account his mother had written him about the cholera epidemic in Sligo in 1832. According to *The Daily Telegraph* it was 'a collection of delicate and forcible allegories'.

In 1889 *The People* newspaper serialised a work called *The Snake's Pass* set in the west of Ireland about the search for a lost treasure buried in a shifting and treacherous bog. Several provincial newspapers also serialised the story and it was published in book form by Sampson Low in 1890. The press were unaminous in their praise and the poet Tennyson told his son to write a letter of congratulations to Stoker. Prime Minister Gladstone amazed Stoker, when he met him, by quoting large extracts from the book.

About this time Stoker was called to the Bar of the Inner Temple, London. 'I only took the exams to escape jury service', he jokingly told his friends. His activities were phenomenal and he was also producing a considerable number of articles for various magazines.

While on an acting tour of Scotland he wrote a short story called *The Watter's Mou'* (The Water's Mouth) which he used to introduce a collection of macabre tales published in 1894. Two more books appeared from his pen that year: another collection of tales entitled *Crooken Sands* and a novel entitled *The Man from Shorrox's*. Of the three books, *The Watter's Mou'* became the most popular and went to a second edition immediately. Then came a romance, *The Shoulder of Shasta*, which was strongly criticised by the *Athenaeum* but praised by the *Telegraph*. *Shasta* heralded a number of books that Stoker was to write on romantic love and gallantry in a highly idealised form.

In May, 1897, Stoker's literary career was to reach its peak with the publication of a weird horror fantasy . . . *Dracula*!

Stoker had been raised on his mother's tales of the west of Ireland; tales of mythology and ghost stories, of the banshee (*bean sidhe*) — the old woman of the fairies who wails and shrieks before a death in the family to which she is attached. He had utilised the horrors of the cholera epidemic in the west of Ireland, when people were buried alive because the able were too afraid to come close to see if they were dead or merely unconscious, in his book *Under the Sunset*. His knowledge of Irish folklore and mythology also comes to the fore in *The Snake's Pass*. Similarly, these influences helped him to fashion *Dracula*.

As a young man Stoker had also read Le Fanu's story

'Carmilla', set around a lonely castle in Styria, Austria, about the Countess Karnstein, a 150 year old vampire who is tracked to her tomb and destroyed by plunging a stake through her heart. Stoker, while in London, became friendly with another Gothic writer, Hall Caine, a Manxman, who reawakened Stoker's memory by tales of Manx Gaelic legends. When *Dracula* appeared it was, in fact, dedicated 'to my dear friend Hommy-Beg'. This was Hall Caine whose first name was Tommy. Caine's Manx Gaelic speaking family called him 'little Tommy' — *an Thommy beag* or, in English phonetics, 'an Hommy Beg'.

These were the factors behind Stoker's inspiration to write *Dracula*. He based the character on the 15th Century 'wampyr' Vlad Dracula, a real historical character who ruled in Wallachia. He enlisted the aid of a friend, Arminius Vambery, Professor of Oriental Languages at Budapest University. Vambery supplied Stoker with his background material, for Stoker never visited Transylvania in his life. The narrative and style of the book Stoker borrowed from Wilkie Collins by which the story is told through the eyes of several characters.

Stoker dropped one chapter of *Dracula* before publication. This was felt to be too close to Le Fanu's 'Carmilla'. The chapter, as a complete story, was published after Stoker's death by George Routledge & Son in 1914 as *Dracula's Guest and Other Weird Stories*.

The Daily Mail summed up the general press reaction to the book:

'In seeking a parallel to this weird, powerful and horrible story, one's mind reverts to such tales as *The Mysteries of Udolpho, Frankestein, Wuthering Heights, The Fall of the House of Usher* and *Margery Quelher*. But *Dracula* is even more appalling in its gloomy fascination than any of these.'

Dracula went to nine editions before 1912. Since it was published in America in 1899 it has never been out of print. It has been translated into the major languages of the world and, in 1933, an Irish translation was made by Seán Ó Currin. First filmed in 1922, the films and film spin-offs have been too numerous to count. In May, 1897, a stage adaptation was performed at the Lyceum and for nearly forty years *Dracula* became a money-spinning play. The history of how this novel has become part of world mythology is ably recounted in Peter Haining's *The Dracula Scrapbook* (New English Library, 1976).

Stoker's next literary attempt was rather a flop. In 1898 he published *Miss Betty*, an idealised love story. His literary contributions to various magazines continued and his publishers were pressing him for a sequel in the *Dracula* mould. In 1902 a new uncanny tale emerged as *The Mystery of the Sea*. Conan Doyle wrote to Stoker: 'I found the story admirable: it has not the fearsomeness of *Dracula*, but it is beautifully handled.' Then came a gruesome tale of an attempt of an Egyptian princess to raise herself from the dead after 5,000 years. It was set in London and Cornwall and entitled *The Jewel of the Seven Stars* (1903).

But Stoker wanted to leave the realms of horror fantasy and pursue his romantic ideals. *The Man* was published in 1905 and was a pure melodrama full of flamboyant themes of honour and gallantry. A totally rewritten version of the tale was published by Cupples and Leon of New York as *The Gates of Life* in 1908.

Just before the publication of *The Man*, Stoker's friend and mentor, Henry Irving, died and Stoker paid tribute to him in a two volume biographical work entitled *Personal Reminiscences of Henry Irving* which was published by Heinemann in 1906. *The Times* of London described it as Stoker's 'literary memorial'.

Again, in 1908, Stoker insisted on returning to idealised love as the theme of *Lady Athlyne*. In the same year came *Snowbound*, published by Collier, a collection of twelve stories ranging from high drama to broad comedy and featuring the adventures of a theatrical touring company. Then Stoker made an effort to combine his romanticism with the demand for another story of the *Dracula* type and in *The Lady of the Shroud* (Heinemann, 1909) he achieved a distinct success. He went back to non fiction and explored his interest in historical hoaxes and swindles in *Famous Imposters*, published by Sidgwick and Jackson in 1910, and which is still reprinted from time to time.

In spite of the output of articles in a diverse number of English and American journals and his seeming indefatigable activities, Stoker was a sick man. He had contracted tertiary syphilis. Daniel Farson, one of his biographers and his great-nephew, suggests that he contracted the disease in Paris where, it was rumoured, he used to take money to the exiled Oscar Wilde. The disease was worsening and Stoker went to his favourite retreat in Cruden Bay, Cornwall, where he began work on what was to be his last novel. It was another uncanny tale entitled *The Lair of the White Worm*, published by William Rider in 1911. It was to be his second most successful novel and was well greeted by the critics. 'Let no one read it before going to bed', advised the *Daily Telegraph*.

On April 20, 1912, Stoker died at his home at 26 St. George's Square, London. The death certificate included the word 'exhaustion' brought about by his disease. Stoker was 64 years old. *The Times* obituary recorded: 'Bram Stoker was the master of a particularly lurid and creepy kind of fiction represented by Dracula and other novels'.

Harry Ludlam, another biographer of Stoker, wrote:

'In creating Count Dracula, Bram Stoker took a widespread superstition, endowed it with the fruits of his imagination and gave it lasting currency in the twentieth century.'

In this anthology I have chosen a story which I consider as Stoker at his most horrific — 'The Burial of the Rats'. I read this in my early 'teens and could not sleep for weeks! But don't let me deter you from reading on. . . .

THE BURIAL OF THE RATS
Bram Stoker

EAVING PARIS BY THE ORLEANS ROAD, cross the Enceinte, and, turning to the right, you find yourself in a somewhat wild and not at all savoury district. Right and left, before and behind, on every side rise great heaps of dust and waste accumulated by the process of time.

Paris has its night as well as its day life, and the sojourner who enters his hotel in the Rue de Rivoli or the Rue St. Honore late at night or leaves it early in the morning, can guess, in coming near Montrouge — if he has not done so already — the purpose of those great waggons that look like boilers on wheels which he finds halting everywhere as he passes.

Every city has its peculiar institutions created out of its own needs; and one of the most notable institutions of Paris is its rag-picking population. In the early morning — and Parisian life commences at an early hour — may be seen in most streets standing on the pathway opposite every court and alley and between every few houses, as still in some American cities, even in parts of New York, large wooden boxes into which the domestics or tenement-holders empty the accumulated dust of the past day. Round these boxes gather and pass on, when the work is done, to fresh fields of labour and pastures new, squalid hungry-looking men and women, the implements of whose craft consist of a coarse bag or basket slung over the shoulder and a little rake with which they turn over and probe and examine in the minutest manner the dustbins. They pick up and deposit in their baskets, by aid of their rakes, whatever they may find, with the same facility as a Chinaman uses his chopsticks.

Paris is a city of centralisation — and centralisation and classification are closely allied. In the early times, when centralisation is becoming a fact, its forerunner is classification. All things which are similar or analogous become grouped together, and from the grouping of groups rises one whole or central point. We see radiating many long arms with innumerable tentaculae, and in the centre rises a gigantic head with a comprehensive brain and keen eyes to look on every side and ears sensitive to hear — and a voracious mouth to swallow.

Other cities resemble all the birds and beasts and fishes whose appetites and digestions are normal. Paris alone is the analogical apotheosis of the octopus. Product of centralisation carried on to an *ad absurdum*, it fairly represents the devil fish; and in no respects is the resemblance more curious than in the similarity of the digestive apparatus.

Those intelligent tourists who, having surrendered their individuality into the hands of Messrs. Cook or Gaze, 'do' Paris in three days, are often puzzled to know how it is that the dinner which in London would cost about six shillings, can be had for three francs in a cafe in the Palais Royal. They need have no more wonder if they will but consider the classification which is a theoretic speciality of Parisian life, and adopt all round the fact from which the chiffonier has his genesis.

The Paris of 1850 was not like the Paris of to-day, and those who see the Paris of Napoleon and Baron Hausseman can hardly realise the existence of the state of things forty-five years ago.

Amongst other things, however, which have not changed are those districts where the waste is gathered. Dust is dust all the world over, in every age, and the family likeness of dust-heaps is perfect. The traveller, therefore, who visits the environs of

Montrouge can go back in fancy without difficulty to the year 1850.

In this year I was making a prolonged stay in Paris. I was very much in love with a young lady who, though she returned my passion, so far yielded to the wishes of her parents that she had promised not to see me or to correspond with me for a year. I, too, had been compelled to accede to these conditions under a vague hope of parental approval. During the term of probation, I had promised to remain out of the country and not to write to my dear one until the expiration of the year.

Naturally the time went heavily with me. There was not one of my own family or circle who could tell me of Alice, and none of her own folk had, I am sorry to say, sufficient generosity to send me even an occasional word of comfort regarding her health and well-being. I spent six months wandering about Europe, but as I could find no satisfactory distraction in travel, I determined to come to Paris, where, at least, I would be within easy hail of London in case any good fortune should call me thither before the appointed time. That 'hope deferred maketh the heart sick' was never better exemplified than in my case, for in addition to the perpetual longing to see the face I loved there was always with me a harrowing anxiety lest some accident should prevent me showing Alice in due time that I had throughout the long period of probation, been faithful to her trust and my own love. Thus, every adventure which I undertook had a fierce pleasure of its own for it was frought with possible consequences greater than it would have ordinarily borne.

Like all travellers I exhausted the places of most interest in the first month of my stay, and was driven in the second month to look for amusement whithersoever I might. Having made sundry journeys to the better-known suburbs, I began to see that there was a *terra incognita*, in so far as the guide book was concerned, in the social wilderness lying between these attractive points. Accordingly I began to systematise my researches, and each day took up the thread of my exploration at the place where I had on the previous day dropped it.

In the process of time my wanderings led me near Montrouge and I saw that hereabouts lay the Ultima Thule of social exploration — a country as little known as that round the source of the White Nile. And so I determined to investigate philosophically the chiffonier — his habitat, his life, and his means of life.

The job was an unsavoury one, difficult of accomplishment, and with little hope of adequate reward. However, despite reason, obstinacy prevailed, and I entered into my new investigation with a keener energy than I could have summoned to aid me in any investigation leading to any end, valuable or worthy.

One day, late in a fine afternoon, toward the end of September, I entered the holy of holies of the city of dust. The place was evidently the recognised abode of a number of chiffoniers, for some sort of arrangement was manifested in the formation of the dust heaps near the road. I passed amongst these heaps, which stood like orderly sentries, determined to penetrate further and trace dust to its ultimate location.

As I passed along I saw behind the dust heaps a few forms that flitted to and fro, evidently watching with interest the advent of any stranger to such a place. The district was like a small Switzerland, and as I went forward my tortuous course shut out the path behind me.

Presently I got into what seemed a small city or community of chiffoniers. There were a number of shanties or huts, such as may be met with in the remote parts of the Bog of Allan — rude places with wattled walls, plastered with mud and roofs of rude thatch made from stable refuse — such places as one would not like to enter for any consideration, and which even in water-colour could only look picturesque˙ if judiciously treated. In the midst of these huts was one of the strangest adaptations — I cannot say habitations — I had ever seen. An immense old wardrobe, the colossal remanant of some boudoir of Charles VII, or Henry II, had been converted into a dwelling-house. The double doors lay open, so that the entire menage was open to public view. In the open half of the wardrobe was a common sitting-room of some four feet by six, in which sat, smoking their pipes round a charcoal brazier, no fewer than six old soldiers of the First Republic, with their uniforms torn and worn threadbare. Evidently they were of the *mauvais sujet* class; their bleary eyes and limp jaws told plainly of a common love of absinthe; and their eyes had that haggard, worn look of slumbering ferocity which follows hard in the wake of drink. The other side stood as of old, with its shelves intact, save that they were cut to half their depth, and in each shelf of which there were six, was a bed made with rags and straw. The half-dozen of worthies who inhabited this structure looked at me curiously as I passed; and when I looked back after going a little way I saw their heads together in a whispered conference. I did not like the look of this at all, for the place was very lonely, and the men looked very, very villainous. However, I did not see any cause for fear, and went on my way, penetrating further and further into the Sahara. The way was tortuous to a degree, and from going round in a series of semi-circles, as one goes in skating with the Dutch roll, I got rather confused with regard to the points of the compass.

When I had penetrated a little way I saw, as I turned the corner of a half-made heap, sitting on a heap of straw, an old soldier with threadbare coat.

'Hallo!' said I to myself; 'the First Republic is well represented here in its soldiery.'

As I passed him the old man never even looked up at me, but gazed on the ground with stolid persistency. Again I remarked to myself: 'See what a life of rude warfare can do! This old man's curiosity is a thing of the past.'

When I had gone a few steps, however, I looked back suddenly, and saw that curiosity was not dead, for the veteran had raised his head and was regarding me with a very queer expression. He seemed to me to look very like one of the six worthies in the press. When he saw me looking he dropped his head; and without thinking further of him I went on my way, satisfied that there was a strange likeness between these old warriors.

Presently I met another old soldier in a similar manner. He, too, did not notice me whilst I was passing.

By this time it was getting late in the afternoon, and I began to think of retracing my steps. Accordingly I turned to go back, but could see a number of tracks leading between different mounds and could not ascertain which of them I should take. In my perplexity I wanted to see someone of whom to ask the way, but could see no one. I determined to go on a few mounds further and so try to see someone — not a veteran.

I gained my object, for after going a couple of hundred yards I saw before me a single shanty such as I had seen before — with, however, the difference that this was not one for living in, but merely a roof with three walls open in front. From the evidence which the neighbourhood exhibited I took it to be a place for sorting. Within it was an old woman wrinkled and bent with age; I approached her to ask the way.

She rose as I came close and I asked her my way. She immediately commenced a conversation; and it occurred to me that here in the very centre of the Kingdom of Dust was the place to gather details of the history of Parisian rag-picking — particularly as I could do so from the lips of one who looked like the oldest inhabitant.

I began my inquiries, and the old woman gave me most interesting answers — she had been one of the ceteuces who sat daily before the guillotine and had taken an active part among the women who signalised themselves by their violence in the revolution. While we were talking she said suddenly: 'But m'sieur must be tired standing,' and dusted a rickety old stool for me to sit down. I hardly liked to do so for many reasons; but the poor old woman was so civil that I did not like to run the risk of hurting her by refusing, and moreover the conversation of one who had been at the taking of the Bastille was so interesting that I sat down and so our conversation went on.

While we were talking an old man — older and more bent and wrinkled even than the woman — appeared from behind the shanty. 'Here is Pierre,' said she. 'M'sieur can hear stories now if he wishes, for Pierre was in everything from the Bastille to Waterloo.' The old man took another stool at my request and we plunged into a sea of revolutionary reminiscences. This old man, albeit clothed like a scarecrow, was like any one of the six veterans.

I was now sitting in the centre of the low hut with the woman on my left hand and the man on my right, each of them being somewhat in front of me. The place was full of all sorts of curious objects of lumber, and of many things that I wished far away. In one corner was a heap of rags which seemed to move from the number of vermin it contained, and in the other a heap of bones whose odour was something shocking. Every now and then, glancing at the heaps, I could see the gleaming eyes of some of the rats which infested the place. These loathsome objects were bad enough, but what looked even more dreadful was an old butcher's axe with an iron handle stained with clots of blood leaning up against the wall on the right hand side. Still, these things did not give me much concern. The talk of the two old people was so fascinating that I stayed on and on, till the evening came and the dust heaps threw dark shadows over the vales between them.

After a time I began to grow uneasy. I could not tell how or why, but somehow I did not feel satisfied. Uneasiness is an instinct and means warning. The psychic faculties are often the sentries of the intellect, and when they sound alarm the reason begins to act, although perhaps not consciously.

This was so with me. I began to bethink me where I was and by what surrounded, and to wonder how I should fare in case I should be attacked; and then the thought suddenly burst upon me, although without any overt cause, that I was in danger. Prudence whispered: 'Be still and make no sign,' and so I was still and made no sign, for I knew that four cunning eyes were on me. 'Four eyes — if not more.' My God, what a horrible thought! The whole shanty might be surrounded on three sides with villains! I might be in the midst of a band of such desperadoes as only half a century of periodic revolution can produce.

With a sense of danger my intellect and observation quickened, and I grew more watchful than was my wont. I noticed that the old woman's eyes were constantly wandering towards my hands. I looked at them too, and saw the cause — my rings. On my left little finger I had a large signet and on the right a good diamond.

I thought that if there was any danger my first care was to avert suspicion. Accordingly I began to work the conversation round to rag-picking — to the drains — of the things found there; and so by easy stages to jewels. Then, seizing a favourable opportunity, I asked the old woman if she knew anything of such things. She answered that she did, a little. I held out my right hand, and, showing her the diamond, asked her what she thought of that. She answered that her eyes were bad, and stooped over my hand. I said as nonchalantly as I could: 'Pardon me! You will see better thus!' and taking it off handed it to her. An unholy light came into her withered old face, as she touched it. She stole one glance at me swift and keen as a flash of lightning.

She bent over the ring for a moment, her face quite concealed as though examining it. The old man looked straight out of the front of the shanty before him, at the same time fumbling in his pockets and producing a screw of tobacco in a paper and a pipe, which he proceeded to fill. I took advantage of the pause and the momentary rest from the searching eyes on my face to look carefully round the place, now dim and shadowy in the gloaming. There still lay all the heaps of varied reeking foulness; there the terrible blood-stained axe leaning against the wall in the right hand corner, and everywhere, despite the gloom, the baleful glitter of the eyes of the rats, I could see them even through some of the chinks of the boards at the back low down close to the ground. But stay! these latter eyes seemed more than usually large and bright and baleful!

For an instant my heart stood still, and I felt in that whirling condition of mind in which one feels a sort of spiritual drunkenness, and as though the body is only maintained erect in that there is no time for it to fall before recovery. Then, in another second, I was calm — coldly calm, with all my energies in full vigour, with a self-control which I felt to be perfect and with all my feeling and instincts alert.

Now I knew the full extent of my danger: I was watched and surrounded by desperate people! I could not even guess at how many of them were lying there on the ground behind the shanty, waiting for the moment to strike. I knew that I was big and strong, and they knew it, too. They knew also, as I did, that I was an Englishman and would make a fight for it; and so we waited. I had, I felt, gained an advantage in the last few seconds, for I knew my danger and understood the situation. Now, I thought, is the test of my courage — the enduring test: the fighting test may come later

The old woman raised her head and said to me in a satisfied kind of way:

'A very fine ring indeed — a beautiful ring! Oh, me! I once had such rings, plenty of them, and bracelets and earrings! Oh! for in those fine days I led the town a dance! But they've forgotten me now! They've forgotten me! They? Why they never heard of me! Perhaps their grandfathers remember me, some of them!' and she laughed a harsh, croaking laugh. And then I am bound to say that she astonished me, for she handed me back the ring with a certain suggestion of old-fashioned grace which was not without its pathos.

The old man eyed her with a sort of sudden ferocity, half rising from his stool, and said to me suddenly and hoarsely:

'Let me see!'

I was about to hand the ring when the old woman said:

'No! no, do not give it to Pierre! Pierre is eccentric. He loses things; and such a pretty ring!'

'Cat!' said the old man, savagely. Suddenly the old woman said, rather more loudly than was necessary:

'Wait! I shall tell you something about a ring.' There was something in the sound of her voice that jarred upon me. Perhaps it was my hyper-sensitiveness, wrought up as I was to such a pitch of nervous excitement, but I seemed to think that she was not addressing me. As I stole a glance round the place I saw the eyes of the rats in the bone heaps, but missed the eyes along the back. But even as I looked I saw them again appear. The old woman's 'Wait!' had given me a respite from attack, and the men had sunk back to their reclining posture.

'I once lost a ring — a beautiful diamond hoop that had belonged to a queen, and which was given to me by a farmer of the taxes, who afterwards cut his throat because I sent him away. I thought it must have been stolen, and taxed my people; but I could get no trace. The police came and suggested that it had found it way to the drain. We descended — I in my fine clothes, for I would not trust them with my beautiful ring! I know more of the drains since then, and of rats, too! but I shall never forget the horror of that place — alive with blazing eyes, a wall of them just outside the light of our torches. Well, we got beneath my house. We searched the outlet of the drain, and there in the filth found my ring, and we came out.

'But we found something else also before we came! As we were coming toward the opening a lot of sewer rats — human ones this time — came towards us. They told the police that one of their number had gone into the drain, but had not returned. He had gone in only shortly before we had, and, if lost, could hardly be far off. They asked help to seek him, so we turned back. They tried to prevent me going, but I insisted. I was a new excitement, and had I not recovered my ring? Not far did we go till we came on something. There was but little water, and the bottom of the drain was raised with brick, rubbish, and much matter of the kind. He had made a fight for it, even when his torch had gone out. But they were too many for him! They had not been long about it! The bones were still warm; but they were picked clean. They had even eaten their own dead ones and there were bones of rats as well as of the man. They took it cool enough those others — the human ones — and joked of their comrade when they found him dead, though they would have helped him living. Bah! what matters it — life or death?'

'And had you no fear?' I asked her.

'Fear!' she said with a laugh. 'Me have fear? Ask Pierre! But I was younger then, and, as I came through that horrible drain with its wall of greedy eyes, always moving with the circle of the light from the torches, I did not feel easy. I kept on before the men, though! It is a way I have! I never let the men get it before me. All I want is a chance and a means ! And they ate him up — took every trace away except the bones; and no one knew it, nor no sound of him was ever heard!' Here she broke into a chuckling fit of the ghastliest merriment which it was ever my lot to hear and see. A great poetess describes her heroine singing: 'Oh! to see or hear her singing! Scarce I know which is the divinest.'

And I can apply the same idea to the old crone — in all save the divinity, for I scarce could tell which was the most hellish — the harsh, malicious, satisfied, cruel laugh, or the leering grin, and the horrible square opening of the mouth like a tragic mask, and the yellow gleam of a few discoloured teeth in the shapeless gums. In that laugh and with that grin and the chuckling satisfaction I knew as well as if it had been spoken to me in words of thunder that my murder was settled, and the murderers only bided the proper time for its accomplishment. I could read between the lines of her gruesome story the commands to her accomplices. 'Wait,' she seemed to say, 'bide your time. I shall strike the first blow. Find the weapon for me, and I shall make the opportunity! He shall not escape! Keep him quiet, and then no one will be wiser. There will be no outcry, and the rats will do their work!'

It was growing darker and darker; the night was coming. I stole a glance round the shanty, still all the same! The bloody axe in the corner, the heaps of filth, and the eyes on the bone heaps and in the crannies of the floor.

Pierre had been still ostensibly filling his pipe; he now struck a light and began to puff away at it. The old woman said:

'Dear heart, how dark it is! Pierre, like a good lad, light the lamp!'

Pierre got up and with the lighted match in his hand touched the wick of a lamp which hung at one side of the entrance to the shanty, and which had a reflector that threw the light all over the place. It was evidently that which was used for their sorting at night.

'Not that, stupid! Not that! The lantern!' she called out to him.

He immediately blew it out, saying: 'All right, mother I'll find it,' and he hustled about the left corner of the room — the old woman saying through the darkness:

'The lantern! the lantern! Oh! That is the light that is most useful to us poor folks. The lantern was the friend of the revolution! It is the friend of the chiffonier! It helps us when all else fails.'

Hardly had she said the word when there was a kind of creaking of the whole place, and something was steadily dragged over the roof.

Again I seemed to read between the lines of her words. I knew the lesson of the lantern.

'One of you get on the roof with a noose and strangle him as he passes out if we fail within.'

As I looked out of the opening I saw the loop of a rope outlined black against the lurid sky. I was now, indeed, beset!

Pierre was not long in finding the lantern. I kept my eyes fixed through the darkness on the old woman. Pierre struck his light, and by its flash I saw the old woman raise from the ground beside her where it had mysteriously appeared, and then hide in the folds of her gown, a long sharp knife or dagger. It seemed to be like a butcher's sharpening iron fined to a keen point.

The lantern was lit.

'Bring it here, Pierre,' she said. 'Place it in the doorway where we can see it. See how nice it is! It shuts out the darkness from us; it is just right!'

Just right for her and her purposes! It threw all its light on my face, leaving in gloom the faces of both Pierre and the woman, who sat outside of me on each side.

I felt that the time of action was approaching; but I knew now that the first signal and movement would come from the woman, and so watched her.

I was all unarmed, but I had made up my mind what to do. At the first movement I would seize the butcher's axe in the right-hand corner and fight my way out. At least, I would die hard. I stole a glance round to fix its exact locality so that I could not fail to seize it at the first effort, for then, if ever, time and accuracy would be previous.

Good God! It was gone! All the horror of the situation burst upon me; but the bitterest thought of all was that if the issue of the terrible position should be against me Alice would infallibly suffer. Either she would believe me false — and any lover, or any one who has ever been one, can imagine the bitterness of the thought — or else she would go on loving long after I had been lost to her and to the world, so that her life would be broken and embittered, shattered with disappointment and despair. The very magnitude of the pain braced me up and nerved me to bear the dread scrutiny of the plotters.

I think I did not betray myself. The old woman was watching me as a cat does a mouse; she had her right hand hidden in the folds of her gown, clutching, I knew, that long, cruel-looking dagger. Had she seen any disappointment in my face she would, I felt, have known that the moment had come, and would have sprung on me like a tigress, certain of taking me unprepared.

I looked out into the night, and there I saw new cause for danger. Before and around the hut were at a little distance some shadowy forms; they were quite still, but I knew that they were all alert and on guard. Small chance for me now in that direction.

Again I stole a glance round the place. In moments of great excitement and of great danger, which is excitement, the mind works very quickly, and the keeness of the faculties which depend on the mind grows in proportion. I now felt this. In an instant I took in the whole situation. I saw that the axe had been taken through a small hole made in one of the rotten boards. How rotten they must be to allow of such a thing being done without a particle of noise.

The hut was a regular murder-trap, and was guarded all around. A garroter lay on the roof ready to entangle me with his noose if I should escape the dagger of the old hag. In front the way was guarded by I know not how many watchers. And at the back was a row of desperate men — I had seen their eyes still through the crack in the boards of the floor, when last I looked — as they lay prone waiting for the signal to start erect. If it was to be ever, now for it!

As nonchalantly as I could I turned slightly on my stool so as to get my right leg well under me. Then with a sudden jump, turning my head, and guarding it with my hands, and with the fighting instinct of the knights of old, I breathed my lady's name, and hurled myself against the back wall of the hut.

Watchful as they were, the suddeness of my movement surprised both Pierre and the old woman. As I crashed through the rotten timbers I saw the old woman rise with a leap like a tiger and heard her low gasp of baffled rage. My feet lit on something that moved, and as I jumped away I knew that I had stepped on the back of one of the row of men lying on their faces outside the hut. I was torn with nails and splinters, but otherwise unhurt. Breathless I rushed up the mound in front of me, hearing as I went the dull crash of the shanty as it collapsed into a mass.

It was a nightmare climb. The mound, though but low, was awfully steep, and with each step I took the mass of dust and cinders tore down with me and gave way under my feet. The dust rose and choked me; it was sickening, foetid, awful; but my climb was, I felt, for life or death, and I struggled on. The seconds seemed hours; but the few moments I had in starting, combined with my youth and strength, gave me a great advantage, and, though several forms struggled after me in deadly silence which was more dreadful than any sound, I easily reached the top. Since then I have climbed the cone of Vesuvius, and as I struggled up that dreary steep amid the sulphurous fumes the memory of that awful night at Montrouge came back to me so vividly that I almost grew faint.

The mound was one of the tallest in the region of dust, and as I struggled to the top, panting for breath and with my heart beating with a sledge-hammer, I saw away to my left the full red gleam of the sky, and nearer still the flashing of lights. Thank God! I knew where I was now and where lay the road to Paris!

For two or three seconds I paused and looked back. My pursuers were still well behind me, but struggling up resolutely and in deadly silence. Beyond, the shanty was a wreck – a mass of timber and moving forms. I could see it well, for flames were already bursting out; the rags and straw had evidently caught fire from the lantern. Still silence there ! Not a sound! These old wretches could die game, anyhow.

I had no time for more than a passing glance, for as I cast an eye round the mound preparatory to making my descent I saw several dark forms rushing round on either side to cut me off on

my way. It was now a race for life. They were trying to head me
on my way to Paris, and with the instinct of the moment I
dashed down to the right-hand side. I was just in time, for,
though I came as it seemd to me down the steep in a few steps,
the wary old men who were watching me turned back, and one,
as I rushed by into the opening between the two mounds in
front, almost struck me a blow with that terrible butcher's axe.
There could surely not be two such weapons about!

Then began a really horrible chase. I easily ran ahead of the
old men, and even when some younger ones and a few women
joined in the hunt I easily distanced them. But I did not know
the way, and I could not even guide myself by the light in the
sky, for I was running away from it. I had heard that, unless of
conscious purpose, hunted men turn always to the left, and so
I found it now; and so, I suppose, knew also my pursuers, who
were more animals than men, and with cunning or instinct had
found out such secrets for themselves; for on finishing a quick
spurt, after which I intended to take a moment's breathing
space, I suddenly saw ahead of me two or three forms swiftly
passing behind a mound to the right.

I was in the spider's web now indeed! But with the thought
of this new danger came the resource of the hunted, and so I
darted down the next turning to the right. I continued in this
direction for some hundred yards, and then, making a turn to
the left again, felt certain that I had, at any rate, avoided the
danger of being surrounded.

But not of pursuit, for on came the rabble after me, steady,
dogged, relentless, and still in grim silence.

In the greater darkness the mounds seemed now to be
somewhat smaller than before, although — for the night was
closing — they looked bigger in proportion. I was now well
ahead of my pursuers, so I made a dart up the mound in front.

Oh joy of joys! I was close to the edge of this inferno of
dustheaps. Away behind me the red light of Paris was in the
sky, and towering up behind rose the heights of Montmartre —
a dim light, with here and there brilliant points like stars.

Restored to vigour in a moment, I ran over the few
remaining mounds of decreasing size, and found myself on the

level land beyond. Even then, however, the prospect was not inviting. All before me was dark and dismal, and I had evidently come on one of those dank, low-lying waste places which are found here and there in the neighbourhood of great cities. Places of waste and desolation, where the space is required for the ultimate agglomeration of all that is noxious, and the ground is so poor as to create no desire of occupancy even in the lowest squatter. With eyes accustomed to the gloom of the evening, and away now from the shadows of those dreadful dustheaps, I could see much more easily than I could a little while ago. It might have been, of course, that the glare in the sky of the lights of Paris, though the city was some miles away, was reflected here. Howsoever it was, I saw well enough to take bearings for certainly some little distance around me.

In front was a bleak, flat waste that seemed almost dead level, with here and there the dark shimmering of stagnant pools. Seemingly far off on the right, amid a small cluster of scattered lights, rose a dark mass of Fort Montrouge, and away to the left in the dim distance, pointed with stray gleams from cottage windows, the lights in the sky showed the locality of Bicêtre. A moment's thought decided me to take to the right and try to reach Montrouge. There at least would be some sort of safety, and I might possibly long before come on some of the cross roads which I knew. Somewhere, not far off, must lie the strategic road made to connect the outlying chain of forts circling the city.

Then I looked back. Coming over the mounds, and outlined black against the glare of the Parisian horizon, I saw several moving figures, and still a way to the right several more deploying out between me and my destination. They evidently meant to cut me off in this direction, and so my choice became constricted; it lay now between going straight ahead or turning to the left. Stooping to the ground, so as to get the advantage of the horizon as a line of sight, I looked carefully in this direction, but could detect no sign of my enemies. I argued that as they had not guarded or were not trying to guard that point, there was evidently danger to me there already. So I made up my mind to go straight on before me.

It was not an inviting prospect, and as I went on the reality grew worse. The ground became soft and oozy, and now and again gave way beneath me in a sickening kind of way. I seemed somehow to be going down, for I saw round me places seemingly more elevated than where I was, and this in a place which from a little way back seemed dead level. I looked around, but could see none of my pursuers. This was strange, for all along these birds of the night had followed me through the darkness as well as though it was broad daylight. How I blamed myself for coming out in my light-coloured tourist suit of tweed. The silence, and my not being able to see my enemies, whilst I felt that they were watching me, grew appalling, and in the hope of some one not of this ghastly crew hearing me I rasised my voice and shouted several times. There was not the slightest response; not even an echo rewarded my efforts. For a while I stocd stock still and kept my eyes in one direction. On one of the rising places around me I saw something dark move along, then another, and another. This was to my left, and seemingly moving to head me off.

I thought that again I might with my skill as a runner elude my enemies at this game, and so with all my speed darted forward.

Splash!

My feet had given way in a mass of slimy rubbish, and I had fallen headlong into a reeking, stagnant pool. The water and the mud in which my arms sank up to the elbows was filthy and nauseous beyond description, and in the suddenness of my fall I had actually swallowed some of the filthy stuff, which nearly choked me, and made me gasp for breath. Never shall I forget the moments during which I stood trying to recover myself almost fainting from the foetid odour of the filthy pool, whose white mist rose ghostlike around. Worst of all, with the acute despair of the hunted animal when he sees the pursuing pack closing on him, I saw before my eyes whilst I stood helpless the dark forms of my pursuers moving swiftly to surround me.

It is curious how our minds work on odd matters even when the energies of thought are seemingly concentrated on some terrible and pressing need. I was in momentary peril of my life:

my safety depended on my action, and my choice of alternatives coming now with almost every step I took, and yet I could not but think of the strange dogged persistency of these old men. Their silent resolution, their steadfast, grim, persistency even in such a cause commanded, as well as fear, even a measure of respect. What must they have been in the vigour of their youth. I could understand now that whirlwind rush on the bridge of Arcola, that scornful exclamation of the Old Guard at Waterloo! Unconscious cerebration has its own pleasures, even at such moments: but fortunately it does not in any way clash with the thought from which action springs.

I realised at a glance that so far I was defeated in my object, my enemies as yet had won. They had succeeded in surrounding me on three sides, and were bent on driving me off to the left-hand, where there was already some danger for me, for they had left no guard. I accepted the alternative — it was a case of Hobson's choice and run. I had to keep the lower ground, for my pursuers were on the higher places. However, though the ooze and broken ground impeded me my youth and training made me able to hold my ground, and by keeping a diagonal line I not only kept them from gaining on me but even began to distance them. This gave me new heart and strength, and by this time habitual training was beginning to tell and my second wind had come. Before me the ground rose slightly. I rushed up the slope and found before me a waste of watery slime, with a low dyke or bank looking black and grim beyond. I felt that if I could but reach the dyke in safety I could there, with solid ground under my feet and some kind of path to guide me, find with comparative ease a way out of my troubles. After a glance right and left and seeing no one near, I kept my eyes for a few minutes to their rightful work of aiding my feet whilst I crossed the swamp. It was rough, hard work, but there was little danger, merely toil; and a short time took me to the dyke. I rushed up the slope exulting; but here again I met a new shock. On either side of me rose a number of crouching figures. From right and left they rushed at me. Each body held a rope.

The cordon was nearly complete. I could pass on neither side, and the end was near.

There was only one chance, and I took it. I hurled myself across the dyke, and escaping out of the very clutches of my foes threw myself into the stream.

At any other time I should have thought that water foul and filthy, but now it was as welcome as the most crystal stream to the parched traveller. It was a highway of safety!

My pursuers rushed after me. Had only one of them held the rope it would have been all up with me, for he could have entangled me before I had time to swim a stroke; but the many hands holding it embarrassed and delayed them, and when the rope struck the water I heard the splash well behind me. A few minutes' hard swimming took me across the stream. Refreshed with the immersion and encouraged by the escape, I climbed the dyke in comparative gaiety of spirits.

From the top I looked back. Through the darkness I saw my assailants scattering up and down along the dyke. The pursuit was evidently not ended, and again I had to choose my course. Beyond the dyke where I stood was a wild, swampy space very similar to that which I had crossed. I determined to shun such a place, and thought for a moment whether I would take up or down the dyke. I thought I heard a sound — the muffled sound of oars, so I listened, and then shouted.

No response; but the sound ceased. My enemies had evidently got a boat of some kind. As they were on the up side of me I took the down path and began to run. As I passed to the left of where I had entered the water I heard several splashes, soft and stealthy, like the sound a rat makes as he plunges into the stream, but vastly greater; and as I looked I saw the dark sheen of the water broken by the ripples of several advancing heads. Some of my enemies were swimming the stream also.

And now behind me, up the stream, the silence was broken by the quick rattle and creak of oars; my enemies were in hot pursuit. I put my best leg foremost and ran on. After a break of a couple of minutes I looked back, and by a gleam of light through the ragged clouds I saw several dark forms climbing the bank behind me. The wind had now begun to rise, and the water beside me was ruffled and beginning to break in tiny waves on the bank. I had to keep my eyes pretty well on the ground before me, lest I should stumble, for I knew that to stumble was death. After a few minutes I looked back behind me. On the dyke were only a few dark figures, but crossing the waste, swampy ground were many more. What new danger this portended I did not know — could only guess. Then as I ran it seemed to me that my track kept ever sloping away to the right. I looked up ahead and saw that the river was much wider than before, and that the dyke on which I stood fell quite away, and beyond it was another stream on whose near bank I saw some of the dark forms now across the marsh. I was on an island of some kind.

My situation was now indeed terrible, for my enemies had hemmed me in on every side. Behind came the quickening roll of the oars, as though my pursuers knew that the end was close. Around me on every side was desolation; there was not a roof or light, as far as I could see. Far off to the right rose some dark mass, but what it was I knew not. For a moment I paused to think what I should do, not for more, for my pursuers were drawing closer. Then my mind was made up. I slipped down the bank and took to the water. I struck out straight ahead so as to gain the current by clearing the backwater of the island, for such I presume it was, when I had passed into the stream. I waited till a cloud came driving across the moon and leaving all in darkness. Then I took off my hat and laid it softly on the water floating with the stream, and a second after dived to the right, and struck out under water with all my might. I was, I suppose, half a minute under water, and when I rose came up as softly as I could, and turning, looked back. There went my light brown floating merrily away. Close behind it came a rickety old boat, driven furiously by a pair of oars. The moon was still partly obscured by the drifting clouds, but in the partial light I could see a man in the bows holding aloft ready to strike what appeared to me to be that same dreadful pole-axe which I had before escaped. As I looked the boat drew closer, closer, and the man struck savagely. The hat disappeared. The man fell forward, almost out of the boat. His comrades dragged him in but without the ax, and then as I turned with all my energies bent on reaching the further bank, I heard the fierce whirr of the muttered 'Sacre!' which marked the anger of my baffled pursuers.

That was the first sound I had heard from human lips during all this dreadful chase, and full as it was of menace and danger to me it was a welcome sound for it broke that awful silence which shrouded and appalled me. It was as though an overt sign that my opponents were men and not ghosts, and that with them I had, at least, the chance of a man, though but one against many.

But now that the spell of silence was broken the sounds came thick and fast. From boat to shore and back from shore to boat came quick questions and answers, all in the fiercest whispers. I looked back — a fatal thing to do — for in the instant someone caught sight of my face, which showed white on the dark water, and shouted. Hands pointed to me, and in a moment or two the boat was under weigh, and following hard after me. I had but a little way to go, but quicker and quicker came the boat after me. A few more strokes and I would be on the shore, but I felt the oncoming of the boat, and expected each second to feel the crash of an oar or other weapon on my head. Had I not seen the dreadful axe disappear in the water I do not think that I could have won the shore. I heard the muttered curses of those not rowing and the laboured breath of the rowers. With one supreme effort for life or liberty I touched the bank and sprang up it. There was not a single second to spare, for hard behind me the boat grounded and several dark forms sprang after me. I gained the top of the dyke, and keeping to the left ran on again. The boat put off and followed down the stream. Seeing this I feared danger in this direction, and quickly turning, ran down the dyke on the other side, and after passing a short stretch of marshy ground gained a wild, open flat country and sped on.

Still behind me came on my relentless pursuers. Far away, below me, I saw the same dark mass as before, but now grown closer and greater. My heart gave a great thrill of delight, for I knew that it must be the fortress of Bicêtre, and with new courage I ran on. I had heard that between each and all of the protecting forts of Paris there are strategic ways, deep sunk roads, where soldiers marching should be sheltered from an enemy. I knew that if I could gain this road I would be safe, but in the darkness I could not see any sign of it, so, in blind hope of striking it, I ran on.

Presently I came to the ege of a deep cut, and found that down below me ran a road guarded on each side by a ditch of water fenced on either side by a straight, high wall.

Getting fainter and dizzier, I ran on; the ground got more broken — more and more still, till I staggered and fell, and rose again, and ran on in the blind anguish of the hunted. Again the thought of Alice nerved me. I would not be lost and wreck her life: I would fight and struggle for life to the bitter end. With a great effort I caught the top of the wall. As, scrambling like a catamount, I drew myself up, I actually felt a hand touch the sole of my foot. I was now on a sort of causeway, and before me I saw a dim light. Blind and dizzy, I ran on, staggered, and fell, rising, covered with dust and blood.

'Halt la!'

The words sounded like a voice from heaven. A blaze of light seemed to enwrap me, and I shouted with joy.

'Qui va la?' The rattle of musketry, the flash of steel before my eyes. Instinctively I stopped, though close behind me came a rush of my pursuers.

Another word or two, and out from a gateway poured, as it seemed to me, a tide of red and blue, as the guard turned out. All around seemed blazing with light, and the flash of steel, the clink and rattle of arms, and the loud, harsh voices of command. As I fell forward, utterly exhausted, a soldier caught me. I looked back in dreadful expectation, and saw the mass of forms disappearing into the night. Then I must have fainted. When I recovered my senses I was in the guard room. They gave me brandy, and after a while I was able to tell them something of what had passed. Then a commissary of police appeared, apparently out of the empty air, as is the way of the Parisian police officer. He listened attentively, and then had a moment's consultation with the officer in command. Apparently they were agreed, for they asked me if I was ready now to come with them.

The Burial of the Rats. 1850.

Jeanette O'Donne. dec 78.

'Where to?' I asked, rising to go.

'Back to the dust heaps. We shall, perhaps, catch them yet!'
'I shall try!' said I.

He eyed me for a moment keenly, and said suddenly:
'Would you like to wait a while or till tomorrow, young
Englishman?' This touched me to the quick, as, perhaps, he
intended, and I jumped to my feet.

'Come now!' I said; 'now! now! An Englishman is always
ready for his duty!'

The commissary was a good fellow, as well as a shrewd one;
he slapped my shoulder kindly. 'Brave garçon!' he said. 'Forgive
me, but I knew what would do you most good. The guard is
ready. Come!'

And so, passing right through the guard room, and through a
long vaulted passage, we were out into the night. A few of the
men in front had powerful lanterns. Through courtyards and
down a sloping way we passed out through a low archway to
a sunken road, the same that I had seen in my flight. The
order was given to get at the double, and with a quick, springing
stride, half run, half walk, the soldiers went swiftly along. I felt
my strength renewed again — such is the difference between
hunter and hunted. A very short distance took us to a low-lying
pontoon bridge across the stream, and evidently very little
higher up than I had struck it. Some effort had evidently
been made to damage it, for the ropes had all been cut, and one
of the chains had been broken.. I heard the officer say to the
commissary:

'We are just in time! A few more minutes, and they would
have destroyed the bridge. Forward, quicker still!' and on
we went. Again we reached a pontoon on the winding stream;
as we came up we hard the hollow boom of the metal drums as
the efforts to destroy the bridge was again renewed. A word of
command was given, and several men raised their rifles.

'Fire!' A volley rang out. There was a muffled cry, and the
dark forms dispersed. But the evil was done, and we saw the far
end of the pontoon swing into the stream. This was a serious
delay, and it was nearly an hour before we had renewed ropes
and restored the bridge sufficiently to allow us to cross.

We renewed the chase. Quicker, quicker we went towards the dust heaps.

After a time we came to a place that I knew. There were the remains of a fire — a few smouldering wood ashes still cast a red glow, but the bulk of the ashes were cold. I knew the site of the hut and the hill behind it up which I had rushed, and in the flickering glow the eyes of the rats still shone with a sort of phosphorescence. The commissary spoke a word to the officer, and he cried:

'Halt!'

The soldiers were ordered to spread around and watch, and then we commenced to examine the ruins. The commissary himself began to lift away the charred boards and rubbish. These the soldiers took and piled together. Presently he started back, then bent down and rising beckoned me.

'See!' he said.

It was a gruesome sight. There lay a skeleton face downwards, a women by the lines — an old woman by the coarse fibre of the bone. Between the ribs rose a long spike-like dagger made from a butcher's sharpening knife, its keen point buried in the spine.

'You will observe,' said the commissary to the officer and to me as he took out his notebook, 'that the woman must have fallen on her dagger. The rats are many here — see their eyes glistening among that heap of bones — and you will also notice' — I shuddered as he placed his hand on the skeleton — 'that but little time was lost by them, for the bones are scarcely cold!'

There was no other sign of any one near, living or dead; and so deploying again into line the soldiers passed on. Presently we came to the hut made of the old wardrobe. We approached. In five of the six compartments was an old man sleeping — sleeping so soundly that even the glare of the lanterns did not wake them. Old and grim and grizzled they looked, with their gaunt wrinkled bronzed faces and their white moustaches. The officer called out harshly and loudly a word of command, and in an instant each of them was on his feet before us and standing at 'attention!'

'What do you here?'

'We sleep,' was the answer.

'Where are the other chiffoniers?' asked the commissary.

'Gone to work.'

'And you?'

'We are on guard!'

'Peste!' laughed the officer grimly, as he looked at the old men one after the other in the face and added with cool and deliberate cruelty: 'Asleep on duty! Is this the manner of the Old Guard? No wonder, then, a Waterloo!'

By the gleam of the lantern I saw the grim old faces grow deadly pale, and almost shuddered at the look in the eyes of the old men as the laugh of the soldiers echoed the grim pleasantry of the officer.

I felt in that moment that I was in some measure avenged.

For a moment they looked as if they would throw themselves on the taunter, but years of their life had schooled them and they remained still.

'You are but five,' said the commissary; 'where is the sixth?' The answer came with a grim chuckle.

'He is there!' and the speaker pointed to the bottom of the wardrobe. 'He died last night. You won't find much of him. The burial of the rats is quick!'

The commissary stooped and looked in. Then he turned to the officer and said calmly:

'We may as well go back. No trace here now; nothing to prove that man was the one wounded by your soldier's bullets! Probably they murdered him to cover up the trace. See!' again he stooped and placed his hands on the skeleton. 'The rats work quickly and they are many. These bones are warm!'

I shuddered, and so did many more of those around me.

'Form!' said the officer, and so in marching order, with the lanterns swinging in front and the manacled veterans in the midst, with steady tramp we took ourselves out of the dustheaps and turned backward to the fortress of Bicêtre.

* * *

My year of probation has long since ended, and Alice is my wife. But when I look back upon that trying twelvemonth one of the most vivid incidents that memory recalls is that associated with my visit to the City of Dust.

'M.P. SHIEL WAS AN IRISHMAN who also exploited the obsession with war.' In these words Brian Aldiss, in his history of Science Fiction and Fantasy, *Billion Year Spree* (1973), dismisses one of the most controversial writers of his day. Aldiss was referring to the fact that during the late 19th Century there arose a thirst from the public to read 'future war stories' of how mankind would wipe itself out in a final world conflagration. And this was long before the First World War and long before the ultimate weapon, the atomic bomb, was ever thought of.

'For a writer as strange as Shiel,' continues Aldiss, 'there was perhaps no recourse but to science fiction.' But he dismisses Shiel (whose name he consistently mis-spells through as Sheil) too lightly. 'He was scarcely the worst writer in the field,' he grudgingly admits, 'the competition for that honour being too fierce, but his prose is prize-winningly grotesque'.

Nevertheless, Shiel still has a large following today. Three of his novels are always listed as being historically important and influential literary works of science fiction: *The Yellow Danger* (1898), *The Lord of the Sea* (1901) and, most importantly, *The Purple Cloud* (1901).

The writers of his day were unanimous in their praise of Shiel's work. The critic and writer Hugh Walpole described Shiel as 'A flaming genius. At his best he is not to be touched.' J.B. Priestley wrote: 'If by genius we mean amazing ideas,

flashes of real imagination, wild originality, then we must grant it him'. H.G. Wells thought his talent was 'colossal' and 'brilliant'. The Welsh fantasy writer Arthur Machen described him as 'Poe, perhaps, but Poe with an unearthly radiance'. When reviewing Shiel's *Shapes in the Fire* (1896) in the London *Times* Machen elaborated 'here is a wilder wonderland than Poe ever dreamed of'. Arnold Bennett thought him to be 'a scholar, a linguist, an inventor, a stylist'. Dashiell Hammett thought of him more simply as 'a magician' while L.P. Hartley called him 'a master of the written word'. Rebecca West summed up all the praise by saying 'Sensible people ought to have a complete set of Shiel'.

Yet today it is very popular to condemn the works of Shiel entirely out of hand in the way Brian Aldiss has dismissed him for he held views that are unacceptable in our more enlightened age. Those views notwithstanding Shiel does remain, in the words of Edward Shanks, 'one of the most remarkable minds and imaginations of our time . . . a poet and a prophet'.

Of Matthew Phipps Shiel there is surprisingly little biographical data available. The late John Gawsworth, (1912-1970) the noted poet, essayist and bibliographer who became Shiel's literary executor, included a sketch on him in *Ten Contemporaries: Notes towards their definitive biography* (1932). He did announce in 1948 that he was going to write a biography of Shiel but, unfortunately, never completed it. In 1948 A. Reynolds Morse published a bibliography *The Works of M.P. Shiel*.

Shiel was born of Irish parents on July 21, 1865, in the West Indies. His father was a Methodist preacher. The family then returned to Dublin. Shiel eventually studied at London University where he took a BA and then specialised in medicine, giving it up in order to teach mathematics. Throughout the rest of his life his hobbies remained chemistry and the working out of mathematical problems.

Shiel had always wanted to write and, in fact, published his first article when he was thirteen years old. He wrote to the American critic Carl Van Vechtan: 'I find no little amusement in writing fiction, but like better mathematics, chemistry and generally manage to have some sort of laboratory wherever I go.'

Shiel also dabbled in toxicology, astronomy, sociology, religion and politics.

In politics one must certainly agree with Brian Aldiss that 'If ever there was a Fascist, Shiel was he. He was as violently anti-Semitic as he was anti-Asian. If ever there was a dangerous vision, in the full sense of that sometimes misapplied term, it is contained in '*The SS*'. Prophetically enough, Shiel wrote a short story entitled 'The SS' about an eponymous Society of Sparta which destroys thousands of people all over the world to make the race eugenically pure. Everyone with any disease or disability is obliterated. Although it is evident that Shiel believed in the philosophical theories which he expounded, the story can also be seen as a terrible forewarning of the activities of that other 'SS' in Nazi Germany.

Certainly Shiel was an admirer of health, strength and youth, to the extent of mysticism. He believed that a strong healthy man in touch with nature virtually achieved a divine under-standing and became a superman. It was his custom to run several miles before breakfast each morning and he was an avid mountaineer, climbing most of the peaks in Europe.

He spent a good deal of his life living in Palermo, in Sicily, but spent the last years living in Chichester, near his friend John Gawsworth.

His first book was published in 1895, when he was thirty. It was a collection of horror fantasy tales called *Prince Zaleski* of which Dorothy L. Sayers has declared that their 'curious and elaborate beauty recaptures in every arabesque sentence the very accents of Edgar Allen Poe'. The stories concern a detective who is weirdly Gothic pastiche of Sherlock Holmes. *The Rajah's Sapphire*, published the following year, was worked by Shiel from a plot given to him by the famous journalist W.T. Stead who was to drown in the Titanic disaster. The same year *Shapes in the Fire*, another collection of short stories, enhanced his reputation as a master of the macabre.

Shiel's work was now appearing in serialised form in the famous *Strand Magazine* and *Pall Mall Magazine*. He was also a friend of Louis Tracy (who wrote the classic *The Final War*, 1896) and actually wrote Chapter 29 of Tracy's book *An American Emperor* which was being serialised in *Pearson's Weekly* in 1896 also. Tracy was writing it episode by episode and one week he fell ill and asked Shiel to stand in for him.

In 1898 Shiel published *The Yellow Danger*, the story of a menace out of Asia, the threat of a Chinese empire which wipes out half the world before being wiped out itself by the British who thus become rulers of the world. The Victorian 'Yellow Peril' music-hall joke emanated from this book. It was a theme to which Shiel returned several times with *The Yellow Wave* (1905) and *The Dragon* (1913) which Victor Gollancz republished in 1929 as *The Yellow Peril*.

Shiel also wrote several 'future war' tales at a time when people indulged in fantasies about the end of the world or how future wars would be fought and with what inventions. H.G. Wells' *The War in the Air* has become a surviving classic of the many hundreds of tales of such wars. The real exponents of these stories were writers like George Griffith whose book *The Outlaws of the Air* (1895) provided the inspiration for Wells' book — which he acknowledges in chapter one.

By 1901 Shiel had published seven books which had established him as a leading fantasy writer. That year came his tour de force, a book which is regarded as one of the great classics of Science Fiction and which, incidentally, is by far his most readable novel — *The Purple Cloud*. In this novel Shiel adapts the theme used by Mary Shelley in her novel *The Last Man* (1826). A doctor goes on an expedition to the North Pole. He is separated from his comrades and when he finally returns from near death in the Arctic wastes he finds that he is the last man left alive in the world . . . everyone has been destroyed by a cloud of purple gas. He sets off in despair to explore the world and eventually finds another survivor . . . but the end of the novel comes with the cloud of purple gas being blown indestructibly towards them.

In 1948 Paramount Pictures purchased the film rights of *The Purple Cloud* but it was not until 1959 that the film was released entitled *The World, The Flesh and The Devil*. There were only three actors — Harry Belafonte, Inger Stevens and Mel Ferrer. One cannot help thinking that the scriptwriter had an extraordinary sense of humour when adapting Shiel's novel. The film was a revolution in American racial tolerance for it featured a negro as the 'good' last man and a white man as the 'bad' last man with a blonde last woman opting for the 'good' man. The picture was released to great critical acclaim.

The writer and critic, Sam Moskowitz, has observed: 'It is indeed ironical that a man (flawed but occasionally brilliant) who was anti-Semite, anti-Christian, anti-Negro, anti-Oriental, ardent believer in Aryan superiority, and a war lover is to be posthumously ennobled as an apostle of peace and racial tolerance every time *The World, The Flesh and the Devil* is shown, as it will be for many years to come.'

In the same year that *The Purple Cloud* was published, 1901, his third classic *The Lord of the Sea*, concerning the rise of an English dictator, was also printed.

By the time he died, Shiel had written some 30 odd books of which 25 were novels. Many of them were of the macabre such as *The Weird O, It, The Evil That Men Do* (1904), *Dr. Krsinki's Secret* (1929) and *The Black Box* (1930). He wrote a little non fiction but in 1919 translated Charles Henry Schmitt's book on *The Hungarian Revolution*. He also wrote poetry and in 1936 his friend, John Gawsworth, edited a collection entitled simply *Poems*.

In 1947 the newspapers reported: 'On February 17, aged 81, the Irish romantic novelist, M.P. Shiel, died at Chichester. He was writing with unique *verve* right up to the end.'

The year after his death Gawsworth edited a memorial volume *The Best Short Stories of M.P. Shiel* for Gollancz and in 1950 a volume of Shiel's essays on *Science, Life and Literature* was published.

In the early 1960's the works of Shiel enjoyed another spate of popularity and titles such as *The Purple Cloud, The Lord of The Sea* and *The Isle of Lies* (1908) were reissued in hardbound and then paperback editions. It would seem that Edward Shanks was right when he said years earlier 'others will come after us who will from time to time demand that his work shall be available for them to read'.

To introduce his work I have chosen 'Xélucha' which H.P. Lovecraft has described as attaining a high level of horrific magic. 'Xélucha', says Lovecraft, 'is a noxiously hideous fragment'. It is one of Shiel's earlier pieces and is a fine example of the work of this strange but brilliant man, a man whose genius is marred by his intolerant comments and the violence of his racialism.

Carl Van Vechtan has stated that Shiel was not merely a manufacturer of wild romances in the manner of Jules Verne: 'One perceives that here there is a philosophic consciousness . . . it will become evident that Shiel may be compared more reasonably with the H.G. Wells of the early romances.' Like H.G. Wells, Shiel's niche in literary history is secure.

XÉLUCHA
M.P. Shiel

"He goeth after her . . . and knoweth not . . ."
(From a Diary)

HREE DAYS AGO! by heaven, it seems an age. But I am shaken — my reason is debauched. A while since, I fell into a momentary coma precisely resembling an attack of *petit mal*. "Tombs, and worms, and epitaphs" — that is my dream. At my age, with my physique, to walk staggery, like a man striken! But all that will pass: I must collect myself — my reason is debauched. Three days ago! it seems an age! I sat on the floor before an old cista full of letters. I lighted upon a packet of Cosmo's. Why, I had forgotten them! they are turning sere! Truly, I can no more call myself a young man. I sat reading, listlessly, rapt back by memory. To muse is to be lost! of *that* evil habit I must wring the neck, or look to perish. Once more I threaded the mazy sphere-harmony of the minuet, reeled in the waltz, long pomps of candelabra, the noonday of the bacchanal, about me. Cosmo was the very tsar and maharajah of the Sybarites! the Priap of the *detraqués*! In every unexpected alcove of the Roman Villa was a couch, raised high, with necessary footstool, flanked and canopied with *mirrors* of clarified gold. Consumption fastened upon him; reclining at last at table, he

could, till warmed, scarce lift the wine! his eyes were like two
fat glow-worms, coiled together! they seemed haloed with
vaporous emanations of phosphorus! Desperate, one could see,
was the secret struggle with the Devourer. But to the end the
princely smile persisted calm; to the end — to the last day — he
continued among that comic crew unchallenged choragus of all
the rites, I will not say of Paphos, but of Chemos! and Baal-
Peor! Warmed, he did not refuse the revel, the dance, the
darkened chamber. It was utterly black, rayless; approached by
a secret passage; in shape circular; the air hot, haunted always
by odours of balms, bdellium, hints of dulcimer and flute; and
radiated round with a hundred thick-strewn ottomans of
Morocco. Here Lucy Hill stabbed to the heart Caccofogo,
mistaking the scar of his back for the scar of Soriac. In a bath
of malachite the Princess Egla, waking late one morning, found
Cosmo lying stiffly dead, the water covering him wholly.

"But in God's name, Mérimée!" (so he wrote), "to think of
Xélucha dead! Xélucha! Can a moon-beam, then, perish of
suppurations? Can the rainbow be eaten by worms? Ha! ha!
ha! laugh with me, my friend: *'elle derangera l'Enfer'*! She will
introduce the *pas de tarantule* into Tophet! Xélucha, the
feminine! Xélucha recalling the splendid harlots of history!
Weep with me — manat rara meas lacrima per genas! expert as
Thargelia; cultured as Aspatia; purple as Semiramis. She
comprehended the human tabernacle, my friend, its secret
springs and tempers, more intimately than any *savant* of
Salamanca who breathes. *Tarare*— but Xélucha is not dead!
Vitality is not mortal; you cannot wrap flame in a shroud.
Xélucha! where then is she? Translated, perhaps — rapt to a
constellation like the daughter of Leda. She journeyed to
Hindostan, accompanied by the train and appurtenance of a
Begum, threatening descent upon the Emperor of Tartary. I
spoke of the desolation of the West; she kissed me, and
promised return. Mentioned you, too, Mérimée — 'her
Conqueror' — Mérimée, Destroyer of Woman.' A breath from
the conservatory rioted among the ambery whiffs of her
forelocks, sending it singly a-wave over that thulite tint you
know. Costumed cap-à-pie, she had, my friend, the dainty little

completeness of a daisy mirrored bright in the eye of the browsing ox. A simile of Milton had for years, she said, inflâmed the lust of her Eye: 'The barren plains of Sericana, where Chineses drive with sails and wind their cany wagons light.' I, and the Sabaeans, she assured me, wrongly considered Flame the whole of being; the other half of things being Aristotle's quintessential light. In the Ourania Hierarchia and the Faust-book you meet a completeness: burning Seraph, Cherûb full of eyes. Xélucha combined them. She would reconquer the Orient for Dionysius, and return. I heard of her blazing at Delhi; drawn in a chariot by lions. Then this rumour — probably false. Indeed, it comes from a source somewhat turgid. Like Odin, Arthur, and the rest, Xélucha — will reappear."

Soon subsequently, Cosmo lay down in his balneum of malachite, and slept, having drawn over him the water as a coverlet. I, in England, heard little of Xélucha: first that she was alive, then dead, then alighted at old Tadmor in the Wilderness, Palmyra now. Nor did I greatly care, Xélucha having long since turned to apples of Sodom in my mouth. Till I sat by the cista of letters and re-read Cosmo, she had for some years passed from my active memories.

The habit is now confirmed in me of spending the greater part of the day in sleep, while by night I wander far and wide through the city under the sedative influence of a tincture which has become necessary to my life. Such an existence of shadow is not without charm; nor, I think, could many minds be steadily subjected to its conditions without elevation, deepened awe. To travel alone with the Primordial cannot but be solemn. The moon is of the hue of the glow-worm; and Night of the sepulchre. Nux bore not less Thanatos than Hupnos, and the bitter tears of Isis redundulate to a flood. At three, if a cab rolls, by, the sound has the augustness of thunder. Once, at two, near a corner, I came upon a priest, seated, dead, leering, his legs bent. One arm, supported on a knee, pointed with rigid accusing forefinger obliquely upward. By exact observation, I found that he indicated Betelgeux, the star *"a"* which shoulders the wet sword of Orion. He was hideously swollen, having perished of dropsy. Thus in all

Supremes is a *grotesquerie*; and one of the sons of Night is —
Buffo.

In a London square deserted, I should imagine, even in the day,
I was aware of the metallic, silvery-clinking approach of little
shoes. It was three in a heavy morning of winter, a day after my
rediscovery of Cosmo. I had stood by the railing, regarding the
clouds sail as under the sea-legged pilotage of a moon wrapped
in cloaks of inclemency. Turning, I saw a little lady, very
gloriously dressed. She had walked straight to me. Her head was
bare, and crisped with the amber stream which rolled lax to a
globe kneaded thick with jewels, at her nape. In the redundance
of her decolleté development, she resembled Parvati, mound-
hipped love-goddess of the luscious fancy of the Brahmin.

She addressed to me the question:

"What are you doing there, darling?"

Her loveliness stirred me, and Night is *bon camarade*. I
replied:

"Sunning myself by means of the moon."

"All that is borrowed lustre," she returned, "you have got it
from old Drummond's *Flowers of Sion*."

Looking back, I cannot remember that this reply astonished
me, though it should — of course — have done so. I said:

"On my soul, no; but you?"

"You might guess whence *I* come!"

"You are dazzling. You come from Paz."

"Oh, farther than that, my son! Say a subscription ball in
Soho."

"Yes? . . . and alone? in the cold? on foot . . .?"

"Why, I am old, and a philosopher. I can pick you out
riding Andromeda yonder from the ridden Ram. They are in
error, M'sieur, who suppose an atmosphere on the broad side
of the moon. I have reason to believe that on Mars dwells a
race whose lids are transparent like glass; so that the eyes are
visible during sleep; and every varying dream moves imaged
forth to the beholder in tiny panorama on the limpid iris.
You cannot imagine me a mere *fille*! To be escorted is to admit
yourself a woman, and that is improper in Nowhere. Young
Eos drives an *équipage à quatre*, but Artemis 'walks' alone.

Get out of my borrowed light in the name of Diogenes! I am going home."

"Far?"

"Near Piccadilly."

"But a cab?"

"No cabs for *me*, thank you. The distance is a mere nothing. Come."

We walked forward. My companion at once put an interval between us, quoting from the *Spanish Curate* that the open is an enemy to love. The Talmudists, she twice insisted, rightly held the hand the sacredest part of the person, and at that point also contact was for the moment interdict. Her walk was extremely rapid. I followed. Not a cat was anywhere visible. We reached at length the door of a mansion in St. James's. There was no light. It seemed tenantless, the windows all un-curtained, pasted across, some of them, with the words, To Let. My companion, however, flitted up the steps, and, beckoning, passed inward. I, following, slammed the door, and was in darkness. I heard her ascend, and presently a region of glimmer above revealed a stairway of marble, curving broadly up. On the floor where I stood was no carpet, nor furniture: the dust was very thick. I had begun to mount when, to my surprise, she stood by my side, returned; and whispered:

"To the very top, darling."

She soared nimbly up, anticipating me. Higher, I could no longer doubt that the house was empty but for us. All was a vacuum full of dust and echoes. But at the top, light streamed from a door, and I entered a good-sized oval saloon, at about the centre of the house. I was completely dazzled by the sudden resplendence of the apartment. In the midst was a spread table, square, opulent with gold plate, fruit dishes; three ponderous chandeliers of electric light above; and I notice also (what was very *bizarre*) one little candlestick of common tin con-taining an old soiled curve of tallow, on the table. The im-pression of the whole chamber was one of gorgeousness not less than Assyrian. An ivory couch at the far end was made sun-like by a head-piece of chalcedony forming a sea for the sport of emerald ichthyotauri. Copper hangings, panelled with mirrors in iasperated crystal, corresponded with a dome of flame and copper; yet this latter, I now remember, produced upon my glance an impression of actual grime. My companion reclined on a small Sigma couch, raised high to the table-level in the Semitic manner, visible to her saffron slippers of satin. She pointed me a seat opposite. The incongruity of its presence in the middle of this arrogance of pomp so tickled me, that no power could have kept me from a smile: it was a grimy chair, mean, all wood, nor was I long in discovering one leg somewhat shorter than its fellows.

She indicated wine in a black glass bottle, and a tumbler, but herself made no pretence of drinking or eating. She lay on hip and elbow, *petite*, resplendent, and looked gravely upward. I, however, drank.

"You are tired," I said, "one sees that."

"It is precious little than *you* see!" she returned, dreamy, hardly glancing.

"How! your mood is changed, then? You are morose."

"You never, I think, saw a Norse passage-grave?"

"And abrupt."

"Never?"

"A passage-grave? No."

"It is worth a journey! They are circular or oblong chambers of stone, covered by great earthmounds, with a 'passage' of slabs connecting them with the outer air. All round the chamber the dead sit with head resting upon the bent knees, and consult together in silence."

"Drink wine with me, and be less Tartarean."

"You certainly seem to be a fool," she replied with perfect sardonic iciness. "Is it not, then, highly romantic? They belong, you know, to the Neolithic age. As the teeth fall, one by one, from the lipless mouths — they are caught by the lap. When the lap thins — they roll to the floor of stone. Thereafter, every tooth that drops all round the chamber sharply breaks the silence."

"Ha! ha! ha!"

"Yes. It is like a century-slow, circularly-successive dripping of slime in some cavern of the far subterrene."

"Ha! ha! This wine seems heady! They express themselves in a dialect largely dental."

"The Ape, on the other hand, in a language wholly guttural."

A town-clock tolled four. Our talk was holed with silences, and heavy-paced. The wine's yeasty exhalation reached my brain. I saw her through mist, dilating large, uncertain, shrinking again to dainty compactness. But amorousness had died within me.

"Do you know," she asked, "what has been discovered in one of the Danish *Kjökkenmöddings* by a little boy? It was ghastly. The skeleton of a huge fish with human —."

"You are most unhappy."

"Be silent."

"You are full of care."

"I think you a great fool."

"You are racked with misery."

"You are a child. You have not even an instinct of the meaning of the word."

"How! Am I not a man? I, too, miserable, careful?"

"You are not, really, *anything* — until you can create."

"Create what?"

"Matter."

"That is foppish. Matter cannot be created, nor destroyed."

"Truly, then, you must be a creature of unusually weak intellect. I see that now. Matter does not exist, then, there is no such thing, really — it is an appearance, a spectrum — every writer not imbecile from Plato to Fichte has, voluntary or involuntary, proved that for good. To create it is to produce an impression of its reality upon the senses of others; to destroy it is to wipe a wet rag across a scribbled slate."

"Perhaps. I do not care. Since no one can do it."

"No one? You are mere embryo ——"

"Who then?"

"*Anyone*, whose power of Will is equivalent to the gravitating force of a star of the First Magnitude."

"Ha! ha! ha! By heaven, you choose to be facetious. Are there then wills of such equivalence?"

"There have been three, the founders of religions. There was a fourth: a cobbler of Herculaneium, whose mere volition induced the cataclysm of Vesuvius in 79, in direct opposition to the gravity of Sirius. There are more fames than *you* have ever sung, you know. The greater number of disembodied spirits, too, I feel certain ——"

"By heaven, I cannot but think you full of sorrow! Poor wight! come, drink with me. The wine is thick and boon. Is it not Setian? It makes you sway and swell before me, I swear, like a purple cloud of evening ——"

"But you are mere clayey ponderance! — I did not know that! — you are no companion! your little interest revolves round the lowest centres."

"Come — forget your agonies ——"

"What, think you, is the portion of the buried body first sought by the worm?"

"The eyes! the eyes!"

"You are *hideously* wrong — you are so *utterly* at sea ——"

"My God!"

She had bent forward with such rage of contradiction as to approach me closely. A loose gown of amber silk, wide-sleeved, had replaced her ball attire, though at what opportunity I could not guess; wondering, I noticed it as she now placed her palms far forth upon the table. A sudden wafture as of spice and orange-flowers, mingled with the abhorrent faint odour of mortality over-ready for the tomb, greeted my sense. A chill crept upon my flesh.

"You are so *hopelessly* at fault ——"

"For God's sake ——"

"You are so *miserably* deluded! Not the eyes *at all*!"

"Then, in heaven's name, what?"

Five tolled from a clock.

"*The Uvula!* the soft drop of mucous flesh, you know, suspended from the palate above the glottis. They eat through the face-cloth and cheek, or crawl by the lips through a broken tooth, filling the mouth. They make straight for it. It is the *deliciae* of the vault."

At her horror of interest I grew sick, at her odour, and her words. Some unspeakable sense of insignificance, of debility, held me dumb.

"You say I am full of sorrows. You say I am racked with woe; that I gnash with anguish. Well, you are a mere child in intellect. You use words without realization of meaning like those minds in what Leibnitz calls 'symbolical consciousness." But suppose it were so ——"

"It is so."

"You know nothing."

"I see you twist and grind. Your eyes are very pale. I thought they were hazel. They are of the faint bluishness of phosphorus shimmerings seen in darkness."

"That proves nothing."

"But the 'white' of the sclerotic is dyed to yellow. And you look inward. Why do you look so palely inward, so woe-worn, upon your soul? Why can you speak of nothing but the sepulchre, and its rottenness? Your eyes seem to me wan with centuries of vigil, with mysteries and millenniums of pain."

"Pain! but you know so *little* of it! you are wind and words! of its philosophy and *rationale* nothing!"

"Who knows?"

"I will give you a hint. It is the sub-consciousness in conscious creatures of Eternity, and of eternal loss. The least prick of a pin not Paean and Aesculapius and the powers of heaven and hell can utterly heal. Of an everlasting loss of pristine wholeness the conscious body is sub-consious, and 'pain' is its sigh at the tragedy. So with all pain — greater, the greater the loss. The hugest of losses is, of course, the loss of Time. If you lose that, any of it, you plunge at once into the transcendentalisms, the infinitudes, of Loss; if you lose *all of it* ——"

"But you so wildly exaggerate! Ha! ha! You rant, I tell you, of commonplaces with the woe ——"

"Hell is where a clear, untrammelled Spirit is sub-conscious of lost Time; where it boils and writhes with envy of the living world; *hating* it for ever, and all the sons of Life!"

"But curb yourself! Drink — I implore — I *implore* — for God's sake — but *once* ——"

"To *hasten* to the snare — *that* is woe! to drive your ship

upon the *lighthouse* rock — that is Marah! To wake, and feel it
irrevocably true that you went after her — *and the dead were
there* — and her guests were in the depths of hell — *and you did
not know it!* — though you *might* have. Look out upon the
houses of the city this dawning day: not one, I tell you, but in
it haunts some soul — walking up and down the old theatre of
its little Day — goading imagination by a thousand childish
tricks, vraisemblances — elaborately duping itself into the
momentary fantasy *that it still lives*, that the chance of life is
not for ever and for ever lost — yet riving all the time with
under-memories of the wasted Summer, the lapsed brief light
between the two eternal glooms — riving I say and shriek to
you! — riving, *Mérimée, you destroying fiend* ——"

She had sprung — *tall* now, she seemed to me — between
couch and table.

"Mérimée!' I screamed, " — *my* name, harlot, in your maniac
mouth! By God, woman, you terrify me to death!"

I too sprang, the hairs of my head catching stiff horror from
my fancies.

"Your name? Can you imagine me ignorant of your name, or
anything concerning you? Mérimée! Why, did you not sit
yesterday and read me in a letter of Cosmo's?"

"Ah-h . . .," hysteria bursting high in a sob and laughter from
my arid lips — "Ah! ha! ha! Xélucha! My memory grows palsied
and grey, Xélucha! pity me — my walk is in the very valley of
shadow! — senile and sere! — observe my hair, Xélucha, its
grizzled growth — trepidant, Xélucha, clouded — I am not the
man you knew, Xélucha, in the palaces — of Cosmo! You are
Xélucha!"

"You rave, poor worm!" she cried, her face contorted by a
species of malicious contempt. "Xélucha died of cholera ten
years ago at Antioch. I wiped the froth from her lips. Her nose
underwent a green decay before burial. So far sunken into the
brain was the left eye ——"

"You are — *you are Xélucha!*" I shrieked; "voices now of
thunder howl it within my consciousness — and by the holy
God, Xélucha, though you blight me with the breath of hell
you are, I shall clasp you, — living or damned ——"

I rushed toward her. The word "Madman!" hissed as by the tongues of ten thousand serpents through the chamber, I heard; a belch of pestilent corruption puffed poisonous upon the putrid air; for a moment to my wildered eyes there seemed to rear itself, swelling high to the roof, a formless tower of ragged cloud, and before my projected arms had closed upon the very emptiness of inanity, I was tossed by the operation of some Behemoth potency far-circling backward to the utmost circumferance of the oval, where, my head colliding, I fell, shocked, into insensibility.

. . . .

When the sun was low toward night, I lay awake, and listlessly observed the grimy roof, and the sordid chair, and the candlestick of tin, and the bottle of which I had drunk. The table was small, filthy, of common deal, uncovered. All bore the appearance of having stood there for years. But for them, the room was void, the vision of luxury thinned to air. Sudden memory flashed upon me. I scrambled to my feet, and plunged and tottered, bawling, through the twilight into the street.

LORD DUNSANY (1878-1957)

AMONG THE GREAT MASTERS of the supernatural tale is Edward John Moreton Drax Plunkett, the 18th Baron Dunsany of County Meath. He was an outstanding dramatist whose supernatural plays anticipated the theatre of the absurd and a virtuoso writer of short stories and essays. The writer and critic L. Sprague de Camp (*Literary Swordsmen and Sorcerers*, 1976) has observed: 'Although he had predecessors, such as the many exploiters of Arthurian legend and lost-Atlantis theme, Dunsany was the second writer (Morris being the first) fully to exploit the possibilities of heroic fantasy — adventurous fantasy laid in imaginary lands with pre-industrial settings, with gods, witches, spirits and magic, like children's fairy tales but on a sophisticated, adult level'.

His was one of the most original talents in literature, and, in addition to being one of the great formative influences in the development of the fantasy genre, he was the author of many of the best fantasy tales ever written. Heroic fantasy had been revived by William Morris (1834-96) but Dunsany adapted it to the short story form of which Seán Ó Faoláin acclaimed him 'a master'.

Edward John Moreton Drax Plunkett was born on July 24, 1878, in Co. Meath. He was of an Ascendancy family claiming the second oldest title in the Irish peerage. The Plunketts adhered to Catholicism through the worst of the persecutions until, in 1713, the then Baron Dunsany was converted to Protestantism. Among Dunsany's ancestors was the saint, Oliver Plunkett. Because the 17th Baron, his father, was separated from his wife, Dunsany spent his childhood between Dunsany Castle in Co. Meath and his mother's home, in Regency House, called Dunstall Priory, in Kent, England. Following the family tradition he was educated at Cheam School, Eton and Sandhurst. From Sandhurst he took a commission in the Coldstream Guard and was sent to Gibraltar. During the Boer War of 1899-1902 he saw action in South Africa. His younger brother entered the Royal Navy about this time and was to become Admiral Sir Reginald Drax Plunkett.

Dunsany succeeded to his father's title in 1899 but it was a title he had little liking for and which he said was 'of the greatest disadvantage' to him in literary life. Dunsany was certainly a strange representative of the Protestant landlord class, an atheist who in no way conformed to the traditional ideas of landlord or aristocrat. He was a gaunt 6ft 2ins and wore a wispy moustache. He was called the worst dressed man in Ireland and seemed to permanently wear a suit of shapeless, baggy tweeds into whose pockets he stuffed countless penciled notes.

When he was not off on his hunting trips to Africa, or merely following his favourite pastime of travelling, he chose to live in Castle Dunsany, a Norman Castle which had been partially rebuilt in the 18th Century. His wife, Lady Beatrice Villiers, daughter of the Earl of Jersey, was once quoted as saying: 'If you're going to modernise a castle, the eighteenth century is the best time to do it'. Behind the bookcases in the great library at Dunsany are a priest hole and secret staircase left over from Cromwellian days.

Dunsany began his writing career at the age of 27, in 1905, with the publication of *The Gods of Pegana* and in it he created a new universe, the first original detailed cosmogony in English literature since William Blake. Great primeval gods appeared from nothingness and formed a cosmos, lesser gods emanated or congealed, forces of nature assumed personality and warred with one another, as neomyth succeeded neomyth in brilliant profusion. The book brought him immediate literary recognition.

In successive books such as *Times and the Gods* (1906); *The Sword of Welleran* (1909); *A Dreamer's Tale* (1910); *The Book of Wonder* (1912) and *Tales of Wonder* (1916) Dunsany created a world of private amazement in terms of myth and legend. Within their ambience there took place many stories of heroes, demigods, petty gods, ephemeral beings and creatures of twilight which have not been equalled outside of Greek or Irish mythology.

Without his creations and undoubted influence on the fantasy genre, it could be argued that there would never have been a Tolkien's *Lord of the Rings*.

Before he died, aged 79, on October 25, 1957, in a Dublin nursing home, Dunsany had published over sixty books and revolutionised fantasy fiction.

Yet in spite of his great literary output he once commented that he spent more of his life soldiering than writing. Certainly in 1914 he was among the first to volunteer for active service in World War One. He was commissioned in the Inniskillen Fusiliers and was training his company in Dublin during Easter Week, 1916. When word came of the uprising, Captain Lord Dunsany and a fellow officer, tried to make their way to Dublin Castle. Refusing to halt at a road block manned by men of the Irish Republican Army, he was fired upon and wounded in the face. The insurgents took him to a hospital where he remained until the insurrection was crushed.

As one might expect from a man of his background, Dunsany was an ardent Unionist in politics and remained pro-British throughout the subsequent War of Independence. It is ironic to note that one of the leaders of the insurrection, who was to be executed shortly after by the English, was a distant relative — the young poet Joseph Mary Plunkett. Joseph Plunkett's father, the Papal Count George Noble Plunkett, took up his son's cause during the War of Independence and became a member of the Irish revolutionary government.

By the end of 1916 Dunsany was out of hospital and fighting at the Front in France. He was an extremely active man who

enjoyed big game hunting and playing cricket. He became
shooting champion of Ireland. But he was also a reflective
man and a chess enthusiast who won the chess championship
of Ireland and even managed to take the world chess championship.

His literary standing created a demand for him as a lecturer
at universities and from 1919 he was making regular lecture
tours of America. In 1940 he was Byron Professor of English
at the University of Athens, a post from which he beat a hasty
retreat when the Germans marched in to annex Greece. During
the Second World War he remained in Kent, England, and enlisted in the Home Guard.

During his early writing career, Dunsany built up a reputation as the exponent of fantasy in the short story form.
Before the First World War he also gained a reputation as
a playwright attached for a time to the new Irish revivalist
drama of Lady Gregory, W. B. Yeats and J. M. Synge. By
1911 his name was prominent in the Irish renaissance and at
one time he agreed to finance some of Yeats' literary projects.
Among his better known plays were *A Night at an Inn* (performed at the Abbey in 1919) which is a supernatural tale of
four men who steal an effigy of an Indian god and meet a far
worse revenge than anything they could imagine. Two other
plays, *The Glittering Gate*, in which two burglars try to break
into heaven, and *Cheezo*, about a young man whose clerical
career is faltering because he cannot believe in eternal
damnation, enhanced Dunsany's career. In his plays he anticipated the theatre of the absurd, whose greatest living exponent
is the Nobel Prize winning Dubliner, Samuel Beckett.

His connection with Yeats and Synge was not altogether a
happy one. He had little enthusiasm for Yeats' poetic antiquari-
anism or for Synge's romantic realism. Dunsany essentially
created his own worlds which he used as a medium through
which to savagely attack elements of the real world which he
did not like. The growing friction between Yeats and Dunsany came to a head when in 1932 Yeats founded the Irish
Academy of Letters and ostentatiously omitted Dunsany on
the grounds that Dunsany did not write about Ireland but about

imaginary places. Dunsany was stimulated to write *The Curse of the Wise Woman*, an excellent fantasy with an Irish locality. He evened his score with Yeats by publicly announcing the formation of a society to honour medieval Italian writers which would omit Dante because 'Dante did not write about Italy, but of a very different place. Most unsuitable.'

During the 1920's and 1930's Dunsany continued his fantasy work but began to experiment with novel size works. There was *The King of Elfland's Daughter* (1924), *The Charwoman's Shadow* (1926) and *The Blessing of Pan* (1927) which proved to be the most outstanding. The latter novel, in which the god Pan emerges to awaken ecstasy in a dreary village, was a great success. During the '20's Dunsany began to leave aside fantasy, although in 1953 he published a rather untypical work entitled *The Last Revolution* which is concerned with self reproducing and intelligent machines.

His new development was on his famous Jorkens tales, a series of stories based on his own travels narrated by a drunken old liar at a London club in order to cadge drinks. Dunsany wrote a good deal of poetry, novels and stories of contemporary Irish life, aesthetic essays, books of reminiscences and three volumes of autobiography – *Patches of Sunlight; While the Sirens Slept* and *The Sirens Wake*.

L. Sprague de Camp has said: 'Dunsany was a writer's writer. Although well known in his lifetime and having much influence on his young colleagues, he never became an actual bestseller, even though some of his plays had considerable success.'

Among the writers that Dunsany influenced enormously was the famous and tragic American H. P. Lovecraft (1890-1937) who recognised Dunsany as the greatest literary influence in his life. Lovecraft wrote that Dunsany was 'unexcellent in the sorcery of crystalline singing prose, and supreme in the creation of a gorgeous and languorous world of iridescently exotic vision'. So impressed was Lovecraft that he sent Dunsany a sixty-four line poem dedicated to him.

The word Dunsanian has become descriptive today of a type of fantasy fiction expounded by such writers as Lovecraft, Clark Ashton Smith, Robert E. Howard and James Branch Cabell.

But Dunsany also gave encouragement to writers outside his genre. He discovered and encouraged the Meath poet Francis Ledwidge who was killed in Flanders in 1917. Ledwidge, born in Slane in 1891, was working as a labourer when Dunsany hailed his talent as a poet. Dunsany also actively encouraged the Irish novelists Mary Lavin and Anne Crone.

As examples of his horror-fantasy at its best, I have chosen 'The Ghost of the Valley' and 'Autumn Cricket'. The choice was hard but only because of the excellence of the material which had to be discarded.

Dunsany's fantasy books were illustrated by Sidney H. Sime (1867-1942) who, in the later books, became more than simply an illustrator. He became a source of inspiring stories in Dunsany. When Sime died Dunsany wrote of him: 'There was in his pictures a sombre grandeur showing all the majesty of night or the mysteries of dark forests, like a joke played by a god whom nobody worships . . . and yet his sombre shadows . . . are always lit by the rays of his merry humour. Now that vast imagination has left us, having enriched our age with dreams that we have not entirely deserved . . .'

The obituary could equally apply to Dunsany.

THE GHOST OF THE VALLEY
Lord Dunsany

WENT FOR A WALK ONE EVENING under old willows whose pollarded trunks leaned over a little stream. A mist lay over the stream and filled the valley far over the heads of the willows and hid the feet of the hills. And higher than that I saw a pillar of mist stand up from the rest, its head above the level of the grass slopes, where they ended under th edge of the darkening woods. So strange it seemed standing there in the dim of the evening, that I moved nearer to see it, which I could not clearly do where I was, nearly a hundred yards away, because of the rest of the mist; but as I moved towards it, and less and less of the river-mist was between us, I saw it clearer and clearer, till I stood at the feet of that tall diaphanous figure.

One by one lights appeared where there had been none before: for it was that hour when the approach of night is noticed in cottages, and the flower-like glow of windows here and there was adding a beauty and mystery to the twilight. In the great loneliness there, with no-one to speak to, standing before that towering figure of mist that was as lonely as I, I should have liked to have spoken to it. And then there came to me the odd thought. Why not? There was no one to hear me, and it need not answer.

So I said "What are you?" and so small and shrill was the

answer, that at first I thought it was birds of the reeds and
water that spoke. "A ghost," it seemed to be saying. "What?"
said I. And then more clearly it said, "Have you never seen
ghosts before?"

I said that I never had, and it seemed to lose interest in me.
To regain its attention if possible, I said that I had sometimes
seen queer things in the twilight which very likely were ghosts,
although I did not know it at the time. And there seemed to
come back into the tall grey figure some slight increase of intensity, as though its lost interest were slowly returning, and in
tones that sounded scornful of my ignorance it said, "They
probably were."

"And you?" I enquired again.

"The ghost of this valley," it said.

"Always?" I asked.

"Not always," it said. "Little more than a thousand years.
My father was the smoke from one of those cottages and my
mother was the mist over the stream. She of course was here
always."

It was strange to hear so tall a figure talking with so tiny a
voice: had a waterhen been uttering its shrill cry near me it
would have drowned the voice of the ghost, which barely
emerged from the chatter of waterfowl farther away.

"What was it like in this valley," I asked, "when you were
young?"

For a while the tall shape said nothing, and seemed to be in-
dolently turning its head, as though it looked from side to
side of the valley. "The heads of the willows were not cut,"
it said. "But that was when I was very young. They were cut
off soon after. And there were not so many cottages. Not
nearly so many, and they were all of thatch at first. They lit
their fires in the evenings all through the autumn. My mother
loved the autumn: it is to us what spring is to you. My father
rose up then from one of the chimneys, high over the thatch,
and the wind drifted him and so they met. He remembered
the talk of the firesides long ago, but only a few centuries
more than a thousand years. My mother can remember for

ever. She remembers when there were no huts here and no men. She remembers what was, and knows what is coming."

"I don't want to hear about that," I said. Something like a cackle of laughter seemed to escape from the ghost. But it may have been only the quacking of far-off ducks, which were flighting at that hour.

"What do you do yourself?" I asked.

"I drift," it said, "whenever there is a wind. Like you."

"Drift," I said. "We don't drift. We have our policies." I was about to explain them to the ghost, when it interrupted.

"You all drift before them helplessly," it said. "You and your friends and your enemies."

"It is easy for you to criticise," I answered.

"I am not criticising," it said. "I am just as helpless. I drift this way and that upon any wind. I can no more control the winds than you can turn Destiny."

"Nonsense," I said. "We are masters of all Creation. We have made inventions which you would never understand down there by your river and the smoke of the cottages."

"But you have to live with them," it said.

"And you?" I asked.

"I am going," it said.

"Why?" I asked it.

"Times are changing," it said. "The old firesides are altering, and they are poisoning the river, and the smoke of the cities is unwholesome, like your bread. I am going away among unicorns, griffons and wiverns."

"But are there such things?" I asked.

"There used to be," it replied.

But I was growing impatient at being lectured to by a ghost, and was a little chilled by the mist.

"Are there such things as ghosts?" I asked then.

And a wind blew then, and the ghost was suddenly gone.

"We used to be," it sighed softly.

"Autumn Cricket"   Jeanette A. Dunne. Dec 78

AUTUMN CRICKET
Lord Dunsany

 N ONE OF THOSE SHORT JOURNEYS by car that one sometimes takes nowadays I happened to pass after nightfall the once-famous cricket field of Long Barrow. They play there still in the summer, though not so much as they used to do; but this was autumn, when it would be deserted by day, and at night there was nothing there but grey mists that had strayed from a neighbouring stream that winds along under the willows at one end of the ground. Perhaps it was the contrast between the activity for which that field had been famous and the loneliness of it in that autmn night that made me feel for a moment a sense of desolation. And then my head-lights flashed on the face of an old man sitting on a wooden bench by the side of the field and gazing out into the mists whose shapes floated up from the stream and rose every now and then in little wraiths, as a breeze in the cold night played with them for a while and soon dropped them again. Somehow this solitary figure there seemed to increase the loneliness. Then just before the light left him, to sweep on and illuminate hedges and branches of trees, the old man began to clap. Sitting all alone on that wooden bench, looking over an empty field, he was unmistakably applauding something. I went on in the car, and that was all the story I had to tell, a field at night

covered with mist, nothing else there, and a man beside it clapping; and not a very likely story either. But I told it, such as it was, to a friend next day who knew Long Barrow, living nearer to it than I do, and this is what he told me. "O, that would have been old Modgers," he said. "He used to be groundsman there but retired on account of age long ago, and has a cottage almost beside it."

"What was he doing there at that hour?" I asked.

"Well, that's the trouble," he said. "It's not good for him at that age to be out in the cold like that, and we can't stop him, unless we have him legally restrained."

"But surely you can't shut a man up," I said, "merely to prevent him from going out in the cold."

"It's more than that," he said. "The old man thinks there's a cricket match going on there every night, and he goes out to look at it."

"Who does he think is playing?" I asked.

"W. G. Grace," he replied, "and Gunn, and a lot of other famous players, all of them men he has seen on that ground and all of them dead. We are trying to have him certified. And then they'll be able to keep him it at night."

"Will he like that?" I said rather lamely.

"No," he said. "He wants to go and see ghosts playing cricket. But it's the only way to stop him. His wife can't do it."

"Can you do it on that?" I asked.

"His doctor says so," said Meadly. That was my friend's name. "He says he has given him very detailed accounts of the games that he watches, even to the score of each ghost."

So I imagined that I was never likely to see any more of old Modgers.

And then one day only a week or so later, when autumn was a little colder and mistier, I was passing that way after night-fall again, and there was the same old man sitting on his old wooden bench that was still by the side of the ground, and gazing steadily, just as he had before, at the wisps of mist that breezes lifted over the rest and let fall again into the greyness that went all the way to the stream. So they had not certified the old man, and he was still out there of a night in the cold.

Next day I decided to go to Meadly's house to ask him more of the story, the beginnings of which he had told me. I rang his bell and he came to the door himself, and I apologized for disturbing him, and told him that old Modgers was still there at night.

"Come in," he said cheerily, "and have some tea, and I'll tell you about him."

And I went into his smoking-room with him and sat down in a comfortable chair, and he said: "The trouble was that one doctor cannot certify a man, It takes two. That is the law. And the old fellow found out that he was going to be certified, and when the second doctor turned up he wouldn't say a word about ghosts. So, in spite of the evidence of his own doctor, we have been unable to get him into an asylum."

"Well, I suppose we'd all try to escape that if we could," I said.

"It isn't the asylum that he jibs at," said Meadly, "but he won't leave his ghosts. You see, he's somewhere in his late eighties, and kept that ground for nearly fifty years and played on it before that; and to give up cricket is to him what giving up much more important things would be to others, and he thinks he's still watching it. Of course, if we could prove that, we could get him certified. But we can't. His doctor had the whole story from him; but that is not enough. We've asked his wife to wrap him up as much as possible. And she does that, but we can't stop him."

"Perhaps it would be possible to reason with him," I said, as tea was brought in by a maid.

"I don't think so," he said.

"I'd like to try," I told him. "He can't want to be frozen to death."

"Men don't like to be killed by any of their follies," said Meadly, "but they don't like to give them up. And I suppose more good advice is wasted on asking them if they wouldn't like to do so than on anything in the world."

"Still, I'd like to try," I said.

And so I added myself to the number of those who ask men to give up the harmful things they like most in life, one in every hundred thousand of whom succeed. So why shouldn't I? I went over by bus next night to Long Barrow an hour or two after sunset and walked alone to the cricket-ground. And sure enough he was on his usual bench, looking out over the famous ground at the first thin wisps of mist that were coming up from the stream and nearing the lonely pitch. I went up to the wooden bench and sat down beside him. He hastily looked all round, evidently to satisfy himself that two men were not within hearing, and not till he had thoroughly scrutinized the misty darkness did he say anything to me. But then he spoke.

"They are just coming in to bat," he said. "That's Gunn, and that's W.G."

"So I see," I replied.

"You know them, then," he asked.

"By sight," I said.

"They often play here," he told me.

"Do you watch them often?" I asked.

"Whenever they play," he said.

"Is it a good thing to be out so late with all this mist rising?" I asked him.

"They never play by day," he said.

"But are you sure you are warm enough?" I asked.

"I wrap up well," he said. "And I never stay more than two hours, unless it's a very exciting game. And I go to bed as soon as I get home."

He stopped to clap then, gazing over the ground towards the approaching mist. And I thought over what he had said, and it seemed to me that if he was really well wrapped up under the good great-coat that he wore, and if he did not stay more than two hours, it might not be so serious as Meadly and others feared, at any rate not till the winter. And so I told Meadly next day. I sat there beside the old fellow for nearly half an hour and heard an excellent summary of a very exciting game, something I suppose that had remained in his memory, which was still fresh and vivid, whatever had happened to the rest of his mind, perhaps overweighted and upset by the sheer power of that part of the brain that stores and preserves past days. It was really a very exciting match. I remember it yet. W. G. won, though that proves nothing, because he nearly always did. I saw Modgers home hale and hearty, and I went to Meadly next day and urged him to leave the old man alone, at least till winter came, and told him that I felt sure he would be all right. And I think I persuaded Meadly. But long before winter was here the old man died.

What happened, as we afterwards heard from his wife, was, only a fortnight later, being a bit older than Meadly had thought, he reached his 90th birthday. And old Mrs Modgers told us that on that very evening, while they were having a bit of a supper and a glass of wine with which to celebrate the occasion, the mist having risen, as it always did in the autumn, but no higher than one of their windows, old Modgers had glanced out of the window and suddenly said they had made him an honorary member, and honorary member of the ghosts who used to play at Long Barrow, because he was ninety. And Modgers had said that this was a great honour, because he was the only living man that had been invited to play at night on that ground. And they were going to play that night, Modgers had said; and the Doctor himself, that is Dr. Grace, had invited Modgers to play for him. So Modgers had gone; she couldn't stop him. And this time he wouldn't even dress up warm.

"Well," she said, "he went out there with his bat, for he had an old bat that he still kept in a cupboard, and he said he wouldn't want pads, because the ball they were using wasn't as hard as all that, and he went out to the pitch and bent down like as if he was batting, and began hitting about."

"But surely," Meadly said to her, "he didn't run."

"He seemed to be hitting boundaries," said Mrs. Modgers. "I stayed and watched the whole time, but he wouldn't allow me to bring him home. He seemed to be hitting boundaries, and so did the gentleman opposite to him, who-ever that may have been, or perhaps I should say *whatever*, seeing they was all ghosts, but for him. But after he had hit about twenty of them he seemed to get tired and not to be able to hit so far, and then he had to run. I couldn't stop him. And after a while he took off his hat two or three times and looked round about him, seemingly very pleased. And I think he had got his century. And that was when it happened. Of course a man of his age couldn't run like he did, and dropped dead. I could do nothing."

We both made those vain attempts that people sometimes make with words, trying to comfort Mrs. Modgers. But, though we knew we could bring her no comfort whatever, we both of us saw a gleam on her face that seemed, faint though it was, to shine from a hidden smile, as she said, "They were never able to shut him up. And he'll be able to play at Long Barrow now with the Doctor and Mr. Gunn whenever he likes."